THE CRITICS ARE ENCHANTED BY THE POWER OF *MERLIN'S LEGACY!*

DAUGHTER OF FIRE:

"Any collection of the Arthurian legend would be lacking without it."

—Heartland Critiques

DAUGHTER OF THE MIST:

"Sorcery, enchantment, mystery and romance blend together perfectly. Like Mary Stewart and Marion Simmer Bradley, Quinn Taylor Evans weaves a spell that enchants, absorbs and enlightens the reader."

—Kathe Robin, *Romantic Times*

DAUGHTER OF LIGHT:

"As powerful and enthralling as the first two books. Enchantment, magic, passion and love all swirl together with evil and danger in a tale that is absolutely unforgettable!"

—Laurel Gainer, *Affaire de Coeur*

And now, the magic continues . . .

MERLIN'S LEGACY: SHADOWS OF CAMELOT

MERLIN'S LEGACY:

SHADOWS OF CAMELOT

Quinn Taylor Evans

Zebra Books
Kensington Publishing Corp.
http://www.zebrabooks.com

ZEBRA BOOKS are published by

Kensington Publishing Corp.
850 Third Avenue
New York, NY 10022

Zebra and the Z logo Reg. U.S. Pat. & TM Off.

First Printing: October, 1997
10 9 8 7 6 5 4 3 2

Printed in the United States of America

Love is a rare gift that can neither be bought or sold,
not for gold coins, land, or even a crown.
It must be given from the heart.

If you find such a love, seize it,
fight to the last breath to keep it.
For life is not worth living without it.

PART ONE

SHADOWS

One

Spring, 1068
The Camden Forest, in the West Country

A red squirrel, which had been foraging acorns in the thick carpet of rotting vegetation on the forest floor, abruptly shot up the trunk of a gnarled oak barking with alarm. A rabbit suddenly sat up, ears twitching nervously, while overhead a glossy, black jackdaw, disturbed from its thievery of a nearby nest screeched a frantic warning and took to wing as a gray wolf loped into the clearing.

The wolf was lean and powerfully built, blending with the shadows of the forest. Its eyes were black as night and gleaming as it paused and smelled the cool, morning air, searching for a scent.

The rabbit darted into a hollow log. Safe in the branches overhead, the squirrel kept up its incessant chatter while the jackdaw screeched and swept low, defending the pillaged feast of shattered eggs in the ransacked nest.

The wolf ignored both the squirrel's noisome scolding and the jackdaw's aerial attacks, long ears casting forward as it finally caught a different scent that came from the edge of the forest, the scent of humans.

Dark eyes gleamed. The wolf crossed the clearing in

long strides, abandoning the easy kill of the rabbit, closing in on new prey.

The sky was cloudless, an intense shade of blue beneath a white-hot sun that made one forget the long winter past.

Overhead, a meadowlark called, a clear, musical sound amid the lazy drone of bees aswarm in wild rhododendron. A breeze stirred, like an invisible hand stroking the tall grass in the meadow, bringing with it the sound of conversation and children's laughter.

Wagons and carts stood empty beneath the thick canopy of redbud and alders. Horses were tethered nearby, dozing with eyes closed in the shade of the trees, tails occasionally twitching back and forth at flies.

Baskets of food, casks of wine, and hogsheads of rich, dark ale brought from the castle had been set beneath the trees in anticipation of the return of the hunters and the midday meal.

The baskets had been opened, the food laid out on long low tables also brought from the castle. Women spoke in quiet tones over needlework and sleeping babies, while keeping a watchful eye over older children who played at mock battle some distance away. Occasionally there was laughter at some joke, usually at the expense of the men and lovers who hunted far afield.

Old Meg stirred from her dozing, roused by some distant voice she felt rather than heard, like an echo of memory both ancient and new, felt in the blood with each beat of her heart.

Instinctively, she opened her sightless eyes though she was guided more by the sounds around her, at once calmed by the quiet, undisturbed conversations and child's playful laughter that bespoke no danger, and at the same time unable to ignore a sudden chill in the warm, spring air.

Though no sound was made, still she sensed the movement beside her as the girl, Amber, stood suddenly.

Guided by that inner sense that saw in other ways, she reached a thin, heavily veined hand with the accuracy of those who are sighted and gently clasped the girl's slender arm.

"What is it, child?"

" *'Tis young master, Kaden,* " came the reply, heard not in spoken words but through the connection of the girl's thoughts with her own in the old way, for Amber could not speak.

"He is chasing butterflies."

Years before, Amber alone survived the brutal slaughter of her entire village by Norse raiders. Cruelly abused by her captors, she was found huddling in the burned out ruins of her family's hut. Wounded in body and spirit, she had retreated into a world of silence.

Only one person had been able to lure the girl out of her sad world of painful memories and make her smile again. The handsome young conjuror who pretended to be a fool—Truan Monroe.

Truan had befriended Amber, easing her sadness with simple tricks—flowers that appeared out of the air or coins plucked from behind her ear—and he had earned her trust when the girl trusted no one.

With him, the girl felt safe and protected. They shared jokes and he told her stories that brought smiles to her face at his foolishness. But Meg suspected, with that uncanny sense of things, that there was more to the fool than he let others see, some secret that he kept from everyone. Then, it seemed something happened between the two and the tentative friendship had suddenly ended, and Amber had retreated into sadness once more.

Joy and fragile hope had turned to pain and sadness once more, and the jester no longer laughed as he once had. Truan Monroe, fierce warrior, conjuror of poor sleight-of-hand tricks, and even worse jokes. At best, a terrible balladeer who could not carry a tune in a bucket. He was a contradiction unto himself. All was not what it seemed with Truan Monroe.

Beside her, the slender arm slipped from old Meg's grasp. She sensed at once Amber's exasperation and sudden amusement, as if the girl had laughed aloud.

"The butterflies fly just far enough to stay beyond his reach," Amber said through the connection of their thoughts.

"Wise creatures," Meg replied. Then added with growing apprehension, "do not let him wander far." For she knew well enough the curiosity and temperament of the toddler. She had been nursemaid to the child's mother, Lady Vivian.

At a year and a half Kaden was a robust, hearty child with the natural curiosity of the mortal world around him, and a growing awareness of his unusual heritage.

Even now, blind as she was, the old woman sensed the child purposefully wandering away from them on those stout legs, guided by that curiosity. Amber had also grown uncomfortable with the child's stubbornness.

"I'll bring him back before he wanders too far. 'Tis almost time for the men to return."

In the girl's reply, Meg heard the girl's unspoken hope that she might have a moment alone with Truan Monroe after his recent return from his home across the Irish sea. He had spent many weeks there, returning for reasons he had revealed to no one.

Then, he had returned only a few days earlier with no more word than when he had left as to the reason for either. He had simply told Lord Stephen that he would serve him as long as he could, leaving when he deemed it necessary. Like a pilgrim warrior.

The toddler ran on sturdy legs in pursuit of a bright blue butterfly that fluttered just beyond his reach amid clumps of heather and yellow gorse at the edge of the meadow.

Each time he was almost within reach, the butterfly flew off on a lazy, zigzagging course, as if guided by some sort of uncanny instinct of self-preservation.

Finally, the butterfly disappeared into a copse of trees that rimmed the edge of the meadow. With a gurgle of laughter, the child followed, completely enraptured.

"Kaden, wait!"

As natural as if she had spoken them, the words formed in Amber's thoughts but would not come, no matter how hard she tried. She ground her teeth in silent frustration as she lifted the hem of her skirt and went after the child.

He was only a few yards ahead, wearing a dark blue tunic and leggings trimmed with silver thread like his father's. His cap of dark hair glinted with shadings of brilliant copper, inherited from his mother.

The forest was cool without the warmth of the sun beating down overhead. Young master Kaden led her a merry chase. But Amber finally caught up with him and, as always, found it impossible to be angry with him.

She smothered a smile behind an expression of mock sternness as she came up behind him. He stood in a small clearing on stout little legs, attention focused on something of great fascination across the clearing. The butterfly no doubt.

"Foolish creature," she silently admonished the butterfly, *"if you let him get his hands on you."* She hoped the butterfly might still manage to escape unscathed for

young master Kaden had not yet learned the fragility of such beautiful things. More than one unwise butterfly had been crushed by his enthusiasm to hold it and show it to his mother.

He had the heart of a poet and the tempcrament of a warrior. The poet would be devastated if the butterfly succumbed. Then she would have to deal with tears, and she didn't know which was more persuasive, his impish laughter or the pools of tears that flooded his remarkable blue eyes when something made him sad.

As she came up behind Kaden, she saw what held his rapt attention, and her blood suddenly went cold in her veins.

The wolf stood just across the clearing, hackles raised beneath a bristling gray coat, head lowered between powerful shoulders, its dark, deadly gaze fixed on the child.

The air froze in her lungs. A scream tore through her brain, but no sound formed in her throat. Only inches away, Amber fought back terror and panic, certain that any sudden movement would cause the wolf to attack.

"Come to me, Kaden." The words repeated themselves over and over in her brain.

"Please, come to me!"

It was not the child, but the wolf that lifted its flat, dark gaze for a fraction of a moment, staring back at her as if it heard. Then it seemed as if the wolf smiled at her, tongue lolling out the side of its mouth, lips pulled back from rows of gleaming fangs.

Kaden turned then, staring up at her with trusting innocence and wide-eyed wonder. In his childish babble he spoke the word for "hound" with no possible understanding that the deadly creature that stood only a few feet away from him was not one of his father's hunting hounds, disciplined to be tolerant of tiny grabbing hands and poking fingers.

There was no place to hide, no place of safety. Their only chance was to run. Amber slowly reached out to the child and beckoned to him with outstretched hand, careful to make no sudden movement. In a simple language of hand signals that Meg had taught her, she implored the child to come to her.

He hesitated, pointing at the wolf and repeating the word, "hound." Amber shook her head, using familiar hand signals to explain that he must come away.

She knew he understood, for he turned back to the wolf and smiled with childish impishness, testing her, unaware of the dangerous game he played. Then he turned back to her and lifted outstretched arms.

She had only a moment to act, scooping Kaden into her arms as she saw the wolf leap. In moments, Amber knew the wolf would be on them. She clasped the child hard against her as she spun around and ran.

She ran blindly in the direction of the meadow. Branches of trees and thick underbrush tore at her clothes and snagged her hair. She felt a sharp sting at her cheek, and bent her head low over the child's head to protect him. Behind her, she heard the creature crashing through the brush after them.

She stumbled, almost fell, and drove back to her feet. Her lungs burned. Every muscle cried out as she forced herself to keep going, knowing that if she stopped or fell, the wolf would immediately be on them. Then through tears and tangled hair, she saw sunlight through the trees ahead and the bright green of the meadow.

On a silent sob, she clutched Kaden so tight against her that he cried out. A branch snagged at her skirt. She stumbled and went down on one knee. As she fought back to her feet, she heard the wolf just behind her.

The wolf hit at the back of her legs. The blow rolled her to the ground. She tried to scream but no sound came out. They were so close to the encampment, yet no one could hear them. Then as deadly fangs slashed at her, she curled herself around the child, protecting him with her body.

Amber felt the tearing pain as the wolf attacked again. She closed her eyes tightly shut, trying to block it out. Then pain gradually gave way to growing coldness that took her past the pain.

She saw the wolf as it attacked and heard the fierce, terrifying sounds it made that seemed almost like cruel laughter. But she no longer felt it. Darkness seeped in at the edges of her vision.

Then she heard a new sound in the forest, a fierce, terrifying sound of rage that grew louder and closer. The wolf ceased its attack. Amber slowly opened her eyes, barely able to breathe for the pain and terror. Only a few feet away two wolves were locked in deadly battle.

She immediately recognized the gray wolf that had attacked her. Its coat looked dull next to the gleaming, midnight black fur of the other wolf.

The two creatures were of an even size and strength, relying on cunning and quickness as they tore at each other, scrabbling for a new foothold as they launched themselves at each other, fell and rolled, then drove back to their feet in a flurry of tangled legs and slashing fangs that quickly drew blood. Then, as if frenzied by the smell and taste of blood, the attack became more desperate and fierce.

Smothered beneath her, Kaden wailed, his terrified cries adding to the frenzy of growling, snarling, and slashing sounds that filled the forest. Then she heard a wild, frenzied cry. It was not a human cry, but the cry of a wounded animal.

Through the haze of growing darkness Amber saw the embattled wolves suddenly part. They stood for a moment, ears flattened against their heads, lips drawn back over fangs, sides heaving beneath bloodied fur. Then the gray wolf slowly backed away.

It limped badly, yet refused to turn tail and run. Only when it finally reached a safe distance and the shelter of dense tree cover did the creature suddenly turn and disappear.

Amber stared at the black wolf, a new fear forcing its way through the pain and terror as the creature slowly turned and came toward her.

It crossed the clearing in long, powerful strides. The sun that burned through the treetops overhead glistened on its jet black fur until it seemed the creature was surrounded by brilliant, golden light.

As it came steadily closer, head down, penetrating gaze fastened on her, she hugged the child fiercely against her and tried desperately to crawl to safety.

"No!" her silent thoughts cried out even as the last of her strength faded and the spreading darkness of unconsciousness swept over her.

"Don't be afraid."

She wasn't certain if she heard the words or imagined them as the creature bore down on her.

The light expanded. The shadows of the forest disappeared. The last thing she saw was the wolf, fierce dark creature with glistening black fur and penetrating eyes.

It closed in on her, in that predatory, stalking gait, leaping through the circle of light. But the creature that emerged slowly took another form.

It was framed by the light as it continued walking toward her, features hidden in shadows. The last thing she saw was long, dark hair that fanned about wide, powerful shoulders, a deadly, penetrating gaze, and the lean predatory stride of a man where the wolf had been.

"You're safe now. I won't let anything hurt you."

The words seemed to whisper through the trees overhead and flow around her. Then her eyes slowly drifted shut. There was no more terror or pain. There was only darkness.

Two

"She cannot hear you," Vivian said gently as Truan bent over Amber. "She is in a place where no mortal voice may reach her."

Across the raised pallet of furs and the pale girl who lay there, still as death, Vivian's gaze met that of the warrior who had ridden as if all the hounds of hell pursued him on the frantic ride back to Camelot, the girl cradled in his arms as if she were as fragile as a newborn babe.

Her keen blue gaze met his. The demeanor of the fool was stripped away, emotions laid bare for all to see in the anguished expression on his lean, handsome features.

"Will she live?" he demanded, and in the fierce anger, she heard a silent, agonized plea.

A highly skilled healer, she felt for the shallow, erratic pulse at the slender throat as the life force ebbed away.

"The wounds are deep," she answered with complete honesty, for there was no certainty of life, not even with her powers. "There has been much loss of blood. I will do what I can."

Truan reached out and seized her by the wrist, his expression anguished. He had no patience for her carefully disguised words and platitudes.

Taken by surprise, not only by the fierceness in his

eyes, but by his unusual strength, which for some reason she could not escape, Vivian flinched and tried to pull away. But even with her extraordinary powers, it was impossible. He was far stronger than she.

"Will she live?" he again demanded, and Vivian sensed that even if the answer was no, he would never accept it.

All about the chamber, tense emotions were drawn to the breaking point. The brutal encounter in the forest had stunned and saddened everyone. Those who hunted accepted the danger of being gored by a wounded boar or stag, but among those who had hunted the forest near Camelot for many years none recalled an encounter with a wolf.

Old Meg shifted uneasily at the brazier where she stirred medicinal herbs into a steaming basin. There was a faint scuffling sound as if some creature fled for cover. By the expressions on the faces of the servants and those who had followed them back to Camelot, they would have liked to do the same.

A warrior approached the pallet. He obviously experienced no such trepidation. He wore leather tunic, breeches, and boots in muted colors that blended with the colors of the forest like the other warriors who had hunted that day. But the mantle about his shoulders was a rich, dark blue. The blue of the royal house of Anjou.

"The lady is my wife, warrior," he reminded Truan in a low, deceptively calm voice. "I highly value every bone in that wrist." In the simple statement was an unspoken threat. "I understand your concern for the girl, but it will be poorly served if you break the wrist of the only one who can help her. And then I will be forced to break your neck."

Rorke FitzWarren, chancellor to the English king, William, carried no weapon. Like the others who had hunted that day, his battle sword had been exchanged for the bow, spear, and pike, far more effective weapons against boar and stag. But he was a proven warrior on many battlefields, including the Battle of Hastings nearly two years earlier, which had seen the defeat of King Harold and led to the conquest of England by William of Normandy, the Conqueror.

"Enough of this," Vivian told them both. "We have no time for this." She looked across at Truan.

"She saved my son's life," she said gently, using her powers to persuade him with every word, for time grew short. "I owe her no less than to save hers. 'Tis a healer's touch she needs, sir warrior, but I cannot help her if you break my arm."

Another warrior stepped to Truan's side. "I have experienced her healing powers myself, my friend. If anyone may save her, the Lady Vivian can, for her powers are great. I carry the scars that are proof of it. You must trust in her for there is no certainty except that Amber will die without it."

Stephen of Valois, son of the king and now master of Camelot, spoke convincingly and without threat. The two men had fought together against Malagraine and the powers of Darkness in recent months past. The bond of friendship and trust forged through blood in battle was a strong one.

Truan's gaze never wavered from that as blue as his own as he stared at Lady Vivian, her beautiful features framed by the fiery fall of coppery hair that had come unbound in that frantic ride back to Camelot.

No threat from her husband, nor the combined strength of ten warriors, could have made him release her. But in that blue gaze he saw tenderness, compassion, and honesty. Eventually, his fingers loosened about her arm.

"She must live!" he said, his voice almost a whisper, the fierceness gone now, but filled with a sort of desperate anguish.

Vivian rubbed her bruised wrist. Though she had felt no true danger from him, still she could not free herself until he chose to release her. That was most unusual. Equally unusual, she had no sense of his thoughts as she did so easily of others as if they willingly spoke their thoughts aloud.

His thoughts were strangely hidden from her, behind some impenetrable wall she could not see through. But there was no hiding his emotions, there for all—both mortal and immortal alike—to see in his fierce protectiveness of the girl.

She had seen such anger in her own husband, most recently a few moments ago, and knew it came from the need to protect when one cared deeply.

Vivian's sister, Cassandra, had spoken of the girl's attachment to Truan Monroe. Only he had been able to make the girl smile and laugh again after she first came to Camelot. But something had happened between them, and he had avoided Amber the past months, looking through her as if she did not exist, retreating from the castle if a chance encounter found them alone.

No one could find the cause for it, for the girl was liked by all at Camelot. In the past months, she had matured from a young girl who had experienced too much harshness of life into a slender young woman of rare beauty and grace.

Though bound by a world of silence brought on by the tragedies she had suffered, she communicated through the use of sign language, which Meg had taught her. The signing language, made by a series of hand movements, allowed her to convey her thoughts to others.

The children of Camelot, like children everywhere,

sometimes found it frustrating to make adults understand them. Amber's language of hand movements gave them the ability to communicate in another way. Even some of the battle-hardened warriors and knights were seen communicating with hand signals, which they found an effective means to silently convey messages.

Yet, no matter what his actions of the past months conveyed, the emotions Vivian saw now made a lie of them all. He cared deeply for the girl.

"I can stop the excessive flow of blood and close the wounds," she gently explained, trying to give him hope. "I will ease the pain so that she cannot feel it, and keep her in deep sleep so that she may recover her strength. That is the easy part."

Truan frowned as he looked across at her. He knew that was no easy task at all. She smiled softly. Then the smile disappeared, replaced by a frown that drew her delicate brows together over somber blue eyes.

"But I cannot give back life where there is none, or summon it back when it is gone. That is the burden of the power which I possess. 'Tis both gift and curse. Nor," she added, pausing, her blue gaze meeting his, "can I give her the will to live. That is within her alone. A choice of the heart and soul that she must make."

And in those words both knew lay Amber's fate. For she had suffered greatly when her family was brutally murdered and her village destroyed. In her shame, pain, and guilt, she had wondered why she alone had been spared, though she had not escaped the brutality the others had suffered. Old Meg once confided the girl wished she had also died that day rather than live with the shame afterward.

"But she is alive now," Truan reminded her, hopefully. "Surely that is a good sign."

Vivian thought of William of Normandy, now king of

England, as he lay close to death after the battle of Hastings. Her husband had ridden across England for two days to find her, following rumors of the fabled healer who was the only one who might save his master. He had abducted her and forced her to return with him and heal the conqueror's wounds.

She had hated William then. He had taken everything from her people in the conquest of Saxon England. But in that conquest, he had given far more back to her through the love and passion she discovered with the man who was now her husband and the son whose life Amber had saved.

Out of war and death had come hope for the future. Her family was reunited, the powers of Darkness were banished from the mortal world, and her father, Merlin, had been released from the curse that had imprisoned him in the world between the worlds.

But she sensed there had been no peace for Truan Monroe, the mysterious warrior who had traveled across the Irish sea and pledged his sword to Stephen all those months ago. Emotions ran deep and true thoughts were hidden. There was far more to this brave, fierce young warrior than anyone knew.

"Aye, 'tis a good sign," she admitted, giving him hope. "Now, bring the candles closer and let me see what must be done."

Leaning over the pallet, she pulled back the mantle Truan had wrapped about Amber when he found her in the woods. It was wet, blood soaking through the heavy dark green wool.

Vivian had practiced the healing arts all her life. The ability to stop the flow of blood and mend flesh with a skillful touch of the hand, the power of the ages flowing through her in a sort of healing energy that seamed the torn edges of wounds back together, and mended shattered bone like the piecing together of fragments of shattered crockery until the whole of the pieces was stronger than before.

She cringed at sight of the damage that had been done, her heart constricting painfully as she sensed with just the touch of her hand near the wound how much pain the girl had suffered to save her son.

Once, near London, Vivian had been attacked by a wild boar. But that had been a creature of the Darkness, with unusual powers that had almost destroyed her. She was startled to discover that these wounds were not unlike those, the precise, methodical slashes meant not to merely cripple and bring down, but to kill and destroy.

She knew enough about animals to know that most creatures did not attack out of viciousness, but killed only when hungry or frightened. And such creatures did not attack humans, but rather chose to avoid humans, if possible.

Not satisfied with the first attack, the creature Amber encountered had struck again and again in a different place each time, for the sheer pleasure of it. What had provoked such an attack?

Cassandra, now lady of Camelot, carried a basin of steaming water laced with medicinal herbs from the brazier. Though she did not possess Vivian's unique skills, she had considerable knowledge of herbal potions and healing ways.

Cassandra had been raised at Tregaron in the West Country before her marriage to Lord Stephen. There, she had been in charge of the care of those who lived at Tregaron. She was knowledgeable in the treatment of ailments such as fever, ague and scurvy, boils, and the usual assortment of cuts, smashed fingers, and other wounds.

She had seen her share of hunting accidents, men

attacked by wild boar and gored by stag. But she paled as the mantle was drawn back, exposing the wounds.

"What sort of creature could have made such wounds?"

"A wolf," Truan replied, his gaze meeting hers across the pallet.

"Those are not the wounds of a wolf," Rorke replied. "Those wounds were made with a weapon."

"I saw the beast," Truan replied with certainty. "It *was* a wolf. Then, it disappeared in the shadows as if it had never been there at all." It was the first time he had spoken of the encounter, which reminded him of another encounter in the forest in the middle of a blinding snowstorm.

That day in the forest he and Lady Cassandra had come upon a creature born of mortal flesh and blood but with the powers of Darkness—a man who took the form of a beast and then disappeared into the shadows. Truan knew her unspoken fear—that the creature had not died in the freezing storm, but might somehow have survived.

"Surely it could not have disappeared completely," Cassandra replied, her expression and the grave tone of her voice telling him that she did indeed remember.

"As if it were made out of air," Truan replied. "Flesh and blood one moment, then gone as if it became one with the mist."

"You must all go now," Vivian told them, taking charge. "There is much to be done." To the old woman, Meg, who stirred another herbal potion at the fire, she said, "Stay with me, I will have need of you." Then she turned to Truan.

"Leave us," she said gently. "There is nothing you can do here." When he glanced down at the pale, silent girl, she assured him, "I will send word as soon as I have finished." This time, it was Vivian who gently took hold of his hand between her own, trying to give him comfort in the connection of her healing touch.

Truan immediately felt the gentle warmth that flowed through her touch and moved along his skin, easing the coldness of dread and fear, which was like an icy hand about his heart. He nodded, then wordlessly turned to leave.

Alone with Amber, Vivian immediately turned her thoughts inward, concentrating on the power deep within her, summoning it, until she felt it move through her. A fiery current that flowed like molten blood through her veins, the power of the Light mending torn muscle and sinew where she touched, seaming the flesh back together, leaving behind a faint pink scar where the wound had been. Then, even before she moved on to the next wound, the scar faded and all but disappeared, leaving behind healthy skin.

Truan paused at the door to the chamber. He glanced back at the pallet where Amber lay so still and silent, her golden hair fanned out across the fur, her shoulders bare above the fur that covered her.

Her blue-green eyes were closed. She had not roused since he found her. Her thoughts were closed, deep in a void of unconsciousness where no pain or memory could reach her.

Still, he wondered, what had she seen in those last moments when he found her, and what would she remember.

He turned, seizing his sword and the shorter hunting knife, his mouth thinned in a determined line, his thoughts already returning to that forest clearing stained with Amber's blood as he strode purposefully from the chamber.

Stephen followed, calling orders to his men. He

paused at the doorway and glanced back at Cassandra. A silent thought passed between them.

She remembered that long ago encounter in the forest, the strange creature Truan had seen, and like an icy hand, fear closed around her heart.

Her step-sister Margeaux, whom she'd been raised with, had died that day after her unborn child had been brutally cut out of her and she was left to bleed to death. The child had been fathered by Malagraine, whose evil had threatened to destroy them all.

What Truan saw that day was not a child, but a man full grown who disappeared in a blinding snowstorm. Neither the child, nor the man he had seen, were ever found, though it was thought neither could have survived, if they were human, for the storm was unlike anything anyone had experienced in the West Country with freezing snow turning everything to ice. If not for Truan, she too would have perished, for her powers were strangely effected by the cold that day. As though some evil inhabited the forest. An evil with powers as strong as her own.

Nothing Cassandra could say would stop them from returning to the forest now, but she drew comfort that they would be together. She trusted her husband's skills as a warrior. He had braved the powers of Darkness, risking his life to save her and their own unborn child. Truan was like a brother to her. He had saved her life once before. She trusted him no less.

The wolf raised its nose and picked up the scent, mixed with pungent cedar, musky oak, and the deeper verdant essence of the forest. Mist clung to its coat, glistening at the ends of dark fur, gleaming eyes set among sharply angled features.

Then a sound—the snap of a twig and the almost indiscernible sound of a footfall in the soft loam that covered the floor of the forest—human sounds, and human scent.

Dark eyes gleamed. The wolf turned and dove into the thick cover of the forest, sweeping under low-hanging branches, bounding over fallen logs, following the scent as a need as old as time burned through the creature's blood—the need to kill. . . .

The candle flames guttered faintly. Cassandra looked up as the warrior slipped silently into the chamber and made his way to the pallet where Amber lay.

Beads of mist glittered in the shaggy mane of dark hair that fell to his shoulders. A thick growth of beard shadowed his jaw. Fatigue lined handsome features set in a grim expression. His dark blue gaze fastened on Amber.

It had been hours since her sister, Vivian, had finished closing the last of the wounds and applied healing poultices, which in time would remove all trace of the injuries. Then, exhausted, Vivian had sought her own chamber to see to the needs of her son, Kaden, and to reassure herself once more that he was indeed all right. With her own son being cared for by old Meg, Cassandra insisted on remaining with Amber.

The girl was pale beneath the layer of furs that covered her against the night chill. She had stirred only once as Vivian closed the wounds, as if in some horrible torment of pain. But it had subsided and then she lay quiet afterward.

"We will not speak of this to anyone, yet," Vivian had whispered, frowning. Without her speaking them aloud, Cassandra had understood Vivian's fears as easily as if she had spoken them.

"You cannot know if her blood has been poisoned," Cassandra insisted. "Perhaps it was a true wolf that attacked her. Then there is no reason for concern."

"I pray you are right, sister. But if not, then we have much to fear, for if it was a creature of the Darkness that attacked her, then there is the possibility that the creature's blood has mixed with hers, the same as if she had been conceived of a creature of Darkness."

Cassandra shivered as she again remembered the encounter in the forest months ago, her step-sister's brutal death, the child cut from her body while she still lived—a child born with the blood of a mortal human and a creature of the Darkness flowing through its veins. She said nothing now of Vivian's fears to Truan.

"The wounds are closed," she said in answer to his unspoken question as he stood beside the pallet and looked down at Amber. "She is sleeping deeply. 'Tis best, so that she can regain her strength."

"Will she live?"

Cassandra stared down at her folded hands thinking how best to answer. "So it seems."

For the first time since entering the chamber, he seemed to relax, weariness appearing at his face.

"You have been here all this time. You must be tired."

She smiled faintly. "Aye, and in some discomfort, but Vivian was near exhaustion and she had not yet seen young Kaden after our return. I told her that I would stay with Amber, and I wished to know that you had safely returned."

"We both returned safely," Truan replied, his handsome mouth thinning to a hard line. She sensed his disappointment. They had not found what they sought in the forest.

"Then you were not able to find the wolf."

His silence was answer enough, and she knew they would return to the forest until the creature was found.

"You spoke of discomfort. Are you unwell?" Truan asked.

" 'Tis a malady that my son can remedy," she said with a faint smile, wincing slightly as she gently laid her hands over her engorged breasts. "I've been away from him too long, while his needs have been temporarily seen to, I fear mine have not. If I do not go to him soon, I fear I shall burst." Her smile deepened.

" 'Tis amazing that with all my powers, I cannot ease this!" With slender hands cupped beneath her breasts, she emphasized the painful fullness of the engorged flesh.

"I think your husband may be able to offer some relief for your discomfort," Truan replied with unembarrassed candor, his manner much eased now that he had seen that Amber still lived and rested comfortably.

"He spoke of little else on the return ride."

Her cheeks flamed with color. The bluntness with which men shared such things never failed to amaze her. But then her husband had felt no reservation about being with her when their son was born, a time when most men usually took to the hunt or battle, or fled far afield, waiting for someone to tell them of it afterward.

But as their child was about to be born, Stephen had refused to be sent from the birthing chamber, watching with awe and humility as his son entered the world. He insisted that he be the first to hold his son, only moments old and still covered with her blood. Since then, in the privacy of their chamber, she often found him watching with that same awe and humility as she nursed the child.

"Do not be embarrassed," Truan told her. "You are fortunate that you have someone with whom you can share such feelings."

"You too will share such things with someone one day," Cassandra replied.

His expression changed, the smile disappearing, replaced by a frown. He shook his head.

"Never."

It was not said in anger, but with grim determination. Cassandra sensed it was not so much by choice as by what he considered to be his fate, as though some great inner struggle went on deep inside him. But when she laid a hand on his arm, and tried to sense his thoughts, he gently smiled. His thoughts were closed to her.

"Your husband and son await, milady. I thank you for your kindness."

When she had gone, Truan slowly approached the pallet where Amber lay. Her breathing was regular and even. Color had returned to her cheeks and her skin was cool to the touch. She rested peacefully except for the small frown that drew her slender brows together as though she might be in pain.

He stroked his fingers across those tiny frown lines, gently massaging them until they disappeared.

Her skin—the first time he had allowed himself to touch her except for earlier in the forest—was like warm satin, the feel of it burning through his memory as he recalled the last time he had touched her. That brief encounter months ago, when he foolishly allowed their friendship to become something more.

Unable to keep his hands off her, unable to deny the even more powerful desires that raged within him, he had kissed her. For a moment giving in to the feelings and emotions that tore at him. Impossible feelings that still remained, but that he kept hidden from everyone. Especially Amber.

Impossible.

Yet, as she lay there in a deep sleep, oblivious to pain

and everything else about her, he couldn't help but think of that kiss. A kiss that should have never been because of the sadness it brought her and the pain it brought him.

"If only it had never happened," Truan whispered. "Then you would not remember it."

In his thoughts, he created an image. Then, closing his eyes, he focused on the image. When he opened his eyes again, he held a feather in his hand. It was a brilliant shade of blue with lighter shadings of green at the ends. The exact color of her eyes.

He lightly stroked the feather across her lips, wanting so much more. If he kissed her now, she would not remember it. She would not even know of it.

"Forgive me, Amber." And in those words, he asked forgiveness for so much more. For lies and deception, for what he was and could never be. Then he kissed her, slowly, tenderly, lowering his mouth to hers, drinking her in, until the taste of her filled his soul like a memory.

Forgive me.

He slept in the chair by the brazier and dreamed. Of wars and battles, of light and darkness, and a recurring image that appeared from out of the shadows and mist— a creature that carried a wrapped bundle in its teeth.

In his dream, he pursued the creature, which eluded capture, always escaping a few steps away. Eventually, he began to close the distance, until it seemed he might actually catch the creature. When it was almost within reach, he saw that the creature was a magnificent black wolf.

Mist glistened at the tips of its thick, dark fur. Equally dark eyes gleamed back at him with a wise, knowing expression as if they shared a secret. Then the creature sprang away, disappearing in the forest, leaving the bundle behind.

He knelt beside the bundle, carefully opening the folds of the rich, brilliant blue cloth wrapped about it with the tip of his sword. A tiny hand emerged, followed by another, small fists waving in the air as the blanket fell open, revealing a naked baby.

It was a boy, strong and healthy, with thick dark hair that molded his head in a lustrous dark cap, and eyes as brilliant in color as the blanket. They were wise eyes, ancient eyes, with the truth of the ages and the promise of the future staring back at him.

In his dream, as he reached for the child, the wolf reappeared, snatching the child, wrapped once more in the blanket, from his grasp. He rose to his feet and with drawn sword went after the wolf.

It stopped at the edge of the clearing, the child wrapped in the blanket, dangling from powerful jaws. In the wolf's dark eyes and in lips pulled back over vicious teeth in a deadly smile, he saw a silent, unspoken challenge.

"If you do not fear the darkness, then follow me . . ."

Three

Follow me . . .

As Amber awakened the words slowly faded. Gradually the dream faded as well, until all she could remember were vague, shadowy images that lingered at the edges of her thoughts. Then, they too were gone.

She slowly pushed up on one elbow. A fire in the brazier burned brightly, glowing golden on pale walls.

She recognized the chamber as one on the upper level, above the main courtyard. It was furnished with only a table, chair, and the pallet, on which she lay. Then she found the feather.

It was brilliant blue, the rich color glistening against the dark fur of the pallet. As she held it to the light, green color shimmered among the blue.

Amber stared at it, wondering where it might have come from for she recalled seeing no such feathers among the hunting birds Lord Stephen kept. Then the feather was momentarily forgotten as she discovered a much warmer heat snuggled below at her feet.

She wiggled her toes and felt a faint stirring. Wiggled them again and received a grunted response. Then a whiskered nose appeared at the edge of the blanket, followed by two beady eyes.

Pippen. He was a small bearlike creature of dubious

origin, with a sleek, dark coat, ringed tail, sharp eyes
that missed nothing, and a puckish disposition. He had
been raised by Lady Cassandra from a cub and considered most of Camelot—at least the vast kitchens and
storerooms with their abundant stores of food—to be
his private domain. Food was his first passion.

Somehow, he had found his way into the chamber
and now burrowed beneath the blankets at her feet.
Comfort was his second passion.

At any given hour of the day he might be found either
rummaging through barrels and hogsheads for anything edible, or burrowing into a cozy nest for a nap.

Amber wiggled her toes again, uncertain why it
seemed important that she could, and immediately received a disgruntled response from Pippen at being un-
ceremoniously dislodged from his warm burrow.

Then, it all came back to her in a rush of painful,
terrifying memories—the picnic in the meadow, Kaden
wandering into the forest, the encounter with the wolf,
and the attack . . .

She moved her legs beneath the layers of warm fur
and felt only a mild twinge of pain, much like that of
overused muscles. She grabbed the edge of the blanket,
threw it back, and immediately shivered at the rush of
cold morning air against her bare skin.

Her nakedness stirred images of other memories of
her clothes being cut away. She lightly ran her fingers
down the length of her right thigh and lower leg, feeling the tender raised patchwork of pale scars.

"I am pleased to see that you are feeling better."

Amber hastily retrieved the furs and pulled them
against her as Lady Vivian entered the chamber, carrying a bowl of steaming liquid that smelled not of vaguely
remembered herbs or medicines, but of rich, hearty

stew, with thick chunks of steaming bread, and apple tartlets in cream sauce that set her mouth to watering.

"I thought perhaps something more substantial today," Vivian suggested as she directed a young serving girl to place the trencher and bowl on the nearby table.

"It will help you regain your strength." She saw the direction of Amber's gaze, a slender ankle exposed at the edge of the fur with a particularly nasty scar now only barely visible in the curve of ankle.

"It required considerable skill to close the wound," Vivian explained, "but I thought it preferable to hobbling about on one leg and a wooden stick." That brought a smile to the girl's face.

How long have I been here? Amber asked, in gestures of the hand signals Meg had taught her.

"Five days," Vivian replied, removing the linen cloth from a basket of warm bread.

"Do you remember anything that happened?"

Amber frowned, struggling with vague memories. *I remember the picnic in the meadow. Kaden had wandered into the forest, and I went after him . . .*

She stared down at the scars on her lower leg, remembering far more that was too horrible to think about.

"They will heal in time and hardly be noticeable," Vivian assured her.

Amber shook her head. Her concern was not over scars. She tried to form the sounds of Kaden's name with her hands but it was difficult for there were no sounds for proper names. She became frustrated with the silence that had taken her voice and the speech that came so easily to others, pounding her clenched fists on the pallet beside her.

Tears sprang into her eyes, anger adding to her frustration. Her inability to speak had prevented her calling Kaden back from the danger that waited in the forest.

Words tumbled through her thoughts. And she could say none of them!

Vivian sensed the girl's anguish and gently took hold of her hands. "It's all right. I can understand your thoughts. You have only to think them the same as speaking."

Amber looked up at her with tear-filled eyes and in her thoughts spoke a single word, the child's name.

"Kaden?"

Vivian wrapped an arm comfortingly around the girl's slender shoulders as she assured her, "Thanks to you, my son is safe. He was unharmed except for a few minor scrapes and bruises which have already healed. I fear you suffered the worst of it." She saw doubt in the girl's expression.

"I assure you, I speak the truth. I have had my hands full the last days keeping him from this chamber. He has grown very fond of you." She felt the girl sag against her.

"I couldn't bear it if anything had happened to him," Amber said through the connection of their thoughts. *"I didn't see the wolf until it was upon him."* She closed her eyes and shivered as the memory returned. *"We would have been killed, if not for the other wolf."*

Vivian was stunned. "There was another wolf?"

It was the first anyone knew there had been two wolves in the forest that day. She handed Amber a cup of a soothing tisane that she had brewed.

Amber sipped the faintly sweet tea slowly. *"It attacked the first wolf and drove it off."* She shivered again at the memory.

"At first I thought I imagined or dreamed of it." She frowned as she recalled the memory. *"It was a little like dreaming it, the sudden explosion of light surrounded by mist in the forest . . ."*

Vivian sensed her hesitation at a part of the memory that she struggled with, as if even now she did not believe it.

"Do you remember something else?"

"It's like waking from a dream and you can only remember part of it," Amber replied, struggling with vague, illusive images. *"You know there is more that you should remember, but cannot."*

The more she tried to remember the more it slipped away from her. Vivian took the empty cup from her.

"It will come back to you in time," she assured her. "When you are ready to remember it."

"And what of the words?" Amber asked. *"Will I ever be able to speak again? Or must I constantly live with this silence, with others thinking me some sort of addle-pated mute who is to be pitied."*

Though Vivian could have used her powers to force the girl to speak, she hesitated, knowing the cure might easily be more dangerous than the malady.

The mind was a fragile thing, made up of wishes, dreams, and secrets. Amber had buried the pain of her loss deep, along with her ability to speak of it. By forcing her to confront the horror of what had happened that long ago day when her family died might easily cause the girl more pain, forcing her to retreat even farther into silence, perhaps even madness.

"I know of no magical cure," Vivian told her gently. "You have the ability to speak. It will return when the pain of *not* speaking is more than the pain of old memories."

Struggling to understand, yet disappointed, Amber nodded. The tisane had eased much of the soreness from her muscles, and now her appetite seemed to be making up for a diet of little more than broth over the past five days.

* * *

"I think you're going to live after all," Vivian laughed as Amber scooped the last crumbs of apple tartlet into her mouth with the same enthusiasm with which she'd launched herself into the meal.

In short order, the girl had consumed a trencher of hearty stew, three hard-boiled eggs, several slices of cheese, a thick slab of ham, and three apple tartlets. It was difficult to tell where it had all gone in such a reed-thin body.

"Now we must see what is to be done about your hair and clothes," she announced. "There was nothing to be saved of your gown."

Amber nodded, eagerly swinging her legs over the side of the pallet. She wobbled unsteadily on her feet and quickly sat down again.

Vivian was immediately beside her, wrapping a supportive arm about her waist. "It's like that at first," she reassured her. "The muscles are still healing. You must give them time to grow strong again." She helped Amber to a nearby chair.

"In a short while you will be as strong as before. Not even the scars will remain." She tucked a thick fur about Amber's legs, then went to the door and summoned servants who had been waiting outside.

They carried in buckets of hot water that steamed in the cool morning air, a bowl of fragrant soap that smelled of the forest, thick linens, and several garments, which they laid across the bed. Then four stout young lads carried in a large iron caldron that closely resembled one of the kettles used in the kitchens.

Amber's uncertainty about the use of the kettle wavered as bucketful after bucketful of water was emptied into the huge pot, then vanished altogether as Vivian assisted her into the steaming bath after the servants had gone.

Vivian added a fragrant powder, which she explained had been ground from pungent dried leaves, and Amber quickly decided she didn't care if she was the main course being offered up for the next meal.

The fragrant powder mixed in the water was like a soothing balm that eased the painful itchiness of the rapidly healing wounds, and the heat eased the ache of bruised muscles.

Afterward, Amber sat before the fire in the brazier her skin aglow from the heated bath and smelling of soap scented with pine oil. Vivian brushed her hair as it dried, the light from the flames in the brazier glowing in the rich gold thickness that fell to her hips.

" 'Tis a small thing," Vivian replied when Amber protested that she was doing the work of a servant. "You saved my son's life. 'Tis a debt I can never repay."

She watched the girl's reflection in the hammered metal used as a reflecting plate.

"The color of your hair 'tis like your name," Vivian said as she brushed. "Amber that flows from the trees in the forest, catching the rays of the sun until it looks like liquid gold."

She paused in the brushing to lay a hand over the soft swell of her stomach. "One day soon I will have a daughter whose hair I will be able to brush just like this." She smiled, as she resumed brushing. "A daughter with dark hair like her father's, and her grandfather's deep blue eyes."

At the surprise in Amber's glance, she shook her head. "Nay, my husband does not know of it yet. He will not be greatly pleased for Kaden's birth was difficult, and he vowed he would not put me through it again. But I have longed for another child. Kaden grows far too spoiled. He must learn the ways of sharing with brothers and sisters. I must simply find the right moment to tell my husband—a moment between battles and warring, when he is most pleased about something and very likely not to yell at me about it."

In the reflecting plate she watched as Amber smoothed the soft, finely woven wool of the gown she now wore. It was a rare shade of blue that brought out the color of her eyes, the softly carded yarn dyed from rare dewberries. She understood the appreciative gesture, known to any woman who has ever received anything so fine.

"It was a gift from Truan," she replied, answering the question in Amber's thoughts. And at the girl's startled expression, explained, "He insisted that you have the gown to replace the one that was ruined. Somehow, he felt responsible."

Amber's thoughts were vivid in the startled expression at her eyes.

"It was Truan who found you," Vivian went on to explain. "If he had not come upon you when he did . . ." Silence hung between them, with only the hiss of pungent wood in the brazier.

A soft frown curved Amber's lips as she struggled again with vague, illusive memories of shadowy images that refused to be remembered.

Vivian finished brushing her hair, plaiting it with lengths of yarn the same color as the gown. When she had finished, she gathered linens and herbal decoctions in her basket.

" 'Tis enough for one day," she told Amber. "You should rest now. You will feel stronger tomorrow. Perhaps the day after you will be ready for a short walk. Meg is most eager to see you," she added, sliding the handle of the basket of herbs and medicines over her arm. "She will bring supper later."

Amber stopped her with a slender hand on her arm as Vivian turned to leave.

"Thank you, for saving my life."

Vivian laid her hand over Amber's and squeezed tightly. "Thank *you*, for saving my son's life."

After she had gone, Amber dozed in the chair before the brazier, the heat wrapping around her, Pippen warming her feet, her fingers closed over a blue feather.

In those last moments before sleep, vague, half-formed images drifted through her thoughts. Shadowy images of a terrifying creature, an explosion of light, and a man where the wolf had been, stepping through a circle of light, reaching for her.

Amber felt much stronger the following day. Strong enough in fact that after the young serving girl from the kitchen collected the empty trencher, she threw back the fur blanket and swung her legs over the edge of the pallet.

She lowered one foot then the other to the smooth stone floor. Then, in tentative steps, she crossed the room to the table.

Pippen watched her progress from the corner of the chamber with a vague disinterested expression while intently polishing off the last of several apples.

"Do not be so smug," she thought. *"You have four legs to waddle upon while I have only two, and those as weak as water reeds."*

Her knees wobbled and would have gone out from under her had she not grabbed the back of the chair for support. Pippen made a chattering noise that sounded suspiciously like laughter.

"Arrogant beast!" Amber thought as she concentrated all her effort at remaining upright. She felt as if she had accomplished something quite remarkable when she crossed the chamber back to the pallet.

Just as Lady Vivian had promised, she felt stronger with each step. She sat on the pallet once more, contemplating yet another day that loomed ahead with those four walls closing in on her.

Meg had brought the morning meal, fussing over her as if she were an invalid. She had brought Kaden with her. Amber was delighted to see the child, who seemed none the worse for his ordeal in the forest.

He was his usual mischievous self, exploring the chamber on tiny legs that were constantly in motion, hands reaching for anything that was just beyond reach with the typical curiosity of a child who has only recently discovered the larger world to be explored, laughing with glee as Pippen played at hide-and-seek, unaware the animal undoubtedly wished only to escape those small grasping hands.

Meg finally removed him with the promise of a visit to the practice yard where he could watch the knights in their contests at mock battle.

Now Pippen was determined to abandon her as well, scratching at the chamber door, eager to be off on his morning rounds of the castle.

She walked to the door, growing more confident of her returned strength with each step. Pippen darted out the door without a backward glance, heading straight for the stairs that led to the main hall below, where at this time of the morning the servants would be clearing the last of the morning meal from the long tables.

The sun was warm on the stones of the floor where it fell through the open shutters. Through the window opening, she heard the now familiar sounds of Camelot—a burst of laughter, the buzz of distant conversations, the occasional bartering and haggling at the marketplace that drifted to her on the morning breeze along with the sound of carts lumbering beyond the walls of the practice yard, and over all, the sound of weapons as Lord Stephen's knights practiced at mock battle in the yard below.

She leaned out the window opening hoping to catch sight of them, but the corner tower blocked her view. The spring air was sweet, the sun warm on her face, but it was not enough. She longed to be outside.

She shivered as the memory of the brutal attack on her village returned. Though she tried to force it back, it came in flashes of images as though she saw them still—the smoldering ruins of the cottages and huts; the bodies of men, women, and children that lay where they had died; the priest dead on the steps of the small church where he had begged the invaders to spare the villagers.

Her father and two older brothers died outside the daub and wattle cottage. Inside, the bodies of her mother and two smaller brothers bloodied the pungent straw on the floor as the Norse barbarians took anything of value—food, clothing, metal tools and weapons—then methodically destroyed the furnishings her father and brothers had skillfully crafted, smashed the weaver's loom where her mother sat of an evening before the open fire, and shattered the small wood cradle. Then they discovered her, crouched in the corner, protecting her younger sister.

She slashed at the barbarian with a carving blade her father had given her when he sent her into the cottage with her mother and the younger children. She might as well have attacked with her bare hands for all the good it did.

Her younger sister was dragged from the cottage,

paralyzed with fear, her eyes wide with horror at the sight of their murdered family. Amber never saw her again. Then their attacker turned to her. He had far different things in mind for her.

Even now, she could not bear to be closed in small, tight places. It reminded her of the horror of that day, when she had been trapped, unable to escape, and all she could do was fix her gaze on the wall of the cottage until it was over.

Now, she closed her eyes, forcing the images back into the dark corners of her memory. She hadn't thought of that day in a very long time, yet it was never very far away. When she opened her eyes they were once more clear and dry.

Perhaps if she had been able to cry that day, to scream and wail for her loss, perhaps in that way she might have been able to exorcise the pain. But there were no tears. Not then, not now. There were only walls that closed in, reminders of things she didn't wish to remember . . .

She slipped quietly out the chamber door, glancing first in one direction then the other to make certain no one saw her, for they would surely make her return to the chamber out of concern. But her need to escape was far stronger than the need for rest.

The morning meal was long past, the halls of the castle empty. As she slowly walked through the passageways she heard the distant sounds of servants in the chambers below replenishing food in the kitchen from the pantry, granary, and smokehouse in preparation for the midday and evening meals.

Her chamber was one of several on the second floor, connected by a covered balcony that looked out onto a small secluded courtyard that opened onto the larger courtyard where she had heard the sounds of mock battle as Lord Stephen's knights practiced with their weapons.

As she approached the end of the hall that connected to the star-chamber where Lord Stephen met with his knights in council, she heard voices.

Old Meg had once said that when one lost the use of one of their senses, the others made up for it. The old woman knew what she spoke of, for though blinded since birth, she possessed uncanny hearing. Robbed of the ability to speak, Amber's hearing was equally acute.

She had learned to listen to the subtle nuances of speech and easily recognized the voices of Lady Cassandra and Lady Vivian in the nursery chamber as she passed by.

She had often joined them there with their sister, Brianna, while the children played. As the children grew tired and napped, they spoke of healing ways, different herbs and medicinals used for different ailments.

These conversations often gave way to gossip of King William and life at court, which she listened to with fascination, the retelling of darker tales in solemn whispers, laughing, sometimes crying, reconnecting the fragile bond of their family as they spoke of Merlin while gazing at their own sleeping babies.

Other times they shared lewd jokes with careful glances in her direction, until old Meg clucked at them like a mother hen.

"What will the girl think?" she had admonished the sisters on more than one occasion. "You make even this old woman blush with your talk."

"What know you of such things?" Brianna asked one morning not long ago.

"I suspect she knows much more than she would care for us to know," Vivian replied, with a sly glance at the old woman.

"Bah!" Meg replied from where she sat in the corner, thin hands busy winding balls of yarn for weaving.

"I have led a solitary life, devoting myself to the teaching of those placed in my care. There is nothing to tell."

"*You* must tell us!" Cassandra encouraged Vivian, when it was obvious the old woman intended to tell them nothing. Vivian's eyes danced with mischief, even as her expression became most solemn.

"Our mother heard it from her mother. She told me that Meg was quite a beauty as a young woman."

This was told even as Meg hunched herself into a tight ball within her chair and muttered about high-spirited young women with nothing better to do than gossip.

" 'Tis said her hair was once as dark and glossy as a raven's wing, her skin fair as a summer morn, and her body that of a lush young maid."

From the corner, Meg sniffed with disapproval and promptly turned her back on the sisters as Vivian continued.

" 'Tis also said that more than one young man fancied mistress Meg, and attempted to lure her to a secret place where they might have their way with her."

Meg pitched a yarn ball into a nearby basket on the floor. It hit with such force that the basket rocked and swayed precariously, drawing the attention of Pippen. When he waddled over to inspect this new diversion, he wandered too near Meg's chair. She chose to vent her displeasure on Pippen with a well-aimed foot at his well-padded backside.

Wise in the ways of such things, and frequently in trouble, Pippen merely scuttled out of her way with amazing speed and made off with a ball of yarn, batting it back and forth between his front paws like a ball, unraveling all Meg's work of the previous several hours.

" 'Tis also said one enterprising young man very

nearly succeeded," Vivian went on to tell them, nimbly removing a sharp needle from Kaden's reach as she sat at her tapestry.

"He befriended her and gave her fine gifts. Then one day, certain of his success and knowing of her skills at healing, he pretended an injury in the stables. When she went to see how badly he was injured, he tried to seduce her."

As if connected by some invisible thread, both Brianna and Cassandra turned to stare at the old woman.

"Then what happened?" they asked in unison.

Vivian leaned forward and lowered her voice discreetly. " 'Tis said that first he kissed her. Then, entranced by her bewitching beauty, put his hands under her skirts. That is when it happened."

"What happened?" the sisters demanded simultaneously.

"He vanished in a puff of smoke," Vivian replied. "Very nearly set the stables on fire."

Cassandra burst into laughter. "Aye," she said, fanning herself with a slender hand. "I have felt such heat."

"And when the smoke had cleared?" Brianna asked. "What happened then?"

"When it cleared the young man was gone, and in his place was an ass."

"She had transformed him?"

"It was thought so, for he was never seen again."

All four of them, including Amber, had turned and stared at Meg. Having had enough of their humor at her expense, the old woman abandoned the chair, and holding her bony frame as erect as possible, swept past them. But it was she who had the last laugh on them.

" 'Twas not that he attempted to seduce me," she informed them with a cool air of disdain as she reached the door of the chamber. " 'Twas the size of his manhood. A wee, disappointing nubbin it was." Then she swept out the door, leaving them all in stunned silence, mouths agape.

Amber heard their soft laughter now as she passed by the chamber. Meg was with them in spite of the previous affront, for she was never far from the babies.

In the main hall below, tables and benches had been cleared to the sides of the great room. Wax had cooled at the candles, a faint smoky pine scent lingering in the air. She heard the gossipy voices of servants as they went about their chores in the kitchens and scullery.

She escaped the main hall, pausing for a moment in the warm, spring sun. It had required a great deal more strength than she anticipated to reach this far. She felt weak, newly mended muscles quivering from the exertion. But she wasn't about to turn back.

After a time, the weakness passed and she made her way slowly along the walkway below the balcony that lined the courtyard where Lord Stephen's knights practiced.

It was a large open courtyard, formed by the wall of the main hall at one end, the sides formed by half walls that lined the walkways of the adjacent buildings. The walls were draped with trailing vines of ivy. Above the walkways were the balconies of the second floor chambers, including the living quarters once occupied by King Arthur, the council rooms, and the great room called the star-chamber.

Large gates stood at the opposite end of the courtyard. They opened onto the rows of cottages, huts, and buildings of the castle inhabitants, protected within the high-towered outer walls.

Camelot had been a ghostly, crumbling ruin when they first came here. But many repairs had been made in the year since. Now it was alive with craftsmen and tradesmen who had brought their families to live once more at Camelot.

They had set up their trades within the outer walls. They were joined daily by crofters, herdsmen, and farmers who brought crops, livestock, game hunted in the forests, and pallets of fresh fish to sell at market.

She often accompanied Cassandra and old Meg to the market, for wandering tradesmen often brought rare herbs or powders from some distant port.

One of Lord Stephen's men always accompanied them into the market, to provide coin and a pair of strong arms for carrying their purchases. On these occasions Truan frequently accompanied them, telling stories of the marketplaces found in the eastern empires where he had traveled.

He told stories of white, marble cities with minarets made of gold where holy men called worshippers to afternoon prayers from atop towers. He told of rich and powerful potentates who carried bags of gold to market on the backs of camels. Occasionally when one of those bags broke open—or was cut open by an enterprising thief—coins spilled to the ground and into the hands of the beggars and poor people.

Meg accused him of telling tales, but he had merely smiled at her, then whirling one hand through the air before Amber, he slowly opened each finger. Tiny golden crystals glittered in the air like golden coins once carried by a powerful potentate.

He told stories of exotic marketplaces in the Byzantine empire where rare spices, herbs, and strange powders and opiates could be found. And where a desert chieftain might purchase a fair-skinned girl with golden hair for a handful of rubies.

As he told the story, he took Amber's hand, cradling it in his. She had felt a strange, stirring warmth low inside as his hand held hers.

Amid the mysterious shadows in his eyes, she also saw a glint of laughter as he passed his other hand over their cupped palms. A smoothly polished, blood-red stone lay nestled in the palm of her hand.

"Bah!" Meg had snorted that day. "The simple tricks and conjurements of a fool. What use is golden dust that blows away on the wind or a worthless colored stone?

"If you wish to work magic, my handsome young friend, then conjure a wheel of bread or a pasty before we die of hunger."

Though Amber knew his conjurements were simple tricks no doubt easily explained by the quick conceal-ment of objects within his sleeves or suddenly seized in fingers quicker than the eye, she had kept the polished blood-red stone. It was hidden away in the chamber she shared with Meg.

But Truan no longer accompanied them to market nor sought her out after the evening meal in the great hall. He had been angry with her ever since that night all those months ago, when she had impulsively kissed him, in a foolish attempt to somehow make him under-stand feelings that she hardly understood herself.

Now he spent most of his time with Lord Stephen's men. Other times he disappeared completely, returning as the gates of Camelot were closed for the night, or not at all.

One night, unable to sleep, she had seen him return-ing just before dawn. He passed so close in the hallway outside her chamber she felt the cold that clung to his mantle, and in the light of a torchère on the wall she saw the mist that glistened in the wild mane of dark hair that fell to his shoulders.

Amber felt compelled to make her presence known, wanting to speak with him about that long ago night in an attempt to preserve their friendship, for he was the only one who seemed to understand her pain.

But she fell back into the shadows as the light of the torchère fell across his features, both handsome and terrifying, his eyes aglow with some strange inner light. As if he was not a creature of this world.

She had allowed him to pass by afraid to make her presence known, afraid of the transformation she had seen in him, for there was nothing about him of the light-hearted jester who always had a joke or humorous story to tell.

"Move yer arse, you addle-pated clot!"

Sir Gavin's harsh remonstrance jolted her from her thoughts and back to the present as she passed close by where he and a younger warrior named Gareth circled round each other with swords drawn.

Gareth was only a few years older than she. The young warrior had been squire to Lord FitzWarren and now trained for knighthood.

"Quit gawking at young ladies and concentrate!" Sir Gavin growled at him. "For if you do not, I will carve you up like a pig on a spit. Methinks there will not be much pleasing to look at then!"

Amber knew that she was the cause of Gareth's distraction. He grinned as he caught her attention, barely side-stepped in time as Sir Gavin swung his broadsword where his head had been, then returned his concentration to staying one step ahead of the heavy blade wielded by the older knight with amazing ease and speed.

The two men circled each other, each striking several well-placed blows deflected in turn by the other's blade.

Perspiration beaded Gareth's forehead and ran down the sides of his face, streaking cheeks recently scraped smooth of pale beard that still grew sparsely.

Though he put forth far less effort at first, Sir Gavin soon became more serious about protecting himself. When Gareth struck an unexpected blow at his unprotected side, Sir Gavin acknowledged his pupil's accomplishment with a snarl of approval.

"Aye, that is more like it!"

Then Gavin faked low with a counter move, spun around unexpectedly, and whacked the younger warrior across the backside with the flat of his blade. Caught by surprise, Gareth stumbled. He recovered and whirled around to confront Gavin's blade poised for another blow.

"As I said, young warrior," Sir Gavin grinned through the grime and sweat at his face as Gareth flushed with embarrassment at being foolishly lulled by self-confidence, "move yer arse, or lose it."

All about them, other warriors laughed good-naturedly, for all had suffered the same humiliation and embarrassment at one time or another during their own training.

"Take up your sword, old man," Gareth challenged. "You've substantially more arse to move than me!"

"Ho!" Gavin snorted with delight as others gathered round to watch. "It seems the young pup has a thirst for more." He grinned with pleasure.

"We'll see who's able to sit on his backside at evening meal, and who must stand."

Amber paused to watch. Since coming to Camelot months earlier, Gareth had become a friend. He often sought her out after evening meals. Though she missed Truan, Gareth's friendship helped fill the void of loneliness.

He was an affable young man with sandy hair, blue eyes, and easy laughter. But Meg had warned her there might be other intentions behind the laughter.

He is a young knight in training and they like to wield their blade, especially when it comes to young girls. He may offer you friendship. Make certain he offers you no more.

But Gareth had not treated her as the other men treated the young girls and unattached women who flirted openly with the knights at Camelot as they went about their chores. Their sideways glances, the undulating sway of their skirts, a stroking hand that slipped beneath a tunic, or whispered invitations left no doubt as to their intentions.

Gareth had always been kind to her, occasionally bringing her small gifts—a length of ribbon, a sprig of lavender, or one of the glossy apples stolen from the pantry.

As others gathered about Gareth and Sir Gavin, she slipped away, determined that she would provide no further distraction. If he was to have any hope of escaping his challenge to Sir Gavin unscathed, Gareth would need all his concentration, not to mention strength, speed, and agility.

She had hoped to find Truan, to thank him for the gift of the gown. But he was not among the other warriors who practiced in the main yard. As she stepped through a covered archway, she found him near the large fountain at the far end of the courtyard. He practiced alone, in a secluded place apart from the rest of the men.

He wore no cumbersome chain mail or protective breastplate, but instead had removed his tunic and wore only leggings and doeskin boots that molded his slender hips and long, muscular legs. Nor did he wear thick, leather gauntlets or helm to protect his hands and head. Whereas the other knights wielded large broadswords which required brute strength meant to cleave a man in two, he preferred a Spanish-made sword, which he wielded with breathtaking speed and agility.

Unlike Gareth who had the slender strength of a youth soon to become the man, Truan's strength was like that of a cat—agile, swift, and deadly, corded muscles rippling beneath skin that glistened like wet gold.

His concentration was intense. He seemed oblivious to everything and everyone about him, completely focused on an enemy only he could see.

No two movements were the same as he sliced and carved the air with amazing grace and speed, pulling back, then lunging again, all the more amazing as he whirled back around and she saw that he practiced with his eyes closed!

Others stopped to watch. No doubt they had seen it before in battle as he fought beside them, but they seemed as awestruck as she by the intense power of each movement, like some sort of exquisite, graceful death dance, which was both terrifying and beautiful to watch.

Amber grew increasingly uneasy. His power was barely controlled, relentless, almost brutal. Fear coiled in her stomach, a fear that echoed from the terror of that long ago day when she had watched as her family was slaughtered.

At that moment, she did not know him. He was no longer the gentle friend who had brought her laughter and friendship. There was no trace of gentleness or kindness in him now.

It was like that time in the hallway when she had seen him return just before dawn, as if a mask had been stripped away revealing the man within, a man who hid behind laughter, jokes, and slight-of-hand tricks.

Suddenly she realized it was a mistake to come there.

She glanced around for someplace she might escape, but it was too late.

As if sensing her presence, he suddenly spun around. Sunlight flashed off the sword. In a terrifying blur of gleaming muscle and flashing steel, Truan thrust the tip of the blade straight at her heart.

A warning cry went out across the yard, frozen in the sudden, terrifying stillness of the yard.

Four

Truan heard the warning shouts across the yard. Yet some inner voice cried a different warning.

Strike! Kill, before you are killed!

Images flashed through his thoughts. Of a sword at his back, and some unseen danger that waited to cut him down. Then, he felt rather than heard another voice.

Do not! For the blood you spill will be your own. The life you take will be your life!

Words moved through his blood like the warmth of the sun, wrapped around the handle of the sword like a powerful, invisible hand, and stayed the blow at that last moment as he spun around.

Eyes still closed, he gradually became aware of the warmth of the sun overhead, the whisper of the wind, and other warning shouts as his senses returned from that faraway place where he had gone as he turned inward into his own thoughts and fought an imaginary enemy. Then, he slowly opened his eyes and stared down the length of the sword.

Half the width of a man's hand, polished steel gleaming beneath the midday sun, the tip of the sword pressed not against the breast plate of a warrior but against pale blue wool drawn taut over a quivering breast.

Truan inhaled deeply, dragging air into his lungs as if he were breaking the surface of water after swimming very deep. Gradually his thoughts cleared and focused as he realized what he had almost done.

Amber stood wordlessly before him. Her eyes were large dark pools, her bloodless features frozen in terror. Her lips were parted on a startled, silent cry. A hair's breadth away from death, she seemed not even to be breathing.

"You idiot! You brainless lackwit!"

Gareth of Montrose, the young knight who had been training nearby with Sir Gavin, was the first to reach them, eyes ablaze with anger. He furiously shoved the blade of Truan's sword aside.

"Who gave you permission to practice here?" he demanded. "You could have killed her!"

No one knew better than Truan the horrible consequences had he not pulled back at the last moment. He hardly needed a wet-behind-the-ears, fuzz-faced boy barely out of swaddling clothes and with more mouth than brains, to remind him of it.

His own anger surfaced, wild and hot. It would have been so easy to cut the boy down for his insults. But that inner voice that warned him to pull up on his sword at the last moment now cautioned that it would be unwise to give in to the anger.

Truan lowered his sword and embedded the tip in the soft earth. He shifted his weight in a casual stance as he leaned forward on arms folded loosely over the hilt of the sword. He smiled affably, yet his gaze never left Amber's.

"I chose a place apart from the others so that I would not endanger anyone. Besides, as you can see," still grinning, he shrugged and made a dismissive gesture toward Amber, "she is not harmed. Only frightened, nothing more. The blame is the child's for venturing in places where she should not."

Only then did she seem to return from that place of terror. She winced as though she had been struck. A startled breath forced its way past her frozen lips. The terror receded, replaced by pain, then a flash of anger as he called her a child.

Better her anger than the mindless terror of moments before, Truan thought, as he added, "You had best return to the nursery, mistress Amber."

What little color she had left drained completely from her face then returned in a furious flush that made the blue of her eyes flash like gemstones. Her slender hands flashed with angry words that tumbled one over the other. When her fingers tangled, she clenched her hands into tight fists as if she wished to strike someone. He had no doubt who that might be.

"You, sir, are no gallant knight!" Gareth spat furiously.

Truan grinned good-naturedly and swept one arm low before him in an exaggerated, mocking bow.

"Merely a fool, as you have pointed out," he replied. "Far more skilled with words than the sword."

"I see the skill in neither. Nor the humor," Gareth replied, his voice taut with anger.

When Truan merely grinned foolishly at him, he made a disgusted sound, and turned to Amber.

"I will escort you back to the main hall where you will be safe." His hand closed over her arm.

Amber stiffened. Her face again drained of all color at the physical contact as terror at being touched replaced the anger of only moments before.

Gareth was much stronger than she. She felt his resistance when she tried to twist free and knew she would have bruises.

The look in her eyes was far different from only moments before. It was a wild, terrified look at being physically touched.

Truan knew where the fear came from, for the old woman had told him of the horrible things the girl had suffered, a trauma so deep and wounding that it had taken from her the ability to ever speak of it. His hand tightened over the handle of his sword.

"Will you allow me to escort you back to the main hall, mistress Amber?" Sir Gavin suggested as he interceded. His gaze met Truan's briefly as he added, "The practice yard is no place for a lady."

Gareth's face flushed with anger as Gavin intervened, yet he dare say nothing to the older knight who outranked him. As his hand loosened at Amber's arm, Truan's hands relaxed about the handle of his sword.

Amber quickly stepped away from Gareth. She glanced up at Truan. In those shimmering blue-green eyes he saw pain, confusion, and questions that he heard as plainly as if she had spoken them. But he dared not answer.

Gavin turned to accompany her but she held out a hand and shook her head adamantly, clearly conveying that she did not wish anyone to do so. She squared her slender shoulders and straightened her back. Her brave defiance tore at Truan, for he knew it was hard won.

"Amber?"

She turned, her emotions exposed for all to see in the expression of fragile hope at the sound of her name.

He grinned, like the fool he needed her to believe he was. Then he winked at her. He waved his hand through the air, then with a flick of his wrist opened his fingers.

"Please accept this small gift as an apology for any distress I may have caused you," he said, with a sarcastic smile. "To add to your collection."

Amber glanced down at the small five-pointed star that lay in the palm of his hand. It was flat and shiny, a fragile crystal that winked and glittered in the sunlight, catching the light in a thousand different colors. It was exactly like the ones he had magically conjured for a group of children only a few days earlier. They had been enchanted by his magical gift, seemingly plucked from the air. She was not.

Tears welled in her eyes. No words were necessary. He knew he had wounded her deeply. Amber turned and fled the practice yard.

Truan watched her go with a sort of fierce desperation, the smile frozen on his face. Then he seized his sword, spun on his heel, and he too left the yard.

Gareth reached for his sword. Sir Gavin clamped a hand over the young knight's arm, restraining him.

"Do not," he told the boy. "You would be dead before you could lift the blade to strike."

"He's a mindless fool."

"Who is the fool?" Gavin asked. "The one who would have others believe it, or the one who believes it?"

Gareth stared after Truan, eager for blood. "You speak in riddles, old man."

Gavin's eyes narrowed at the affront but he let it pass. "It is only a riddle if you chose not to understand it."

Vivian watched from the upper balcony as Amber fled the practice yard. The girl passed through the doors of the main hall below, looking neither to right nor left at those she encountered, but with head down. Without seeing them, Vivian sensed the tears, and the chaos of the girl's emotions, along with the deep, wrenching pain and knew who was the cause of it.

She looked across the yard at the men briefly gathered there, her gaze following one who walked away from the others, the sun gleaming off his dark hair and bronzed body. Beside her, she sensed the old woman who also watched with a deep frown creasing her wrinkled brow, as if she truly saw. And for the first time she sensed the old woman keeping something from her.

She was almost as surprised by that as by the fact that the changeling was capable of it.

"What do you see that I do not?" she asked, trying to fathom the thoughts of the old woman who had been her nurse and faithful companion since she was a babe.

It was old Meg who had carried her from the immortal world where she had been born into the mortal world to the abbey where the outcast monk Poladouras and the old woman had raised her.

Vivian's powers had far surpassed those of the old woman. She had always had the ability to know her thoughts, but she sensed there were thoughts that were somehow hidden from her.

"You know well enough that I am blind," Meg answered. "You see far better than I. Occasionally I sense a wall before I walk into it." She shrugged. "Nothing more."

Vivian snorted. "We have known each other far too long, dear one. Do not play games with me."

She tried again to reach the old woman's thoughts and immediately encountered a powerful resistance.

Meg winced as though in pain and held up a thin, heavily veined hand. "Do not, child. I am old. There is nothing of importance that you do not already know."

But as she released Meg's thoughts, she sensed a single word that whispered from some far away place in the old woman's memory—*brother.*

* * *

Truan did not take his meal in the great hall with the other knights that evening. Nor several nights after that. He left Camelot, not returning for a fortnight, and then once more hiding behind the disguise of the fool, playing at board games with Lord Stephen's men until late at night, drinking too much wine as though bedeviled by demons he did not wish to confront, then leaving in those last hours before dawn, usually in the company of' one of the unattached women who served Lord Stephen's household.

Amber watched it all from afar until she could not bear it any longer. Then she retreated to the chamber she once again shared with Meg or the nursery where she helped care for Lady Vivian and Lady Cassandra's babes.

Yet, no matter how much she tried to forget the friendship they had once shared, she constantly found herself looking for Truan whenever she was in the main hall, trying to understand the changes that had come over him.

He still entertained Lord Stephen's men and their ladies with jokes, illusions, and slight-of-hand tricks. But he continued to treat her as he had that day in the practice yard, like a child, to be humored and then sent off to play with the other children. On the rare occasions when she encountered him alone, he retreated into uncomfortable silence and quickly disappeared.

What had happened? she wondered as she lay on her pallet at night, tears staining the linen cover. What had she done to make him hate her so?

"What is your name?"
The woman turned from the tapestry hung on the

wall, her fingers lingering at the rich threads woven there, finer than anything she had ever seen.

"Mary," she replied, at the same time she reached for the yarn tie that bound her hair. She pulled it free, tossing her head so that the thick, black silk fell loose about her shoulders.

She knew she was not beautiful. But she was sturdily made with full breasts and ample hips. Her hair was her finest feature, tumbling down her back and over her shoulders in a curtain of black silk, the dusky areola of a pendulous breast exposed one moment, then hidden the next in a simple game she played very well.

"Yer a simple gel, Mary child, that's fer certain," her mother had told her a long time ago.

"And ye've no father's name you can claim that might help you along in life. But yer a comely one," she had added, examining young Mary's naked body with a critical eye.

"You must use what you have wisely, and don't squander it. Never give it away, miss. Make a man pay for takin' his pleasure of ye."

Then she instructed Mary in the ways of pleasing a man. But that had all been a long time ago. She had been with many men since, but always of her choosing. Months ago, she had chosen Truan Monroe.

There was more to this warrior with dark, handsome features, crystal blue eyes, and the manner of a fool.

He was lean and strong, for she had seen him in the practice yard. And when others were not watching the smile left his face, replaced by a brooding, intense fierceness that excited her as no other.

And for months she had let him know in subtle ways that she would gladly lift her skirts for him and no other. Now he had come to her, but hardly begging.

The smile was gone, replaced by that fierceness. She

knew he watched as she untied the laces of her bodice, continued to watch as she stroked her hand over the fullness of her breast, tugging on the dusky nipple until it grew taut, still watched as she let the gown fall to the stone floor and stood completely naked before him.

Then she slowly walked toward him where he sat in the chair before the brazier. There was a fierceness in his eyes different from before, not just the wildness of sex, but something more, a deep inner fire that seemed to smolder as she approached closer.

He held back when she knelt before him, slipped her hand, behind his head, and pulled him down for her kiss. She smiled knowingly, and instead trailed kisses down across his chest and hard, flat stomach.

He was perfectly made, long and lean, with gleaming muscles wrapped around long leg bones, skin glowing like dark gold in the light of the flames at the brazier. Her mouth followed her fingers as she untied the lacings of his breeches.

She groaned softly as her mouth closed over him, bringing him to life with her lips and tongue, the groan deepening as his hands went back through her hair and his flesh filled her throat. Her tongue glided the full length of him, the hunger within growing as his flesh grew, the certainty growing as well that he would be sweeter than anything she had tasted.

Truan's hand glided back through her hair, but in his thoughts the warm silk that spilled through his fingers was not black but the color of rich, golden amber.

She offered him her breast, moaning as he suckled her deep into his mouth. But in his imagination the nipple that grew hard and beaded beneath his tongue was pale pink not dusky brown.

Then he turned her and bent low over her like a creature claiming its mate, and it almost seemed that the body that opened eagerly to his was slender as a reed, the folds of flesh he parted were delicate and tender, and the sweet heat within gliding over him as he thrust inside her had only one name.

Amber.

He came violently, her name whispering through his blood. But the woman who cried out beneath him, her lush body racked by wave after wave of pleasure, was not Amber.

Mary wakened as he stirred beside her. When she reached for him, he eased from her side. And when she called his name to beg him back to her bed, she discovered that she was alone.

Five

The feast was to celebrate the summer solstice. All of Camelot was bedecked with garlands of flowers. Banners in the blue and gold colors of the king and the black and silver of Lord Stephen flew from the towers.

The gates had been opened to nearby villagers who brought food, fresh game from the forest, the first harvest of summer crops, rolls of thick coarse wool shorn from herds of sheep earlier in spring, and casks of wine hauled inland from Penzance.

Musicians played and athletic contests were held. At night bonfires burned, lighting up the night sky, while torches glowed from the parapets of Camelot, in final celebration as plans were made for Lady Vivian and Lady Brianna to return with their husbands to London.

From there Lady Brianna and her husband, Tarek al Sharif, would journey to their home in the North Country arriving long before the first chill of winter and the birth of their first child.

Meg was to go with them as far as Amesbury Abbey on the journey to London.

"I am old," she had told Amber, with a shrug of her thin shoulders. "I have lived most of my life in the mortal world. I chose to spend the last of my days in the place that has been my home for most of those years."

She intended to return to the small abbey where Lady Vivian had been raised, there to spend the remainder of her days tending to her gardens.

"I have been away too long. I will have to replant when I return. There is work enough for an old woman." And she would be near enough to Lady Vivian when her second child was born early the following year. So it had been decided.

Amber had decided as well. In spite of the fact that she cared deeply for mistress Cassandra and her baby, there was nothing to keep her at Camelot. No family, nor hope of one. And so, she too decided to return to London.

The trip would take them almost two weeks, traveling at a slow pace through the warm summer days for the comfort of the women and young Kaden. She and several other women at Camelot had already begun packing for the journey.

She hoped she might have a moment alone with Truan to tell him that she was leaving, but in the past few weeks he was gone by first light most days, returning long after she had left the main hall. She heard rumors that he spent a great deal of time with one of the women from the village.

She did not know why the knowledge of it caused her such pain. After what had happened she found the touch of any man abhorrent and repulsive. But Truan never touched her that way. Not even that one time when he had kissed her.

She remembered it even now, a kiss stolen in the shadows. For the first time there was no fear, only the need to reach out and touch someone. And she had then as she kissed him back. But he had abruptly pushed her away from him, ending the kiss, as if he suddenly couldn't bear the touch of her.

But even now, if she closed her eyes, she could remember that intense, brief encounter, the heat of his
mouth on hers, the fiery sweetness of his breath min-
gling with hers, his body straining against her body.

Even though he considered her no more than a child,
it was not a child's body that had answered the strength
in his, nor was it with a child's eyes that she had looked
at him afterward.

She had wanted to tell him that day and so much more,
in words that were imprisoned in her heart and in her
thoughts, and became clumsy when she tried to make
the signing language with her hands. But he would not
listen. He saw her as a child to be humored or merely
tolerated. If only she could go to him as a woman.

Now, through the window opening she heard laughter and conversations, followed by cheering as skilled
marksmen gathered in the courtyard and bested one
another at the longbow. The sun was warm, the bitter
cold winter little more than a memory as if it joined in
the celebration.

Then she saw Truan as he took his place next in the
line to test his marksmanship. The afternoon breeze
molded the thin linen shirt to his shoulders, the deep
V-cut at the neck exposing dark, golden skin beneath.
Silken hair, dark as a raven's wing, fell in unbound
waves to his shoulders.

His legs were spread in an wide stance, weight bal-
anced evenly as he brought the bow up, wrapped long
fingers over the bowstring and drew it back in one fluid
motion of effortless strength and gleaming muscle.

He bent his head slightly to one side and sighted
along the shaft of the arrow, aligning the tip of the
arrow with the target. A gust of wind lifted the mane
of dark hair and Amber held her breath, knowing from

having watched Lord Stephen's men that the slightest breath of wind could alter the path of flight drastically.

His concentration was completely focused. He seemed unaware of anything or anyone else about him, except the target and the tip of the arrow. The air ached in her lungs as Amber waited expectantly.

In her thoughts Amber cried out for him to wait out the wind to take the shot, as the others had. Then she expelled it on a startled gasp with the force of the arrow as it escaped the bow and impaled the target, dead on center.

After the shot had been taken Sir Kay slapped Truan on the back, a broad grin splitting his face in an expression that would look boyish when he was a graybeard of three score years.

"Ho! What fair maid's skirts did you lift this time? For truer arrow never found a target."

"Mistress Mary of the laundry, if rumors are to be believed," Sir Gavin replied, lifting a tankard in salute. "The very same lass who cuffed you upside the head with the mallet the cook uses for tenderizing rough-cut meat, if I'm not mistaken and gave you such a bruise."

"He told me he walked into a door," Sir Rolf joined in, grinning over the edge of his own tankard.

"Oh to be sure, 'twas the door," Gavin rejoined. "We've all had a run-in with that *door!*"

There were explosions of laughter all around amongst the men, but it quickly died as Truan reminded them of the wagers they had made against his skill at the bow.

"I wish to collect now, before you become too fond of King William's wine to recall the amount owed," he told them. Amid much grumbling, they handed over the appropriate coin.

"That is the second time you have won at the bow,"

young Kay grumbled. "Are you certain there is no trick to it?"

Truan shook his head, with a sly smile. "No trick that you shall ever be able to discern, especially after three tankards of wine."

"Then how may one best you, bowman?" the lad asked good-naturedly but with a steeliness in his voice that revealed he would like very much to know, and not nearly as drunk as his companions.

"By drinking not one drop of wine. It dulls the senses and slows one's reactions," Truan informed him. "That is the reason it was so easy for the Roman senators to slay Caesar."

Only then did he accept the tankard of wine offered by one of the men. He downed it all at once, the mellow warmth stealing through his senses and warming his belly. He tied off the leather pouch that now held their coins and tucked it into the front of his shirt.

As he turned, he heard a shriek of childish laughter. Young Kaden had escaped his mother and shot across the yard as fast as his small legs would carry him. With the devil in his eyes and his mother on his trail, his laughter filled the warm summer air as he ran headlong toward the line of warriors testing their skill at the bow and ax.

Oblivious to the dangerous weapons all about, Kaden dove amongst the men, trying to escape Vivian.

Truan caught him just short of disaster, lifting him out of harm's way.

The child was a squirming, wiggling bundle of energy, with bright blue eyes and a thick cap of dark hair. To the casual observer, the warrior and child could have been like father and son.

Only upon closer look were the differences obvious, in the shape of the eyes and the child's high forehead with hair spilling forward like that of his father, Rorke FitzWarren, the Count de Anjou.

"Where are you going, little warrior?" Truan asked the child, who turned a suddenly serious gaze upon him. He had seen that look before, caught somewhere between laughter and tears. But neither laughter nor tears appeared. Instead, a yawn escape as fatigue caught up with the toddler. The child laid his head upon Truan's shoulder and he immediately inserted his thumb into his mouth.

The small chest heaved a big sigh, and in that way of all children when they slow down long enough to discover they are tired, his eyes slowly drifted shut.

"To sleep, I think," Truan said gently, feeling the tiny weight gradually become heavier in his arms. He gently rubbed the small back, feeling the fragile wings of tiny shoulder blades.

He instinctively turned his face into that small cap of hair, snuggling the child at his shoulder, and closed his eyes as he breathed in the sweetness of the warm, small body. He thought of recent dreams that had haunted him—of a child's face turned to him as if in warning—then disappeared, unrecognized. But the child in his dreams was not young Kaden.

"Holding a child comes natural to you," Lady Vivian said as she finally caught up with her son and quietly approached so as not to wake him. " 'Tis not so for all men. Are you certain you have not done this before?"

She laid a hand on her son's back and felt the even rise and fall with each breath amid the occasional snuffling sounds all children make when sleeping—that reassuring sound that every mother listens for.

Truan shook his head. "Fatherhood is for others, but not for me."

"I know of a warrior who once felt as you do, but he

changed his mind," Vivian replied, thinking of her own husband, a fierce warrior who believed as Truan believed, that marriage and fatherhood were for others, but not for him.

Again Truan shook his head, his expression almost sad now. "It can never be," he said adamantly. "For no woman would be willing to bear my child."

Vivian looked at him aghast. Was it possible the man did not know how handsome and appealing he was? Especially when in moments such as this when he was not acting the part of the fool.

"How have you determined this, milord warrior?" she asked.

" 'Tis something I know," he replied and for a moment the sadness in his eyes was so deep and compelling that whatever the reason she knew he believed it. Then it vanished and that flashing smile replaced the sadness as the fool returned and the man she had glimpsed with that great, aching sadness, disappeared.

He laid his hand across his chest, as he began reciting a foolish poem.

"Dear madame, I do not know which is worse

"the smell of your son, or the smell of my horse.

"His breeches sag and droop

"It is clear they are filled with . . ."

Vivian held up her hand to stop him, at the same time she attempted to stifle a giggle.

"So I beg you, madame please," he continued.

"to give some measure of ease

"to those who encounter the young scamp

"for he is both smelly and damp."

As he finished the foolish rhyme, Truan straightened. From the corner of his eye he caught a glimpse of a sudden movement at the upper window at the main hall, a gleam of gold the color of warm honey, and then it was gone.

Amber abruptly stepped back from the opening and flattened herself against the cool stone wall beside the window. She closed her eyes, holding onto that image of the fool holding the child.

Though she was too far away to see the expression on his face, there was no mistaking the loving tenderness as he cradled Kaden against his shoulder.

Why then she thought, could he not find it within him to show some measure of kindness to her?

She wiped the tears from her cheek. As she climbed the stairs to the private chambers with an armful of freshly laundered linens to be packed away for the journey, she caught a glimpse of a rounded shadow passing along the other side of the hall.

Pippen. She thought. At least he did not turn away from her. No doubt he'd been raiding the pantry again and was headed toward her chamber with whatever hoard he'd made off with this time.

As she went in search of the creature, she realized his precocious habits would hardly be welcome at William's court in London. She could just see him bedeviling the Saxon noblemen and their ladies, causing all sorts of mischief. No, he must remain at Camelot but she would miss him terribly when she returned to London.

As she neared her chamber she heard scratching and scrabbling about. Pippen was a burrower. His natural instinct was to bury anything of potential value and return for it later.

She constantly found apples, nuts, and crusts of dried bread, not to mention shiny objects, bits of thread, and pieces of fluff in the most unlikely places. But his favorite hiding place was the niche of loose stones behind a basket at the wall near the hearth.

She saw the overturned basket as she entered the room and shook her head.

"Whatever will become of you?" she thought, going after the creature. *"When I'm no longer here to protect you."*

She whistled softly to Pippen as she reached for the overturned basket.

"If cook finds you first, she'll have your hide on the tanner's wall."

But the creature was not hiding behind the basket nor was he anywhere in the chamber.

Eventually she gave up looking for him and returned to the main hall for there was much to be done in preparation for the feast that night. It was to be the last celebration before their return to London.

"Cease fidgeting, girl! So that I may finish this," Meg scolded as she once more started over the laborious task of plaiting Amber's heavy golden hair into a single thick braid.

"There is no need," Amber replied sullenly in the connection of their thoughts. *"I do not plan to attend the banquet. I prefer to take my supper in my chamber."*

Meg's wise old eyes narrowed thoughtfully as she sensed the sadness in the girl's thoughts.

"You would not wish to disappoint mistress Cassandra or Lord Stephen," Meg said persuasively. "They have been most kind to you these past months. 'Tis a special occasion to celebrate the christening of their son. And 'tis the last time all three sisters shall be together before Brianna leaves for the north country to await the birth of her own child."

"I mean no disrespect," Amber replied, frowning over

her thoughts as though trying to arrange them care-fully. *"'Tis only that I will be needed elsewhere."*

It was a flimsy excuse at best and Meg knew it. "And what of young master Kaden?" the old woman asked. "He is a handful and will be underfoot. Lady Vivian is relying upon you to look after the child, for her respon-sibilities will keep her busy enough. Unless," the old woman added with narrowed gaze, "there is another reason you do not wish to attend the banquet."

Amber glanced up and saw the woman's reflection above hers in the metal plate used for a looking glass, and the speculative expression in those wise, blind eyes that seemed to see far too much. In their milky white depths, which lacked any trace of color, she saw a gentle wisdom and realized the old woman knew she'd lied.

She stood abruptly, abandoning the chair. Her rebel-lious hair uncoiled from the plaited braid to spill loosely over her shoulders, as if it was a live thing, shimmering in the light from the torchère on the wall.

Amber shook her head stubbornly, and completed the undoing of the braid until she stood before Meg in glorious, radiant defiance.

"If I am to be treated as a child, then I shall wear my hair like a child!" she replied through the connection of their thoughts. Then she whirled around and fled the cham-ber and the old woman's probing thoughts, terrified she had failed to hide her true feelings.

As she fled the chamber she heard a burst of laughter from the main hall below that signaled the evening's celebrations had already begun. The aroma of meat roasting at the spit mingled with the pungence of fresh-cut cedar boughs, the fragrance of rare citron and san-dalwood from the burning candles which clustered along walls, and the even rarer spices that flavored the fruit swimming in honied sauces, roast dove in a plum glaze, cakes, and puddings. And overall, the spicy intoxication of mulled wines and dark mead.

She slipped through the shadows at the edge of the hall, seeking a place nearest Lady Vivian and young Kaden.

Tables were already heavily laden with food. Musicians played on the lute and zither. The hounds, exhausted from hunting the past several days, snored in the corner oblivious to the celebration.

There were wild hoots of laughter and shouts of encouragement as Lord Stephen's men began a round of betting with small, brightly painted wooden cubes. They were painted with from one to eight markings on each of eight sides. Then the cubes were placed in a wooden cup. One man began the game, shaking the cubes in the cup, then tossing them down onto the table with a loud smack that caused young Kaden to laugh with excitement each time the cup hit the table.

Then the cup was removed, revealing the cubes called dice on the table. A matching pair of cubes with identical markings face up was hoped for, the higher the matching numbers the better. Three cubes with matching numbers face up was preferable, and harder to come by.

Bets were made among the knights just before the dice were tossed down upon the table, then the cup was removed to a chorus of groans and wild cheers as losers parted with precious coins to the winners who had either the good fortune or some hidden skill in choosing the numbers that turned up.

Kaden was fascinated with the game of dice, and small, fast hands eagerly reached from the edge of the table. Amber had been watching after him and was faster.

Gareth of Montrose smiled as he joined her. He gestured to the men at the table.

" 'Tis no more a game of chance than yon exhibition

is a feat of magic." He pointed across the hall where Lord Stephen and several of his men had gathered. The young master of Camelot was tall, like the king. But there was another who was equally as tall as Lord Stephen. Truan Monroe stood among them, the center of their attention. He was performing some slight of hand trick that held the attention of all.

"Here, I shall show you." Gareth leaned close and explained, whispering low so the others at the table did not hear. "Watch the next round carefully. There will surely be two dice that roll the same number." At her questioning glance he smiled.

"I have seen this game played many times before in London. There are lead weights in the dice so that they tumble and roll just so."

The dice were thrown down once more to loud groans and cheers. Two rolled the side up with five distinct markings. Gareth smiled with satisfaction and downed the tankard of mead. His tankard was quickly refilled by one of the eager serving girls. When he offered it to Amber, she shook her head. She had no taste for the bitter brew.

Lady Vivian joined them, seizing her boisterous son. "It is past his bedtime. If I allow him to remain any longer, he will be cranky and impossible in the morning."

Kaden protested when she hoisted him from his perch on Amber's lap, no doubt sensing that his plans for the evening had just been curtailed. He arched his back and attempted to escape his mother's arms, but she held on firmly. When he protested, she soothed him with gentle thoughts. Soon, he laid his head on her shoulder and plopped a thumb into his mouth.

"I'll put him to bed for you," Amber suggested, making the words with her hands. She was eager to escape the

hall, and constantly seeking Truan's gaze, even just a look to indicate that he still cared for her, and finding only the fool grinning back at her.

Vivian shook her head. "Stay and enjoy the entertainment. There is no need for both of us to miss supper."

Amber glanced across the hall at the men gathered there. Gareth saw the direction of her gaze, the undisguised, heartfelt look that leapt into her eyes as her gaze fastened on Truan Monroe and then the way she quickly looked away before anyone might see it. But he had seen it. He downed the tankard of mead, the strong brew making him reckless and bold. He slammed the tankard down onto the table.

In a voice loud enough for all to hear, but directing his challenge to one man alone, he called out to Truan, "Sir fool! I wager ten pieces of silver that I will discover the trick you play on these good men."

Truan slowly turned around, his gaze narrowing on the young knight, and the slender young woman standing beside him.

He had watched Amber enter the hall earlier, alone, silent, and unnoticed. Like the flame of a candle burns unnoticed in the vast darkness that surrounds it.

She wore her hair unbound, like the younger girls of Camelot. But the youthful innocence was an illusion. Her hair fell in defiant, sensual waves past her shoulders like a silken mantle that shimmered dark gold one moment, then with the light of flames the next.

He wanted to take her in his arms and hold her tight, as he once had. He wanted to kiss away the pain he saw in her eyes. But he dared not. For he couldn't bear to see the betrayal and horror in those eyes when she learned what he truly was and what he was capable of.

She wore the gown he'd given her. It was soft blue, the color of morning sky, and matched her eyes. He caught her glance, briefly, and in that gentle open gaze he saw her true thoughts reflected in the flash of pain and the way she quickly glanced away, as clearly as if she'd spoken her feelings for him aloud.

If you only knew the truth. But he could never say it, not in this lifetime. For the truth would turn any feeling she had for him to fear. Better her pain and anger than that.

And so he smiled back at Gareth foolishly, cupping his hand behind his ear.

"Do I hear the idle gossiping of women?" he asked, loud enough for all to hear, as he mimicked their whispering and simpering mannerisms in a way that made even the women in the hall laugh at his amazing impersonations.

"Or is it the squawking of chickens that have been let loose in the castle?" he suggested as he folded his arms, flapping them like wings, while imitating the squawking of hens in the yard.

Then, he glanced once more at Amber as he pretended to intently listen once again.

"Nay, 'tis neither! 'Tis the noisome chatter of children who should have been put to bed hours ago with the babies of the castle."

The expression on Amber's face tore at his heart as his words had the desired effect. Two bright spots of anger appeared, one on each cheek.

"What you hear, master of fools," Gareth boldly answered, "is a challenge to prove yourself more than a common thief who plucks the coin from one pocket only to have it reappear in another, or a seducer of innocent young maids who woos them with fanciful sleight-of-hand tricks while stealing their virtue."

Gareth removed the short-bladed knife from his belt and thrust it tip-first down onto the table. The gleaming blade embedded in the wood, the handle quivering as he released it, removing all doubt that this was any light-hearted challenge.

Beside him, all color drained from Amber's face, in an expression Truan had never seen before—an expression of pure terror. She shuddered. Her eyes were wide, dark pools as she stared at the blade, painful memories returning at the sight of it. Connecting his thoughts to hers—he experienced all the painful memories of that long ago day when her family had died.

When she attempted to twist free, Gareth restrained her and pulled her back against him.

Silence suddenly engulfed the great hall. There was only the warning hiss of the fire on the hearth and the disquieted whimpering of the hounds as they roused from sleep and sensed the sudden tension in the room.

Young Kaden stirred restlessly in his mother's arms. She quieted him with a gentle touch as she urgently sought to locate her husband, Lord FitzWarren. He stood among the men closest to Truan. If he understood the urgency of her thoughts, he ignored them. She handed her son to Meg.

Truan smiled, but the look in his eyes was far from humorous.

"Name your challenge, sir knight," he called out.

Gareth did not release Amber, but laid a possessive hand upon her shoulder. She shuddered with each breath, her slender shoulders trembling beneath the waves of long golden hair as she struggled with those old memories. A single touch had stolen the fire and anger, and returned the haunted look to her eyes. Gareth smiled with confidence.

"Convince the good people of Camelot once and for all that your tricks and conjurements are genuine, and the silver pieces you have taken from these men are yours."

"By what means that they have not already been convinced of it?" Truan asked, still smiling easily as if it was all a game.

Gareth's gaze fastened on the knife embedded in the table before him. His eyes narrowed with satisfaction.

"You would have everyone believe that the hand is quicker than the eye," he replied. "But none have actually *seen* your tricks, only a coin plucked from a young maid's hair, or a dove that suddenly appears in your hand as if by magic—both easily concealed in the sleeve of one's tunic."

He demonstrated, appearing to pluck yet one more silver coin from behind Amber's ear.

She shrank away at the touch of his hand, reduced to a trembling, terrified creature by his touch.

To prove his point, he then shook two more coins from the length of his sleeve. They dropped into the palm of his hand and he held them aloft, demonstrating how the trick had been played.

"And if I do not?" Truan asked.

Gareth smiled as he stroked a hand across Amber's cheek, aware of the effect on her and the fool who watched.

"Then *all* will know you for the cowardly fool that you are."

"This goes beyond a light-hearted challenge," Rorke FitzWarren muttered to Lord Stephen, nearby.

"I will not allow a knight in my service, to insult one of your men."

Stephen stopped him, with a hand at his arm. "Do not interfere, my friend," he replied, watching Truan with intense interest.

"But the young pup has a wish to let blood," Rorke

argued. "All because of an insult on the practice field, which *he* provoked in the first place."

Stephen shook his head, recalling a conversation months earlier with Truan, after Stephen had returned with Cassandra through the portal in time, certain it was Truan who had opened the portal allowing him to follow her and save her life.

With renewed interest, he replied, "There is far more to this than either of us knows. Let us see what our friend is capable of."

Rorke frowned as Truan announced, "Then choose the means of the challenge."

Gareth's smile deepened as he seized the blade and pulled it from the table.

"Then let the hand be quicker than the eye, so that all may see!" As he turned the knife, seizing it by the blade, all those about Truan cleared a space about him. Except for Rorke FitzWarren. He laid a hand on Truan's arm.

"You have proven yourself in battle. Every man present knows your skill to be true. There is no need for this. *He* is the one who acts the fool."

"He is not the one who matters," Truan replied softly.

Rorke's gaze narrowed. It was not like the young warrior from the remote island across the Irish sea to feel the need to prove himself to a young maid. Particularly when he had his choice among the young women of Camelot to warm his bed. Then Truan grinned and shrugged as if it was not a serious matter at all but merely a contest he couldn't refuse.

"I have never been able to pass up a challenge."

"Even when that challenge might find a knife thrust in your heart. The boy is skilled with a sword, but even better with a knife. He has brought more than one of my knights to his knees with that skill."

Truan shrugged. "I appreciate your concern, milord

FitzWarren. But what is the worst that can happen? That Camelot might be rid of a bothersome fool? The price seems of little concern."

"Enough concern when it is your own blood you speak of," FitzWarren replied.

Truan's smile flashed with devilish humor. "You speak, milord, as if I have already lost."

"I have seen the boy's skill," Rorke repeated.

"Ah, but you have not seen mine. Step aside, milord. If his aim falters I would not wish to have the blade strike you. If his aim is true and I am the one to falter, I would not have your tunic stained with blood."

"You are a fool!" Rorke snapped with disgust, shaking his head as he took several steps back.

"This is the challenge," Gareth declared. "If you are truly capable of plucking a coin from the air then you should be able to pluck this blade from the air before it strikes. If not, your feet had best quickly move you from harm's way."

"And if I succeed," Truan added, "then I shall have the same opportunity with the blade."

Gareth smiled mockingly. "Of course."

"Then let it begin," Truan called out as he bowed mockingly toward Gareth, but his gaze was for Amber as she stood with head bowed beside the young knight.

Gareth whispered something to Amber. When she seemed not to hear, he forced her head back. Her gaze met Truan's briefly. He saw a flicker of recognition and the silent torment that was like a knife in his heart.

There were softly muttered curses all about him. Then, confident that Amber and all the others watched, Gareth took careful aim, drew back his arm, and threw the knife with deadly, bone-chilling accuracy. Straight at Truan's heart.

Six

There were gasps of surprise, as, quicker than the eye, Truan caught the blade between his hands. While everyone stared in amazement, he slowly turned the blade over.

He looked across at Gareth's stunned expression and smiled as he seemed to balance the knife upright on the end of his finger.

"The hand *is* quicker than the eye," he pointed out, then while all about him continued to stare, he slowly withdrew his hand.

The knife did not fall but continued to dangle in the air as though suspended by some invisible thread from the ceiling, slowly turning, the light of the candles and torches reflecting in a blaze of light from the blade.

Most stunned of all, Gareth stared at him with a mixture of disbelief and rage.

" 'Tis an illusion!" he cried out. "He tricks us all!"

"What trick?" Truan innocently asked, spreading his hands wide to show that he did not manipulate the blade. "The knife is your own, thrown by your hand. Unless, you are the one who has deceived us all," he suggested.

Humiliation spread across Gareth's face. The expression in his eyes one of pure rage. He gathered the coins that had been wagered from the table and hurled them at Truan.

Truan held up his right hand. In midflight the coins suddenly stopped and like the knife seemed to hang suspended in midair.

"If the coins are lost, it will make them difficult to spend," Truan quipped, slowly waving his hand through the air. The coins turned as though commanded by the movement of his hand, disappeared, then reappeared in the cupped palm of his hand. He sifted them through his fingers, turned his hand over and dropping them into his pocket to the delight of all about him, who gasped with pleasure at the trick then laughed.

Thoroughly humiliated, Gareth seized Amber by the arm and pulled her back against him.

In the sudden flash of anger in Truan's eyes, Gareth saw what he hoped for, something the fool cared about far more than coins or honor.

"Release her," Truan suggested.

Gareth smiled, his hand tightening over Amber's arm, his attention diverted for a careless moment.

There was a sudden gasp. A woman screamed a warning. Though all watched none could be certain of what he had seen. All were certain of only one thing. Truan's hand never touched the blade where it hung suspended in the air. But they heard it—that unmistakable hiss of a weapon slicing the air with great force, then the lingering quiver as it hit the wall behind Gareth, pinning his sleeve to the wood.

For a moment the younger warrior was too stunned to speak. Then color rose up his neck and blazed across his cheeks. He seized the blade and pulled it from the wood. When he turned back around he looked ready for battle.

Heedless of the danger, Vivian slipped to Amber's

side and pulled the girl behind her. Gareth's vivid gaze met hers. His hand clenched around the handle of the knife. All about the hall hands reached for weapons.

"Enough of these games," Vivian said, laying her other hand over the young warrior's, persuading him with the power of her thoughts.

" 'Tis a time for celebration," she explained, giving him her thoughts, bending his will to hers. "The guests are hungry and thirsty. Surely there is more sport to be found in the practice yard tomorrow than within these walls."

But in his thoughts Vivian encountered a powerful resistance she had not anticipated. Then resistance wavered and disappeared as though snatched away. His hand eased beneath hers at Amber's arm and he released the girl.

"Go now," Vivian whispered, letting her thoughts infuse the girl's.

Amber shuddered as though waking from a horrible nightmare. The eyes that looked back at Vivian were still haunted, but no longer held the look of a lost soul. Eventually Amber nodded, then turned, and left the hall.

Truan watched her escape the hall, grateful to Lady Vivian, for he knew of her powers and suspected far more than mere words had passed between them.

"It is not over, fool," Gareth vowed through tight lips as he spun on his heel and also left the hall, the laughter of Lord Stephen's men ringing in his ears, none of them aware of his threat. But Vivian had heard it. And she had felt it moving through his blood beneath her hand at his arm.

Truan did not go after Amber, but instead remained with Stephen's men. Vivian watched with growing interest as he continued to play the part of the jovial jester—drinking and laughing with Lord Stephen's men, to all outward appearances the encounter with Gareth given no more thought or importance than the gold coins that now filled his pocket.

But Vivian had seen something in his eyes when he confronted Gareth, an emotion briefly revealed in an expression that betrayed his feelings.

He was in love with Amber, with an intensity that came from the very soul. Vivian had no doubt that he would easily have risked his life for the girl, or just as easily taken a life to protect her. But for reasons she did not understand, he refused to reveal those feelings to anyone, *especially* Amber.

How does one catch the wind? Truan thought with growing frustration as he returned to Camelot just before dawn.

He felt it, moving across his senses. He smelled it in a certain lingering presence with every breath he took. But he could not touch it!

He entered the main hall through the laundry, abandoned at this early hour of the day. Yet he felt the shadows move around him, as though they watched as he passed by. Restless and unsettled, he had fled Camelot during the celebration the night before and wandered the countryside like a creature of the night. But somewhere distant as the cock crowed he had returned, his search in vain.

He heard the distinctive sounds of crockery and metal pots in the kitchen as he passed by, followed by the rousing voice of the cook as she called to the young servant girls who helped her prepare food for the household.

He ducked through a side passage, aware that Stephen often rose at this time of the morning. He wished for no encounters that would require explanations, and instead cut through the breezeway that connected the corridors of the chambers on the main floor to the gardens beyond.

The gardens provided a rich abundance of fragrant roses, trailing forsythia, and yellow saffron, which had grown in chaos after so many years of neglect before Lady Cassandra pruned and clipped the wayward, woody vines into submission. Nearest the kitchens were the vegetable gardens with certain pungent flowers and medicinal herbs planted among the rows to thwart the onslaught of pesky insects with voracious appetites.

It was there he found Amber.

She was kneeling amid the fragrant plants, mud and greenery staining the hem of her gown. Her hair was unbound as it had been the night before, sweeping forward over her shoulders and hiding her features as she bent low.

Truan frowned. Though he knew she spent much time in the gardens with Lady Cassandra and Lady Vivian, learning the healing arts, he could not imagine what had brought her there at this hour of the morning. Then he saw the trembling of her slender shoulders and heard the sound of her weeping.

It had taken every last ounce of self-control not to go to her the night before after the confrontation with Gareth. He thought there was nothing worse than the look of fear in her eyes. But now he discovered something far worse. Her tears.

The sound of her weeping tore at him as if some creature had sunk its claws into his very soul and opened a wound.

"Amber," he whispered her name as he had whispered it a thousand times in his thoughts. At first she seemed not to hear him and it occurred to him there was still time to leave before she turned and saw him. But he could not.

On the ground before her lay something dark and furry. As he approached closer, Truan recognized the dark coat with the distinctive ringed markings. He crouched low beside her, lightly stroking the creature's soft fur. It was cold to the touch, there was no sign of life. The beloved pet had been dead for some time.

Once he had owned such a pet, a small silky coated ferret-like creature that had eased the loneliness of a small boy with neither a mother or father to love him.

The animal had been small enough to curl into the front of his tunic, and he had carried it everywhere with him, along with an assortment of odd treasures found during his explorations of the island where he was raised. The wee creature often popped out at the most unpredictable moments, surprising his tutor and tormenting her when it crawled beneath her skirts and tangled her feet. It was a wonder either of them survived past his seventh year.

But they had, and the creature had lived with him until his fourteenth year, curling upon his pillow at night, accompanying him everywhere. But in that way of all living things, the creature had grown old, its muzzle graying with the years. One day he awoke to find it gone.

It was as if the creature had fled with the passing of his childhood. He never saw it again. But for a long time afterward he kept the small cloth the creature had slept upon tucked within his shirt as if he could hold onto the innocence of childhood as long as he could hold onto the piece of cloth.

In time he no longer needed the cloth, nor the creature, but the memories lingered for they were dear to him. As he knew the rascal, Pippen, had been dear to Amber. No doubt, she had found solace in the animal's simple acceptance, as he had found in his pet. And now that had been taken from her, just as everything else had been taken from her.

"He is gone, Amber," he said gently. "There was nothing you could have done." For he understood as well the desperate helplessness one felt at such a loss, as if there might have been something she could have done.

"I will bury him for you here in the garden."

She looked up at him then. Her eyes were softly swollen, her cheeks wet with tears, the expression on her face one of unbearable sadness.

He stood and gently pulled her to her feet. He should not have touched her. For having touched her, there was only one choice and that was to hold her.

He pulled her into his arms. There was no resistance, only the softness of her melting into him as his arms closed around her.

She was small and fragile, her breath shuddering out of her in small, desperate weeping sounds that tore at him, her head cradled against his shoulder, her cheek pressed against his heart.

He closed his eyes, memorizing the feel of her, the way she clung to him, the complete surrender to her sadness as if it would consume her, each breath she took, the feel of her tears through the linen of his shirt.

Then a deep, shuddering breath passed through her. She lifted her head from his shoulder. Tears clung to the tips of her lashes as she looked up at him with such unbearable grief and sadness, but there was no fear of being touched by him.

He gently stroked her cheek, her tears wetting his fingertips. Then, cradling her tear-stained face in his hands, he tenderly brushed her lips with his.

He heard the soft sound she made at the back of her throat, felt her startled breath whisper against his lips, then felt the soft yielding of her mouth in a tentative kiss that claimed his very soul.

In that kiss he felt the past and the future collide, as if something fated had stirred and awakened. He suddenly pushed her away from him.

She was pale, her expression stunned and filled with confusion, her lips softly swollen from the kiss.

"Leave!" he told her fiercely, then more gently, but no less adamant, "Go now. I will see that your pet is buried."

When she still hesitated, he turned on her. "What are you waiting for? Get out of here!"

Unable to speak, her thoughts spoke for her in the connection between them.

What have I done to make you hate me so?

Tears spilled down her cheeks. He couldn't bear to look at her then, to see the pain he had caused her.

He heard the wounded sound she made, and then felt her sorrow deep inside his own soul as she fled the garden.

Though she tried to speak with Truan in the days after, he seemed to have disappeared. Then there was no time to speak with him as the day of their departure for London drew near.

She mourned Pippen. Even the children at Camelot sensed his loss. There was no playful companion scurrying about, stealing their toys, or causing havoc in the kitchens. Even the cook seemed to miss the creature, grumbling that it did no good now that he was gone, she still could not find anything in the vast storerooms.

Days passed swiftly. At night she fell onto her pallet and slept deeply and without dreams, after exhausting days of final preparations and endless packing, which frequently had to be done over after young Kaden set upon the baskets and trunks in Lady Vivian's chambers.

The child was in an especially quarrelsome mood, as if he sensed the sadness that he could not possibly understand, although mistress Vivian insisted it was because he was cutting new teeth. He tried the patience of everyone, including Meg, who was usually more tolerant, having raised the child's mother, who had much the same curiosity about things and temperament.

She encountered Gareth occasionally, but he kept mostly to the practice yard. He approached her once or twice, perhaps to apologize for the confrontation the night of the feast, then quickly disappeared without speaking of it when others were about.

The day of their departure finally arrived. The sky was thick with summer clouds that brought with them an ominous wind, as if they had perhaps delayed too long.

Lord FitzWarren was eager to depart. He wanted to make the first encampment, a sheltered site several kilometers to the east, before first nightfall. The king's knights were mounted upon their warhorses in the courtyard, the drivers sat atop the wagons. Her own belongings had been packed into the second wagon along with Meg's and the bedding for Kaden and the women.

Farewells had been said several times. Vivian and Brianna had bid their sister farewell. Cassandra had vowed to visit London the following spring when Brianna's baby was due and remain long enough to assist the birth of Vivian's second child. There were many tears, until their husbands grew restless and announced that it would be nightfall if they did not leave soon.

Glancing toward the sky, Amber thought it seemed as though night had already descended. She looked for Truan and spotted him among Lord Stephen's men.

He was to accompany them as far as the western borders, then he would return to Camelot.

"It is time," Rorke FitzWarren gently reminded his wife again.

"Where is Meg?" Vivian asked, looking around for the old woman who had gone to fetch young Kaden from the nursery. After he had nearly been trampled beneath the feet of nervous horses earlier in the morning, it had been decided the child would be safer in the nursery, out of harm's way until they were ready to leave.

Amber laid a hand on Vivian's arm. *"I'll tell her that we're ready to leave,"* she told her, making quick words with her hands. *"It will give you more time with your sister before we must say goodbye."*

Vivian watched the slender girl cross the courtyard and frowned softly. Then she turned to Cassandra and they spoke of things each must remember until they were together again, even though they were all as near as the others' thoughts.

"Perhaps I will surprise you," Cassandra replied, for she possessed the gift of traveling through time and though she had vowed to her husband that she would not risk herself in that way again, her eyes danced with mischief. "You may find me in London sooner than you think."

Across the yard Truan's head came up suddenly. He sensed something as he sat astride his horse in the courtyard.

It was like the subtle change of the wind, a sudden coldness that tingled across each nerve ending and made him shiver. He had seen the words Amber made with her slender hands and knew she had gone for the old woman and the child, reminding him that the time for parting drew closer with each passing moment.

He told himself it was for the best. He told himself

that she would find a measure of peace and contentment with Lady Vivian and her family. He could not risk her ever learning the truth, for he could not bear to see the look in her eyes when she saw him as he really was.

That uneasiness moved through his blood and whispered through his thoughts. He grew restless, watching for her return. It was taking too long. She should have returned by now with the child and old woman.

Vivian sensed his uneasiness, then saw him throw the reins carelessly aside and suddenly dismount. Then she sensed the source of his concern. As if a warning moved like an icy hand across her skin, she ran after him.

Truan took the stairs of the main hall two at a time, reaching the second floor chambers in only moments. Vivian burst through the door after him as though she had flown up the steps. She cried out in alarm when she saw the chamber.

Furnishings had been overturned, hangings stripped from the walls and window openings. The brazier had been overturned, and the acrid stench of smoldering wood permeated the air. Amid the destruction, both heard the muffled crying of a child.

Vivian flew across the room, throwing furnishings out of her way, tearing aside tapestries. In the middle of the rubble and destruction she found her son.

Kaden sat on the floor, eyes wide, cheeks colored with anger. He had a scrape on his forehead and one on his arm, but apparently was otherwise unharmed. Vivian scooped him into her arms, holding onto him fiercely. She turned at the sound of others entering the chamber behind them.

"What in God's name happened here . . . ?" Gavin stared at the destruction in the room as he came in behind Rorke FitzWarren, who entered with sword drawn. Several more weapons were drawn as Lord Stephen and his men arrived.

"Something beyond God," Truan said grimly as he crouched on the floor. He shoved aside a heavy trunk and bent over a slender blood-soaked form.

Vivian handed her son over to Cassandra, the sadness in her eyes revealing what she knew she would find there. She knelt beside Truan, slipping her arm beneath the shoulders of the old woman who lay there, the halo of silver-white hair falling back from sunken, withered features.

"Dear old one," Vivian whispered as she cradled Meg in her arms. She sensed the waning heartbeat, the struggle to hold on, the enormous will it took to draw each breath. Blind eyes slowly opened.

Meg reached a feeble, trembling hand up to her, gently stroking Vivian's cheek as she had countless times when Vivian was a child, and in the tenderness of that touch, she gave Vivian her dying thoughts—of the creature she had come upon in the nursery, hiding among the shadows, how it had come at her, how she had fought to protect Kaden.

Vivian gave the dying woman some of her own strength, willing her to hold on, to fight, to live, even when she knew there was no hope of it. Such was the conflict within her—the knowledge that she had the power of immortal life, that she could heal the worst wounds with but a touch, but she could not hold back death.

"Where is Amber?" she asked the dying woman, for she sensed the horror and pain in Meg's thoughts and knew only she had the answer, for Amber was not in the chamber.

The old woman clutched at the front of Vivian's mantle. She stared at Vivian as if she truly saw for the first time.

"The creature has taken her," she replied in a ragged whisper, and on a last shuddering breath, "into the darkness."

Vivian gently eased the old woman down onto the floor. When she looked up, Truan was already gone. Assured that her son was safe, at least for now, Vivian went after him. She found him in the star-chamber.

It was a hallowed place. For it was here that her husband had brought the sword Excalibur, and Tarek al Shaarif had brought the Grail, to join with the power of the Oracle, set into the center of the round table where King Arthur had once sat with his loyal knights and ruled over Camelot, in a time and place that had faded into myth and legend. A place that was very real.

Excalibur gleamed in its place at the table, the tip of the sword aligning in perfect symmetry with the light that reflected off the Grail and the Oracle, a triangle of brilliant light, power, and hope for the future.

Truan stood before the royal seal at the far end of the chamber. It had been carved from the same pale sandstone from which Camelot had been built.

Five hundred years later it had been released from the filth, soot, and grime that had accumulated over the centuries, once more revealing the ancient Latin inscriptions that proclaimed Arthur king of Britain . . . like the light of truth emerging from the darkness.

But now the giant carved medallion as tall as a man, gleamed with a dark wetness that beaded along the intricately carved images and ran across the face of the stone.

"He has taken her," Truan said, "because he knew I would have no choice but to follow." He leaned against the stone seal, beating his fists against the ancient inscription as he repeated fiercely, "He has taken her!"

"Who has taken her?" Vivian demanded, for she sensed nothing of what had happened.

Truan slowly pushed away from the stone. "Gareth has taken her through the portal."

"How could you possibly know that?"

"I know it the same way you know such things."

For the first time in her life, Vivian felt true fear.

"Who are you?" she demanded, attempting to reach inside his thoughts.

"Your thoughts betray you," Truan replied softly. "I sense fear, anger, mistrust . . ." He slowly turned away from the wall and she saw the blood on his hands, as though the stone had been bleeding.

Others had entered the chamber behind them. She drew strength from their presence, especially her sisters, for their power was great.

"Who are you?" she again demanded, hiding the fear behind the anger.

His head slowly came up. Gone was any resemblance to the fool who had entertained them with his wit, tricks, and conjurements. Gone was the foolish smile, replaced with a fierce expression as though some dangerous beast lurked within, disguised by the affable smile and handsome features.

She felt Cassandra's presence behind her, and sensed her disbelief even before she heard her sister's gasp of surprise.

The fool was gone, replaced by the semblance of someone Cassandra had met once before . . . someone he resembled in the chiseled, handsome features, the grim-set mouth, and eyes, that were a remarkable shade of blue.

They were the features of someone she had met on

her journey into that distant time where the battle between the Darkness and Light had begun and where a kingdom had been lost. A young man who possessed that same remarkable eye color that had been passed down to the daughter who now stood beside her, and had also passed from the father to his son.

"Brother," Cassandra answered.

PART TWO
CAMELOT

Seven

Cassandra slowly approached the stone seal. Months earlier, she had used her power to open a portal in this very place. Through that portal she had gone on a quest to fulfill her destiny—to seek the Oracle of Light.

What she had found was another world, a world that existed five hundred years ago, in Arthur's time. Though the place she found resembled Camelot with its sandstone walls, parapets, and the legendary star-chamber, it was not the same.

What she found on the other side of the portal was another Camelot, one that existed in a world ruled by the powers of Darkness, and she had been imprisoned in ice—perhaps doomed to remain there forever entombed with her unborn child had Stephen not followed her on a perilous journey through the portal, which no mortal had ever made before.

Now she rested her hands upon the surface of the stone, sensing with her powers the traces of energy that still lay within the stone seal . . . of those who had recently passed this way.

She turned her senses inward, drawing on the power she had been born with, listening for their essence, reaching out and feeling their presence as it lingered there. The whisper of two souls that had passed this way, one was gentle and innocent—a mortal, human soul, the other was not.

Cassandra felt herself sinking into the stone, become one with it. The portal opened before her a gaping, cavernous passage filled with shadows and sound, voices crying out—perhaps the voices of others who had passed this way through the centuries. But there was no light to guide the way, only the darkness that loomed ahead, pulling at her as though trying to pull her from the mortal world into that world of darkness.

Then she felt the strength of an arm encircling her waist and she was being pulled back. It was like being pulled back from the edge of a precipice.

Stephen held her tightly against him. Holding on, refusing to let her go. He spoke gently, his head lowered beside hers, calling her back with words of love and the sound of their son's name, willing her to return from that place that lay beyond the portal, where she had almost gone again.

Eventually he felt her heart beating steady and strong once more beneath where his arm encircled her under her breasts—a sound that had meant life for their son all those months he lay inside her; a sound that meant life to Stephen each night as he lay beside her. She lifted her head and the eyes that looked back at him were once more clear with recognition and it was as if in that moment his own heart began beating again.

She turned in his arms and laid her head against his chest, the memory of that other time when they had almost lost each other flowing between them urgent and real as they held onto one another, as if it all happened only moments ago.

Stephen knew only too well what waited on the other side of the portal. Once opened, there was no assurance those who passed through would ever find their way back again.

Holding his wife tight against him, he warned Truan, "You must wait! 'Tis too dangerous to go alone."

"You did not wait when you went after Cassandra," Truan replied, his mouth thinned in a hard expression as he finally released the connection to Cassandra's thoughts. Through that connection, he glimpsed what she had seen, experienced what she had experienced, moments before . . . and all those months ago.

Truan laid his hand against the stone seal where Cassandra had stood only moments before. He felt the energy within, like a signal marker left behind that guided the way through. Even now, it faded. He shook his head as he came away from the stone, his fingers wet with the blood that covered it.

"If I delay, the path through the portal will fade," he replied grimly. "And there will be nothing to mark the way they have gone. Amber will be lost forever in that other time. You know that I speak the truth."

Though Stephen wanted to persuade him against it, there was no argument he could offer. He needed no special gift of sight to understand the reasons that his friend had to go after Amber. He understood them in his heart.

Truan wiped the blood from his hands, blood that marked the journey through the portal. But whose blood was it? Gareth's? Or Amber's? For he knew that it was Gareth, or at least the human form of the young knight, who had taken her.

How to catch the wind? he had wondered not long ago as he returned from yet another futile search for a creature born of an unholy union of the Darkness and mortal flesh when Lady Margeaux had lain with Malagraine and conceived a child of evil.

A creature torn from her body by the evil that had sired it; a child only moments old and glimpsed as it fled through a blinding snowstorm; a child of the Darkness who possessed the ability to take the form of man or beast.

In the forest, he had stared into the eyes of Darkness, which had taken the form of a large gray wolf. And for a moment, he had felt a kindred spirit. As if he looked at himself. Two wolves, each with the instinct to kill, the sounds of their struggle shattering the silence of the forest, the blood of both creatures bright on the leaves of the trees and soaking into the earth.

Different, yet the same. Both capable of transforming themselves, both with unimaginable powers that could kill and destroy. Where did the difference between the two of them lie? Who was to say which was good or evil?

He had struggled with those questions all his life, loathing that part of him that was neither man nor beast but a terrifying creature caught somewhere in between. He had been a loner, who struggled with the legacy of the power he'd been born with, trying to run away from *who* and *what* he was.

In a clear pool of water after a rain, in the shimmering crystal orb that the old woman used to see both the past and the future, even in his shadow that fell across the ground with the sun at his back. He could never escape himself.

Until one day, high atop a mountain where he had gone, once more trying to escape, the vision finally came to him, a whisper from the past and a voice of the future that called to him.

He had thought himself dreaming that day, the air too thin for his lungs, the cold wind sweeping over him at that high place, until he thought he might die. Perhaps he even longed for death, hoping that it would release him from the torment of uncertainty.

But as his mortal life faded, his heartbeat growing fainter in his blood, his lungs ceasing their struggle to draw air, he discovered that immortal part that lived within the mortal shell of his human body. It was then he first saw the child of his dreams, looking back at him.

"Follow me," the child whispered as the power within grew stronger, an energy of brilliant light that expanded, bringing with it the knowledge of the ages, the power of the others blessed with that power who had gone before him, the accumulated memory of their existence and experience, as well as images of their past, the present, and glimpses of the future. A past, present, and future that he was part of and could not escape.

He might run from it. He could hide away in some distant cave or high atop a mountain, but if he denied the power of the Light which he had been born to, the powers of Darkness would claim him. And he saw the future that would unfold if that came to pass. A future of unbelievable suffering, death, and destruction for all mankind. For mankind was the embodiment of hope for the powers of the Light.

He was changed when he eventually returned from his journey, much older with the knowledge of the Ancient Ones in his soul. The old priestess who had raised him sensed it immediately. The look in her wise old eyes had been one of both happiness and sadness.

"You have found what you were seeking," she sent him her thoughts with a gentle smile. Then the smile wavered. *"And now you will be leaving me."*

"I will never leave you," Truan had vowed, speaking that long ago day of the heart and soul, rather than the

physical parting, for both knew that it was necessary. *"A part of me will always be here with you."*

The old priestess, Elora, nodded and laid a hand against his cheek. *"When you were given into my care, I knew it was only for a short while, that the day would come when you must leave. I accepted that as I must. And I know that the day has now come. Go now, son of my heart."*

He left the island, journeying far on a quest to understand the mortal world that he'd been born to in that long ago time and place. Eventually, he returned to the island, only to discover that Elora was gone. Dead, some said, having perished on that same mountaintop where he had his vision of the future, for how could an old woman possibly survive in such a place. Others said she had simply walked into the sea until it rolled over her, rising from the surface in a silvery-golden mist. He never saw her again. But he remembered her. Ancient, and yet ageless. Old in his first memory of her, yet unchanged in his last memories of her.

That last time when he left the island he kept his true nature hidden as carefully as he kept his thoughts hidden behind the disguise of a charming, lackwit fool.

It was the fool who first encountered Lord Stephen and his men, swooping down out of a tree like some winged creature to drop at their feet with an inane grin on his face, beginning a quest that had brought him to this moment—his destiny.

Brianna tentatively approached him now. She was like the creatures whose form she often took, instinctively cautious, watchful, holding back. Whereas Vivian, like the power she possessed, was like a force of nature—straightforward, open, unafraid.

But it was Brianna who understood as neither Vivian or Cassandra could with their extraordinary powers, the duality of the spirit that tormented him still, part creature, part human, yet neither, and therefore misunderstood and feared.

She reached out and touched him, her touch as light and fragile as a bird's wing, connecting not in the bond of shared thought, but in the connection of spirit of all creatures who share the bond of instinct.

She suddenly drew her hand back as though she had been burned.

"You possess the power of transformation!"

Truan smiled sadly. "I will not bite you. I never acquired the taste for hawks, their talons are far too sharp."

She smiled tentatively in return, uncertain whether he jested or was being perfectly honest with her.

"Nor have I ever acquired the taste for pesky rodents."

The sadness faded. Truan laughed, shaking his head. "I have missed much not having you around to torment me, little sister." Then the smile faded, replaced by a thoughtful expression. "I have missed much, in not having my family around me."

She looked up at him with wise eyes. "We all have missed much. But you need not be alone. There are those who are capable of accepting us as we are."

He nodded. "Aye. I have the three of you."

It was Vivian, straightforward like that force of nature he compared her to and which was inherently a part of her, who frowned as though she had been contemplating something of great importance that she had now decided upon.

"Our father must be told," she said with a firm nod. "He is as much a part of this as we are."

Truan shook his head. "There is no time." His gaze met Cassandra's. Of all of them, she understood what lay ahead.

"Aye," she said softly. "You must go now, before it is too late."

"Then, you must carry Arthur's sword," Rorke FitzWarren said, removing Excalibur from its place upon the round table. "It possesses great power."

"Nay," Cassandra said softly. "He cannot carry anything with him that existed in Arthur's time. It would alter everything. The past would be changed, thereby changing everything that has followed in the five centuries since his death."

Stephen and FitzWarren exchanged a look, each with the same thought.

"Then that would mean . . ."

"That none of us might exist," Vivian spoke the thought aloud. It was a grave truth that affected them all.

"What of Amber?" Stephen asked. "She does not exist in the past as it has been written, the past that has created the world we now live in. Will her presence there alter the future?"

"That is why you must find her," Cassandra replied, for it was impossible to say how Amber's presence there might affect the past and future."

"If she is alive," Truan said softly, for he could not sense anything except that she had passed through the portal. She had been alive then. But now? He could not be certain.

"Stephen survived the journey through the portal," Cassandra assured him. "It is possible that Amber survived. The way is clearly marked. You must follow before it disappears." She opened her hand. It was covered with blood.

Truan took her hand, cradling it in his. He touched the blood on her fingers, blood that he had also found within the portal.

"Is it her blood?"

"The creature was injured when Meg fought to protect the babies. I sense the life force of all three in the blood found there."

Truan nodded. "I must go now."

"You will not wait for our father?" Vivian asked.

Truan laid his hand against her cheek, feeling the warmth of the fire that moved through her blood in ancient ways.

"Tell him where I have gone."

Cassandra laid a hand on his arm as he stepped before the ancient seal.

"Trust in the power that lies within you. It is the only thing that may save you, and bring you back to us."

Stephen gently pulled her back and held her against his side as he bid his friend, "Safe journey."

Truan turned and laid his hands upon the ancient stone seal. He traced the edges of the images carved there with his fingers as he turned his thoughts inward at the same time he reached out with the power within, expanding his senses beyond the mortal world into that other world that existed beyond the stone in that void of darkness where Amber had gone, her essence left behind in traces of blood.

His hands slowly passed through the stone into the gaping void that waited. It was like diving into a deep, dark pool, the opening of the portal expanding like ripples of water that spread in concentric waves of sight, sound, and texture, piercing the darkness, those glistening drops of blood like signposts that showed the way.

"I have a son?"

Like a man who had taken a blow, Merlin's expression was stunned, filled with disbelief as he stared at Vivian.

She sensed his thoughts in a fragile, volatile connection filled with a torrent of emotions, not the least of which was incredulity, then anger as he turned to her mother, Ninian. The expression on his face revealed that incredulity, along with pain as he realized he had been deceived.

"I have a son? Answer me!" And in the desperate, angry question lay conflict—the need to believe that what Vivian had told him was true along with the deep wounding pain that came from the growing realization that he had been deceived. By someone he loved more than life itself.

And in Ninian's silence, he knew the answer.

"Why was I not told?" he demanded, the anger breaking through in a current of rage followed by wounded words. "How? When?" Then giving way to anger once more. "Why would you keep something like this from me?"

Vivian felt trapped, caught up in something she did not want to be part of. She had been forced to come here, given no choice when Truan made his decision to go through the portal after Amber. But now she wanted to leave, to escape the anger she had never seen before between her parents.

She had been certain that Merlin must know, that like herself and her sisters, Truan had been sent to a place of safety as a child for his own protection from the powers of Darkness. But by Merlin's reaction—the incredulity and rage—she realized that he had not known that he had a son.

In a rage of energy so powerful that it frightened her, Merlin flew across the room, seizing Ninian by the arm.

Though she had been raised in the mortal world by Meg and the monk, Poladouras, Vivian had spent much time in the place where she and her sisters had been born, the world between the worlds where Merlin had been exiled after Arthur was slain and the Darkness ruled the kingdom. Never once in all that time, had she ever seen Merlin raise a hand to Ninian.

Her parents loved one another with a depth of human emotion she could not fully understand as a child. Much of that love extended to her and her sisters, but there was a part of it that always seemed off limits to them, as if it existed only between the two of them. A passion so deep and consuming that at times she and her sisters felt excluded.

Only later when she discovered the passion found in the arms of her husband had she finally understood what her parents shared and realized that it was not possible for another to be part of it. But at the moment, there seemed precious little of that love as Merlin angrily confronted Ninian.

"Tell me the truth, wife," he demanded.

And Vivian knew that Ninian had no choice but to tell the truth for she was a changeling. And though she possessed many powers, they were nothing compared to Merlin's power. If Ninian resisted, he would force the truth from her with the use of that power. But Vivian feared the outcome, for she knew what it meant. If not freely given, it was like a violation of the soul, a wounding so deep and complete that Ninian would never forgive him for it.

"Please . . ." Vivian implored them both.

"Stay out of this, daughter," Merlin said gently. "This is between your mother and me."

Vivian glanced at her mother, whom she favored with her flame red hair and heart-shaped features. She sensed the pain in that gentle heart, saw the turmoil of inner struggle as Ninian held herself as though against some great pain that washed through her and then her slender shoulders sagged as she gave up the struggle.

"I longed to tell you, husband," she said softly. "I wanted to, and yet . . . I could not."

Merlin reached out to her then, his deep love for her reaching out to the pain he sensed within her, wanting desperately to believe that she had done it for the same reasons she had protected their daughters.

"Why?" he asked, gently taking hold of her by the shoulders, turning her toward him. "I shared the knowledge of our daughters, and the pain when we were forced to send them away. Why could you not tell me of my son?"

Ninian slowly lifted her face. Suddenly she seemed much older, lines of unbearable sadness, pain, and regret appearing at her mouth and eyes. She reached up and tenderly touched his face, her fingers trembling.

"All these years we have shared everything, husband. We have lain together and shared our bodies and souls. I have felt you move inside me with a passion so great that I thought I must surely die from it. And you have felt the movement of each child you gave me moving deep within me, including the child I conceived after Brianna was born even though it lived for only a few moments."

Vivian looked up. She had not known that her mother had lost a child.

"You held each in your arms, still wet with my mortal blood," Ninian continued, tears glistening in her eyes, "including that small, dead babe." A tear spilled from her lashes.

Merlin looked at her incredulously. "What are you saying? Is Truan my son or is he not?"

Vivian felt as if her heart was breaking at that moment, so great was Ninian's sadness. She didn't want to hear any more. She wanted only to leave and return to her own husband and hold him and their son. But she could not, for she knew that this too was part of what began when the creature of Darkness took Amber through the portal.

Ninian nodded. "Aye," she said, her voice barely a whisper. "But he is not *my* son."

She stepped away from Merlin. Suddenly she seemed small, fragile, and wounded, as if gathering herself against some deep inner pain.

"What are you saying!" Merlin demanded. "How can this be?"

Ninian took a deep, shuddering breath. Her voice was hardly more than a painful whisper as she said, "He is your son by another."

"That cannot be! I have never betrayed you with another, nor would I have been able to. I was exiled to this place."

"I do not speak of this place. I speak of before. In the mortal world," Ninian said prophetically. "When you loved another."

Merlin was stunned. Vivian wanted him to deny it. Not because she thought Truan had lied. She knew he had spoken the truth. They had all sensed it. Merlin *was* their father. She wanted him to deny it because she could not bear her mother's pain, believing that Merlin had loved another before her.

But her father did not deny it. In his face she saw the anguish of truth. A truth he had buried long ago, not realizing its full consequences. He closed his eyes and hung his head.

"So long ago." His voice broke with emotion. "The beginning of the end. A stolen moment that should never have happened and with such devastating consequences."

"What are you saying?" Vivian asked, glancing from one to the other. This was more than just a lost love, something much more that somehow effected them all.

"Who is Truan's mother?"

Ninian stood silently at the window, sadness and pain lining her beautiful features.

Merlin looked at her with all those same emotions and the last traces of hope, still wanting desperately to believe in her. But her silence condemned her. She had kept this from him all these years.

"Father?"

Merlin's gaze softened as he looked at Vivian. He laid a hand gently against her cheek. "It is not your doing, daughter. It all happened a very long time ago. If I had known . . ." He sighed heavily.

"My son," he repeated. "By what you have told me, his powers are great, and yet he is in perhaps the greatest danger of all. It is a trap, and if it succeeds . . ." He turned then to the door of the cottage, his thoughts already whirling away from them to another place and time.

"Father? Where are you going?"

"I must warn him."

And he was gone, sweeping from the cottage and past the gardens. She knew the place he sought, the place where he had always gone when she was a child.

"Mother?" She turned back to Ninian.

A single tear slipped down Ninian's cheek as she turned from the window. "I have lived all this time in this place. I accepted that I could never leave it. And I came to love it." She looked up at Vivian and smiled softly. "All my babies were born here in this place that most people believe does not exist. We chose to return here afterward."

Vivian knew she spoke of Merlin's release from the

curse of the Darkness that had trapped him here, between the two worlds of the mortals and immortals.

"I cannot stay here now."

Vivian's uneasiness grew. She had never seen her mother like this.

"What are you saying? 'Tis only a misunderstanding. He will come back. I know he will."

Ninian shook her head. "No," she said, with great sadness and certainty. "He will not.

"The wound is too deep, the pain too great. 'Tis a thing that can never be forgiven. I knew it even when I fell in love with him, knowing that he loved another." She shook her head.

"I must go, for I could not bear to see that look on his face, knowing that whatever he had once felt for me had turned to hatred." She looked about the cottage then, slowly, carefully, as if memorizing each tiny detail, committing everything to memory.

She took nothing with her except small mementoes that Vivian and Brianna had made for her as children, and the recent gift Cassandra had given her once their estrangement had healed—a tendril of her son's hair in a clear crystal pendant. Then she left the cottage and never looked back.

"But where will you go?" Vivian asked, tears filling her eyes.

"A place apart where perhaps I may discover what is to be done with the rest of my life."

"How will I find you?"

"We are joined in a way that can never be broken, daughter. I carried each of you under my heart. My blood flows through you. I will be as close as your thoughts."

Eight

Truan was running, then stumbling and falling, pushing back to his feet, constantly following that glistening trail of blood through the passage.

It grew stronger, the scent of it filling his senses, moving through him, pulling him down that passage of swirling light and sound, a chaos of brilliant images speeding past him as though he passed through a shower of falling stars, each of them ablaze with color.

Then he was being pulled toward the center of the light. It exploded around him and he was hurtling through the light to the other side.

He rolled hard, grunting with pain as his shoulder drove into the hard ground beneath him, losing skin in a dozen places. Then he quit rolling, the ground beneath suddenly solid and firm. It took moments longer for his stunned senses to find equal footing and cease hurtling around inside his head, longer still before he painfully drew air back into his lungs and slowly opened his eyes.

Vivid green swayed before him with a slow, undulating motion. He ground his teeth together, forcing his chaotic senses back under control. Gradually, the outline of leaves stirring on a nearby branch took shape. Then more leaves and branches became visible as his eyesight steadied and expanded to take in his surroundings.

Truan turned over on his back, the sudden movement causing his thoughts to fling into chaos again. As they steadied, he opened his eyes once more and stared up at the canopy of trees overhead.

Where was he?

There was a sense of familiarity in the formation of trees and large clustered rocks that lined the clearing, and the course of the stream that meandered through it, as if he might have been here before.

The branches of the trees overhead stirred gently, a breath of wind brushing across his face, bringing with it the sounds of the forest that were also strangely familiar, as if he had heard them before in just that same way, in the agitated bark of a squirrel and the scolding chatter of a jackdaw suddenly followed by an expectant quiet.

A woman's terrified scream rolled him to his knees. Every sense focused on that sound as he pushed to his feet, drew his sword, and set off through the forest just as he had before, in another time.

He heard the scream again and cut across the stream, ducking under low-hanging branches, landing surefooted, not even the whisper of leaves stirring in his wake, silent and deadly as the forest creatures as he pursued that sound and the human scent it belonged to.

He found the clearing at the edge of the forest, moving downwind, the hair raised at the back of his neck, hand clasped over the handle of the sword as he edged closer and heard voices—clear and urgent.

Then he saw the two women across the clearing. One was dark haired with dark gentle eyes, high cheekbones, and a slender jaw. She stood behind the other, who was small and slender, no more than a girl.

The first woman was dressed in fine satin, green stains vivid across the pale luster of costly fabric. Her hair was plaited in a thick dark braid that fell down her back, and on the first finger of her hand she wore a red stone that gleamed like dark blood.

The girl wore her hair loose. Sunlight gleamed off the silken tresses that spilled across her shoulders and down her back in glorious golden tangles. Her gown was simply made but of fine cloth and molded a slender body braced for battle. She held a stout stick before her in small, elegant hands.

Her slender jaw was firmly set, her gaze focused straight ahead, lips slightly parted, her high breasts rising and falling beneath the bodice of her gown with each sharply drawn breath as if she had been running— or perhaps from the fear that he sensed in her.

She motioned the other woman back and as she turned her head slightly, her gaze still fastened on something across the clearing, he saw the brilliant blue-green of her eyes.

He would have known her anywhere—fragile, beautiful, her eyes filled with emotion, her strength showing through the fear and pain.

"Move slowly and with great care," she told the other woman, the smoky softness of her voice stunning him, freezing him to the ground, for a moment blinding him to everything else.

He had imagined her voice a thousand times, heard a whisper of it in the gentleness of her thoughts and in the tender words conveyed in the images she created with the hand language which Meg had taught her.

But the sound of it was like a dream of something imagined and felt but never experienced until this moment. It was soft yet strong, like steel wrapped in velvet. He had found her.

The richly dressed woman clutched Amber's arm, trying to pull her back. Neither woman noticed him, but instead continued staring across the clearing, slowly backing away.

Then, holding the stick before her, Amber pushed the other woman away from her.

"You must go now!" she said urgently.

"I will not leave you!"

Amber shook her head adamantly. "It cannot attack two at once." Her voice rose on a single word, "Run!" as the wolf leapt across the clearing toward them.

The woman did not run, but pulled a slender knife from her belt and held it before her.

The wolf was an enormous creature, all muscle and sinew beneath thick black fur, lips pulled back over deadly fangs, a fierce, terrifying growl rolling from deep inside the massive chest as it attacked.

Amber swung the stick as hard as she could. It struck a glancing blow. The wolf rolled, lunged to its feet, and circled to attack again.

The first blow had stunned her. Her grip was clumsy, numbness spreading all the way from her fingers to her shoulders from the force of the blow as the end of the stick connected with hard shoulder bone instead of the vulnerable chest as she'd intended.

Her hands grew clammy at the thought of the wolf's fangs sinking into her. She had seen hunting dogs set upon a helpless rabbit and imagined the pain of tearing flesh and muscle. But she had heard that after the first blow a sort of numbness set in that spared the prey from experiencing the final agony as it was torn apart.

She was terrified. Fear backed into her throat as the wolf attacked again in a blur of black fur and slashing teeth.

Truan raised his sword and charged into the clearing.

He caught the wolf with a low, glancing blow that swept its legs from under it and sent it rolling head over tail. The animal yelped, a fierce sound that was part surprise, part pain, and all fury as it rolled across the clearing. It immediately leapt to its feet and circled wide, seeking a new point of attack.

"Amber!" he warned low. "Do not move!"

All his senses were focused on the wolf, not a creature of the Darkness as before, but still dangerous. He did not see her stunned expression or the soft frown that drew her brows together at the sound of her name.

He sensed the attack even before the wolf moved, an instinct, part of the bond he shared with all creatures, which moved through his blood in silent warning and raised the hair at the back of his neck.

He reached out through his thoughts, communicating through that instinctual bond, the blood pumping savagely through his veins. There would be but one outcome. Death.

"You do not wish to die this day!" he communicated to the wolf, as clearly as if he had spoken. *"Leave this place, brave warrior of the forest, and live to hunt another day."*

He sensed when the wolf hesitated, a shift in the wary stance, ears no longer flattened against the head but cocked slightly forward as though listening, then the wavering of uncertainty as the sharply angled head lifted.

The wolf stopped its pacing, glancing back through the trees. That sharply angled head swung back and for a moment their gazes met—the gleaming yellow of the wolf and the deep blue of the immortal.

As if some silent agreement had been reached, the beast abruptly turned and left the clearing as quietly as it had entered, with only the silent stirring of low branches to mark the way it had fled.

Amber's heart gradually ceased its frantic beating. Eventually she was able to draw air back into her lungs.

"Did you intend to fight it with your bare hands?"

Her voice pulled Truan back from the edge of conflict, back into his mortal body, back into the present.

He looked down at his hands, only then aware that he no longer held his sword but had cast it aside with all his thoughts focused on the connection of his senses to those of the wolf.

He turned, drawn by the sound of her voice, soft as smoke, far different than he had imagined, with no trace of sadness or painful memories.

In this dangerous place, where events unfolded that affected the future where he had come from, there was no shyness or uncertainty. There was no painful silence or memories of the horrible things she'd endured that had taken away her ability to speak.

Everything had happened just as it happened before when the wolf attacked in the forest. Just as before her gown was torn and there were traces of blood. But she did not seem greatly injured.

"Sir knight?" she asked, looking at him with curiosity. "How is it that you know my name, when I do not know yours?" The last of her fear disappeared, replaced by curiosity.

Only then did he realize that not only did she have no memory of the horrible things she'd suffered, she had no memory of him.

"Or are you perhaps a conjuror who magically appeared at the last moment to save us?"

He coughed to hide his surprise. He sensed that she remembered nothing, including her journey through the portal. Yet she had struck far closer to the truth than she could have imagined.

"Do you even have a name that I may thank you for saving my life?"

He had not counted on this. It changed everything. "I am called Truan."

She smiled. "There that was not so difficult. Was it?"

"More difficult than you know."

"But you managed quite well," she complimented him, mischief dancing in her eyes. "Perhaps you can even remember not to lose your sword next time."

In spite of the grave situation they were in, Truan laughed. This was a creature he had never known, a spirited, brave, beautiful young girl not haunted by the past, but the person Amber might have been if not for the things she had endured.

Only then was he aware of the other woman who slowly walked toward them, brushing leaves and dirt from her gown. She was handsome with a regal bearing in spite of the leaves that clung to her braided hair and the dirt that smudged her cheek, and her smile was radiant, setting her eyes aglow.

Guinevere. As surely as if she had said her name aloud, Truan knew who she was. In his time, the story of Guinevere was wrapped in myth and legend—the daughter of a Celtic king, rich in land, who brought to her marriage to the warrior king of Britain great power and the bright hope for the future of a kingdom meant to last a thousand years.

As the woman who was more legend and myth than soul and substance walked toward him, it was not difficult to see how Arthur and perhaps a few others had lost their hearts to her.

She had been as brave as any warrior, refusing to flee to save her own life, choosing instead to fight off the wolf. But for all her regal beauty and bravery, there was also an air of sadness about her.

He sensed the warriors' approach and quickly retrieved his sword. They were dressed in blue tunics and breeches with polished metal breastplates, their swords gleaming in the midday sun. Eleven warriors who wore the ancient Latin crest hammered in steel at their breastplates and in the decorative hilts of their swords— identical to the inscription on the great seal in the starchamber.

With equal measures of awe and respect, Truan realized who they were—Sirs Bors, Gawain, Lochiel, and Gaheris—royal knights whose names were carved in panels at the round table. Men who were all dead in his time but whose legends lived on.

Sir Bors, the oldest of Arthur's knights, a scholar who fought by cold calculation and mathematical genius.

Lochiel, the lover, whom it was said no maid could resist, who fought the way he wooed a young woman, with sweet seduction and clever escape.

Gaheris, the gentle giant, whose size alone was intimidation enough for most enemies to quit the field before the battle had even begun.

And Gawain, Arthur's nephew, whose bravery and loyalty had become the legend for stories told to young boys in the countless generations that had followed.

"Hold!" Guinevere commanded as the knights advanced, their weapons aimed at Truan! "Do not harm him. It is only by this stranger's sword that we are alive."

One by one, swords were lowered, though not sheathed. Truan smiled inwardly. Arthur's knights would not risk the life of their queen twice. She turned to him.

"We are most grateful, sir warrior," she repeated. "Who is your master? To whom may the king offer his gratitude for your service?"

Her questions caught him unprepared. He reminded

himself that he had traveled five hundred years into the past. A past where Arthur, not William the Conqueror, was king, and where the powers of Darkness waited to claim the kingdom.

Events had been set in motion in this time and place, events that directly affected the future where those he cared for deeply now existed. Great care must be taken, for if he acted foolishly or unwisely, he would put them all at great risk.

He had hoped to find Amber and return with her to their own time and place. In doing so, he had been prepared to deal with Gareth. He had not been prepared for the chance Amber would not even know him, much less wish to return with him.

It all had some purpose, which had not yet revealed itself to him. But he sensed the danger of events moving swiftly and beyond his power to stop them if he did not take great care.

He had once found refuge in the guise of a fool, but Arthur had no need of fools. He did, however, have a need of warriors for he was about to face the greatest battle of his life.

"I owe fealty to no one, milady," he replied, his thoughts forming a plan which might keep him near Amber.

"Everyone in the kingdom owes allegiance to the king," Sir Bors reminded him, and in his words Truan sensed a reminder of his tenuous position.

Only by the queen's intervention had he not already been run through with a sword, which would have presented him with a very complicated situation. For though he would have come to no true harm at the end of a mortal's sword, there could only have been one of two possible outcomes. Either his opponent would be the victor and he would be forced to appear to die on the spot, or he would be the victor. In either case, he would not endear himself to the king, and it would then be impossible to gain entry to Camelot. He chose his words with great care and thought.

"My sword is my master," he replied. "I go where it takes me."

"A mercenary," Gaheris responded, making no attempt to disguise his contempt. "You sell your skills to the highest bidder, no matter if he is the king, or Malagaunt, but whoever has the richest purse."

Leaning upon his sword, Truan gestured widely. "Do I look as if I sell my services to the highest bidder." For his clothes were those of a warrior, tunic, breeches, boots, sword.

"Then perhaps you are a poor warrior."

"Not by what I have seen this day," Guinevere interceded.

"Aye," Amber agreed beside her. "We have seen him face down a wolf with his bare hands and charm."

In her eyes, he saw laughter. He would have laughed too if the truth did not put him in such poor light for his claim as a warrior.

"Perhaps we should test your skill with a sword," Lochiel suggested, towering over them all. "We have only your word of your claim."

"Another time," Sir Bors ended the discussion. "There are only a few hours daylight left. We must reach Camelot before nightfall. You will come with us. The king will wish to speak with you, warrior."

The wagon stood in the roadway that cut through the forest, surrounded by more of Arthur's men. It was enclosed, heavy tapestries meant to protect against the cold drawn back at the window openings.

They were not blue and gold, Arthur's royal colors, but vivid brilliant green, and woven through with scenes that were found in the forest—of animals, trees, the sun, moon, and stars. The pennants that hung from the wagon posts were also green.

"I have no horse," Truan pointed out the obvious as the ladies were escorted to the wagon.

When Sir Bors ordered one of his men to dismount, Guinevere countered the order.

"Ride with us, sir warrior." Beneath the invitation was a subtle command. "It will be only marginally more comfortable than astride a horse, but I would like to know more about a warrior who owes loyalty to no man."

The wagon was large and spacious inside. He sat across from Guinevere. Amber slipped into the seat beside her. The wagon lurched forward and he was forced to brace his feet against the opposite side to maintain his seat.

Outside the wagon, two of Sir Bors's men followed close at each side just beyond the window openings, and within easy striking distance if their new passenger proved to be dangerous.

Across from him, he was aware of the queen's quiet contemplation and Amber's amusement as he constantly readjusted his position to keep from being tossed upon the floor.

"How is it that a warrior of such great skill and independent means finds himself afoot in the forest?" Amber asked, with undisguised curiosity.

The color of the tapestry reflected in her eyes, making them seem more green than blue. Her full, well-curved lips twitched with the smile she tried without success to conceal.

"I have traveled far," he explained without lying, "no horse could have survived such a journey."

"Yet you survived."

He felt himself smile in response to this new, undiscovered Amber, a wonderful beguiling creature no mortal could resist.

"I survived only by the skill of my sword."

"For which we have only your word, and it is yet to be proven," she pointed out.

"These are dangerous times," he said. Then added logically, "Only a fool or someone of adequate skill would dare risk traveling the countryside alone."

The wagon swayed around a bend, lurching sharply over the uneven roadway. She pitched forward and would have been thrown to the floor of the wagon if he hadn't caught her.

His hands were strong yet gentle as they brushed the curve of her breasts and closed around her arms, preventing her from falling to the floor. Instead, she landed against him. Her head came up, and her gaze met his.

He sensed the flash of recognition, that fragment of a moment when some memory whispered to her from the past—her past that lay in the future, five hundred years from now. And for a moment the flirtatious smile wavered on her lips.

He could have forced her to remember, but something held him back. Something within the joy he had found in that smile, something freely given without the memories of her painful past lingering like shadows of sadness in her eyes. This Amber was free of the past, and by the powers of the Ancient Ones, he wanted to hear her laughter not her weeping, he wanted the warmth of her smiles not the haunted expression he saw every time he had touched her.

He returned her to the seat opposite and gently released her. But the warmth of the contact remained on his fingertips, the softness of her breasts, felt through the fabric of her gown. Even now, those soft breasts rose and fell more rapidly than normal, and the laughter in her eyes burned with a different light.

"Tell me of your family," Guinevere suggested, studying him thoughtfully.

"I was born here. I know most of the families in this shire."

Again, he chose his words carefully. And so far as this time and place was concerned, he spoke the truth.

"I have no family."

"No horse, no family, and fealty to no man," Amber remarked.

"Ah, but I do have a sword."

Once again, he was aware that the queen watched him intently.

"Have we perhaps met before, sir warrior?" Guinevere asked. "Perhaps in the service of my father?"

Truan shook his head. "I am new to this place. We have not met before."

"I will accept your answer for now, sir warrior," she replied. "But we will speak of it again."

He nodded. "If it pleases your majesty."

"You are premature, sir warrior," she replied, the smile on her lips fading. "I am not yet the queen."

"But soon enough, milady?" he inquired.

History at its best was handed down through stories told from one generation to the next, or scribes who chose to write what the latest reigning king would allow them to write. But at least this much was known in his time—that Guinevere had been Arthur's queen.

It had also been told that theirs was a great love, marred only by whispered stories about the knight, Lancelot. All of it was conjecture, left to the ages as myth and legend. But whatever truth lay in this past that he was now part of, there was an unexpected sadness in the young woman who sat across from him. She sighed.

"Aye, soon enough." The smile returned, if not with complete humor. "Upon the very moment of our arrival if it is to be decided by the king's advisors, generals, and his seneschal."

He realized then that not all of the legend was merely that—legend. If what she said was true, then the marriage she now traveled to under such tight guard by Arthur's men, was a marriage of title, lands, and power. A power that Arthur believed he controlled, little knowing of the greater powers that manipulated the future of mankind.

"When I saw you in the forest . . ."

In her thoughts he sensed her reaching out for the memory of something she had experienced. Then it was gone. She stared out the window.

"You reminded me of someone."

"I hope that it is a pleasant memory." For he could sense none of it within her thoughts. Her gaze met his and she smiled softly.

"Yes, a memory to last a lifetime."

Nine

It was long after nightfall when they finally reached Camelot.

The first time he had seen Camelot, it had been a place of refuge, a pile of battle-scarred stone ruins, shrouded beneath centuries of neglect and the wasting elements that had laid siege to it. Barely more than a place of myth and legend, so little of its grandeur had survived.

Only the star-chamber with the crumbling ruins of the round table and the stone seal carved with ancient Latin words and names had survived intact.

In the months afterward, through hard work and the skill of hundreds of craftsmen, Camelot had been restored to a semblance of its former grandeur, a place that many still believed existed only in myth and legend, a shining symbol of hope and faith for the future. But that was five hundred years in the future.

This was Camelot as it had been when Arthur, the warrior king, had laid claim to all of Britain by virtue of his vast army and solidified that claim through marriage to Guinevere, daughter of a powerful chieftain.

As they arrived bonfires glowed across the countryside. Across the river, whose course had changed over five hundred years, gleaming sandstone towers rose at the fortress walls like giant sentries standing guard. All along the walls torches had been lit and banners flew in Arthur's royal blue and gold colors in welcome of the new queen.

The wagon lumbered across the bridge, followed by Arthur's knights and warriors. As they passed through the gates, light from torches played across the features of the two young women who sat across from him.

Amber's expression was filled with surprise at the masses of people who had gathered to greet them, a virtual city that dwelled within the massive walls of the fortress castle. Flowers and gold coins showered through the window opening in tribute. She seized one of the flowers, a delicate white rose.

"See how they greet you, milady? Surely it is a sign that you will find happiness and love here."

Guinevere took the rose. She stared at it thoughtfully as she rode steadily toward her destiny and the future that awaited.

"Love is a rare gift that can neither be bought nor sold," she replied thoughtfully. "Not for gold coins, land, or even a crown. It must be given from the heart. If you find such a love, dear Amber, seize it. Fight to the last breath to keep it, for life is not worth living without it."

Then she looked up. Her gaze met Truan's briefly. "Yes, sir warrior, even queens long for love. We are, after all, human, with human feelings, needs, and hopes, no different from any other. Different only in that we cannot chose who we will love. The choice is made for us."

"But if you could chose, milady?" He thought surely she spoke of Lancelot, but as history had recorded, she likely had not even met that brave knight before this day.

She smiled. "Then I would chose a young warrior

with no horse, no land, nor titles, only his sword, his name, and his skill at staring down wolves in the forest."

"These are meager gifts, milady."

"I would trade them for what awaits," she said with such heartfelt honesty and poignancy that he reached out to her.

The wagon lurched to a stop before the wide steps of the main hall. Torches glowed, making it seem like day within the walls of the fortress.

The large fountain within the grand courtyard bubbled with water that spilled through the hands of stone figures sculpted in the Roman style. In the future he had often practiced there with Stephen's men.

Was it only a few weeks ago that he had very nearly injured Amber when she ventured too close? Five hundred years? The blink of an eye or the time it took to draw a breath?

Time. It moved swiftly. The span of centuries traversed in but a few steps through the portal. Yet, here, he sensed, it was as it had been five hundred years ago. Not an illusion of the Darkness, but events as they had unfolded in that long ago place. And he was now part of it.

All of Camelot had come to welcome their new queen, including Arthur who descended the steps surrounded by his other knights, counselors, generals, and his seneschal.

Guinevere seemed to gather herself emotionally. He saw the momentary hesitation as she closed her eyes, the silent gathering of strength, and heard the hasty prayer that whispered through her thoughts. When she looked at him again it was with strength, courage, and gratitude.

"Thank you, sir warrior, for making my journey a pleasant one."

"Do you think they plan to behead me now?" he remarked, not entirely joking for Arthur's reputation as a fierce warrior was also legendary.

" 'Tis not likely once I have spoken to Arthur. He is a reasonable man."

"Then let us hope he is a man in need of all the warriors he can use," he suggested with a grin at both Guinevere and Amber. "But just in case he is not, then I do not intend to be plucked from this wagon and put upon the headsman's block."

Stepping across, he opened the door of the wagon, and quickly stepped down with his sword at his side. He was taller than most of Arthur's knights, except for Lochiel who towered over everyone. His height and the sight of his sword, not yielded in submission, but held securely where he could easily draw it, was enough to stop any who might have considered taking him to the headsman's block.

Before any of Arthur's knights reached the door of the wagon, he extended his hand to Camelot's new queen. In the shadows of the wagon, he saw her take a deep breath. The hand that took his trembled only slightly, then held on with a light, sure strength.

He sensed Arthur's presence as well as that of his knights, advisors, and generals. He sensed as well the questions that formed in the king's thoughts even before he spoke.

"What is this?" the king demanded. "One of my warriors rides in the wagon?"

Many tales had been told of Arthur. Of his noble birth to a family of Roman and Celt descent, their name lost in obscurity, of his prowess on the battlefield, his cunning strategy, the charisma and energy of the boy-warrior who united the warring clans of Britain against the invaders who would lay claim to her; of the brilliant tactician who waged a war of intellect, cunning, and indomitable power over all, including the chieftain who at last yielded his most prized possession—his daughter, Lady Guinevere.

But synonymous with tales of Arthur's conquests and power were stories of his lord high counselor, the engineer, brilliant intellect, some called him priest, wizard, prophet—Merlin.

Truan had glimpsed Merlin briefly at Camelot in the days after Cassandra's return through the portal. But there had been no look of recognition between them, no moment when Merlin looked at him and he sensed the flow of communication in a single word—*son*.

He had known then that the old priestess, Elora, had spoken the truth, his father had no knowledge of him for he would never have been able to conceal it from his thoughts.

Truan knew the circumstances under which his sisters had been raised, kept apart, safe from the powers of Darkness, cloaked by obscurity, the truth known only to a handful and those protected by the Powers of the Light.

He accepted it. But now, in this place and time, he found himself looking for Merlin among Arthur's inner circle of trusted advisors and counselors.

For it was Merlin whom many believed made it possible for Arthur to be king, through wise counseling, bold military encounters that no other field general would have dared, a cunning no mortal was capable of against the invading hordes from the north, and the power to rule both wisely and well. But Merlin was not among those who had come to greet Guinevere.

"A stranger, milord," Sir Bors informed the king. "Encountered in the forest and the reason for our delay."

"If not for this kind stranger, milord," Guinevere spoke up, "we might have been delayed permanently."

Arthur was taller than most men, his dark brown hair close cropped about handsome, aquiline features that revealed his strong Roman heritage. He wore a full beard and mustache, also closely cropped, and the raiment of king in the finely made velvet tunic in deep, rich blue, set with silver at the neck and sleeves. He wore blue leggings and black boots, and a fur-lined blue mantle with silver clasps embossed with the royal insignia.

But his eyes were the eyes of a warrior, wide-set, intelligent, seeing everything in a sweeping glance, narrowing as they returned to Truan in a piercing blue stare that spoke of the fierce, Celt blood that flowed through his veins.

"I had heard there was trouble." He glanced back to Guinevere. "You were not harmed?"

"No, milord. As you can see. I have arrived safely."

"Aye," Arthur remarked, and revealed a glimpse of the man within, a man in the full of his prime not entirely immune to the striking beauty of the young woman chosen for his queen. He had taken her hand in his. He brought it to his lips and kissed it, clearly surprising her.

Whether for outward appearances to his people, or not, he seemed truly relieved that she had arrived unharmed. He smoothed his fingers over her slender ones clasped over his other hand. It was a tender gesture so unfitting a warrior or a king. Guinevere seemed warmed by the gesture.

"I would not wish to give your father cause to lay siege to my borders before the vows are spoken."

She stiffened only slightly, but the smile remained in place. "Of course not, milord."

Arthur turned then, presenting her to those who had crowded into the courtyard and sat atop the walls, eager for a glimpse of their new queen. She stood regally beside him, a slender young woman of unbelievable strength and tenderness who very likely would have chosen otherwise if the choice had been hers to make.

Who had she loved so deeply? Truan wondered, as Arthur then turned to escort her up the steps to the main hall.

"Come then," he said. "You are all weary from your travels. Something to eat and a fire to warm yourselves by." The words were cordial enough, spoken as a courtesy to the lady at his side. But he saw the look that passed between Arthur and Sir Bors, with the silent communication of men who understood each other well. As Arthur's men closed round him, his hand instinctively went to his sword.

"Please, milord," he heard Guinevere's voice over those who closed around him, rich, queenly, filled with a silken authority that she would need in the days, weeks, and years that lay ahead.

"I owe this warrior my life," she explained, forcing them to halt their procession into the hall. "Does the king reward his brave and loyal subjects with punishment for doing what he would have them do?"

Caught in a public dilemma from which there was no easy escape, Arthur perhaps had his first lesson in dealing with the ways of women, particularly women who are queens. She posed the question with great diplomacy, her hand gently laid over Arthur's arm. Perhaps Arthur sensed that in this moment lay the pattern for many other such moments in the future. Wise man that he was, he acknowledged her wisdom and turned back briefly.

"Is this man a loyal subject of Camelot?" he asked. "I have not heard him swear any such fealty."

Truan smiled inwardly as he met Arthur's gaze evenly.

He had sworn fealty to Camelot and Lord Stephen in that other time and place. It was not a lie to speak it again now. He did not go down on his knee as he knew custom demanded, but instead inclined his head in the manner of one man recognizing the status of another.

He heard Lady Guinevere's sudden sharp intake of breath. When he looked up, her face was pale, filled with emotion as she stared at him. In her gaze he sensed a moment of recognition and it clearly unnerved her. The king sensed it as well, that sharp gaze narrowing.

"Are you unwell, milady?"

She recovered and spoke without hesitation. "Nay, milord, 'tis only fatigue, while you keep us all here in the chill night air waiting for words that will not warm us."

Arthur laughed. "True enough, milady." He turned back to Truan. "What say you, warrior? Will you swear fealty or spend the night chained with the hounds?"

"Is there a choice, milord?"

"There is always a choice."

Truan smiled, but his words were for Guinevere, so that she might know that she had a friend she could rely upon for as long as he could stay.

"I swear my loyalty to Camelot, by my sword, my strength, and my sacred honor."

"Well spoken, young warrior. You are welcome at Camelot. But rest assured you shall prove both your skill with the sword, and your loyalty."

Amber followed close behind the king and queen. She turned once, glancing back at Truan, a thoughtful expression on her face. There had been no time for words between them.

Arthur's knights entered the hall before him. He was left to trail behind with the retainers and attendants. As he reached the top of the steps, she slipped from the shadows and laid a hand on his arm. Even though he could not see her clearly for the shadows at the doorway, he knew her touch.

It moved through him like quicksilver, a burning fire that began at the light pressure of her fingers and moved through his blood.

"Sir Bors is the most experienced warrior," she warned, her soft-as-smoke voice reaching through his dreams and senses. "He has great skill. He will wait for you to come to him before he strikes. In that way, he knows what to expect.

"Lochiel is dangerous because of his strength," she went on to explain. "He can wear down six men and still stand to face the next."

He smiled, teeth flashing in the shadows, as he felt himself drawn by that voice, wishing to hear it whispering other words of need and want, sighing as he touched her. His fingers moved up her arm.

"And Gawain?" he asked, not because he needed to know, but because he needed to touch her. His fingers slipped around her arm, gently drawing her closer. There was no resistance, only the flash of blue fire in her eyes from the light of a nearby torch.

"Gawain is known for his bravery. 'Tis thought he would rather die than dishonor himself."

His hand glided farther up her arm, fingers brushing the curve of her breast. "And Gaheris?"

He heard her startled breath. He felt it in the sudden swell of her breast against his fingertips. He sensed the surprise of desire that leapt within her senses and in her thoughts—something she had not expected, nor experienced before.

"The others have pledged their swords and family names to Arthur out of loyalty and honor. Gaheris is the most dangerous of all, for he is the king's nephew.

He has everything to lose and everything to gain, and there is nothing he won't do to prove himself worthy of the king's favor."

"Why do you tell me this?"

"Because . . ." she hesitated, and in her thoughts he sensed the answer. Because she wanted him to stay at Camelot, for reasons she could not even understand. But she did not say that, certain that her thoughts were safe.

Then she smiled, small dainty teeth gleaming in an impish expression.

"Because the woods are full of wolves. And I would not care to be eaten by one." She whirled away from him, the sounds of the welcoming feast reaching her from the hall within.

" 'Tis not the wolves you should fear, Amber," he replied, teeth flashing, as she turned back to him with an odd expression.

"Should I fear you, sir warrior?"

"Never, sweet Amber, for I would never harm you."

She smiled, tentatively, uncertain whether he spoke the truth, or made some jest at her expense.

"Even if you were a wolf?"

Her question startled him. What did she know? What did she remember?

"Not even then, little one. I would sleep by your side and warm you when you slept. I would walk with you through the forest, guiding the way. I would protect you with my life, with my last drop of blood."

She did not laugh at him, but instead reached out and touched his hand.

"Like today in the forest?"

He felt her searching for more, something that peered at her through the darkness that shrouded her memory of her other life.

"Yes, in the forest."

She nodded. "I will always feel safe when you are near, Sir Wolf." Then she was gone, slipping inside the main hall, joining the others.

He saw shadows that moved at him from either side as Arthur's knights closed in on him. He smiled, undaunted by their greater number.

"It would be a shame for Lady Guinevere to find the blood of her knights spilled upon the steps of Camelot," Truan said calmly.

"You are too certain of yourself, warrior," Sir Bors replied.

"I am certain of the outcome."

Truan nodded as he sensed their hesitation, then he, too, stepped through the door into the legend that was Camelot.

Ten

"Convey my gratitude to the king for his hospitality," Truan commented as he surveyed the chamber that was to be his night's lodging, and his prison.

Sir Bors nodded. "It was the king's wish that you be accorded every comfort so that you would need nothing."

Truan turned and met the knight's steady gaze. Nothing, he thought, that would make him feel the need to leave his chamber.

"The king is most generous," he said, a smile curving his mouth.

"And on the morrow," Sir Bors added, motioning the young squire from the chamber, "an audience with the king. He is most curious how a lone warrior came to be afoot in the forest with nothing but the meager clothes on his backside, and an unusual weapon made of . . ." he paused, searching for the word.

"Steel," Truan provided the correct terminology.

The composite metal, forged in fire and hand-made in the middle-empires in another time in the distant future, had been the object of much curiosity and speculation among Sir Bors's men.

In this time and place, metal weapons made from composites of iron and other known substances were presently the finest to be found. Over the next several hundred years such metals would form the core of civilization, except for isolated, more advanced parts of the world.

Steel, a composite of metals far stronger than iron, capable of holding a lethal edge and impervious to shattering under the blows of other weapons on the field of battle, would not be used for at least several hundred years. *If* mankind survived.

"*Steal,*" Sir Bors repeated, using the obvious, incorrect interpretation, but in all fairness the one the knight was most familiar with in his own time. He grunted.

"Aye, *stolen.* No doubt the means by which you came by such a weapon. Use your time wisely, warrior. For it may be your last on this earth."

He had sensed Sir Bors watching him throughout the evening, during the feast in celebration of the new queen's arrival. The goblet of wine at the table before him had never emptied, was never even lifted.

Even when the other knights each took their turn to toast the betrothal of the king, only Sir Bors's wise, scrutinizing gaze never lifted in open admiration of the queen's beauty, but remained steadily fixed on Truan.

In acknowledgment, Truan had raised his own goblet in salute to the knight, his own gaze equally measuring. In Sir Bors he sensed not an enemy against whom he must constantly guard his back, but a watchful guardian whose first duty lay unswervingly with the king.

The dark enemy he had followed through the portal was not to be found in the embodiment of the loyal knight, but in another who remained apart. So he spent his first evening at Camelot searching for shadows.

Amid conversations, beyond the normal ranges of hearing, he heard every word, saw each glance, sensed every thought of those in the royal court. But nowhere among them had he sensed the dangerous, dark presence of an evil heart.

There were many who were not part of the celebration, called far afield by duty. Among them was Gareth. But the question remained, who or what, would he find when he finally confronted the young knight who had gained the trust of those in the future, and then abducted Amber to this time and place? And to what purpose?"

The stout door to the chamber closed behind Sir Bors and the squire with a solid finality. Truan smiled as he heard the anticipated grate of metal against metal as the heavy bolt was secured.

There was no need to try the latch. He'd known even before he was brought to the *guest* chambers that Arthur's guards had been ordered to make certain he did not leave the chamber.

He would have done no less. But he had come here to find answers and he wasn't about to let Sir Bors and his men, or mere stone walls, stop him.

The window proved to be as tightly secured as the door, with no other exits or entrances. The oil lamp burned steadily on the small table near the brazier. But no fuel had been provided. He might be treated as a guest for the benefit of the new queen, but it was clear he was to be provided little comfort until the king had decided what was to be done with him.

It was cold in the chamber, one of several that lined the subterranean caverns of the fortress.

"Guest chamber." He smiled grimly, and muttered with contempt, "dungeons."

In the future, such places became the embodiment of terror and power of man over his fellow man. A place where men were taken and tortured, and never emerged.

On the table sat the rudiments for survival—a ewer

of water, a crust of bread that the rats would no doubt fight him for before morning, and the extravagance of a small oil lamp no doubt so that he could appreciate the luxuriousness of his accommodations.

The smile returned at their foolishness in thinking four walls could imprison him. He considered the options that his prison presented him. The most immediate and simplest brought him back to his current companion who had already appeared, sitting up with curiosity in the corner, beady eyes staring at him, nose twitching as it caught the scent of the bread and fresh meat, in the form of himself.

"Rats," Truan said with disgust, dismissing that option even though the obvious was that if a rat could get into his cell it could escape just as easily. He shuddered.

He'd never cared for rats after a particularly nasty confrontation with one as a child. Experimenting with his newly discovered power of transformation, he'd done as most curious, precocious children and ignored the warnings of the old priestess to use his powers wisely.

Until then he'd always envied the ability of small creatures to come and go as they pleased, sneaking in and out of small places, for the most part, unseen. A wily rat that occupied the woods nearby had been the subject of misguided boyhood interest. And so, giving into that mortal, very human part of himself, he had drawn upon the power within and transformed himself into a rat.

Transformation was one thing, an understanding of the strengths and weakness of the creature of his transformation was quite another. The rat that had once regarded him with wariness had then regarded him as fair game in a territorial battle that very nearly ended his experimentation with transformation, and his brief if foolish life.

He was run aground, deep in the forest, far from Elora's watchful eye and it probably would have all ended there, quite simply because he had neither the experience nor the sense the Ancient Ones gave an ant to figure out the reverse transformation that could have gotten his scrawny neck out of the predicament. If not for the wolf that happened upon the rat.

So preoccupied was the rat with him, that it let down its guard. And in that careful balance of nature, that one moment cost his adversary its life.

It might well have cost his life as well, for one rat hardly provided a satisfying meal for a wolf. But there had been another presence in the forest that day, a presence of swirling light and energy that lit the dark shadows as though the sun had permeated the depths of the woods. An energy the wolf had sensed, that raised the hackles upon its back, a powerful presence felt in the quivering of the leaves on the branches of the trees and in the sighing of the wind as though voices whispered.

The wolf backed away from his hiding place. Eventually he heard other sounds, the sound of a force moving toward them through the forest. The wolf's ears flattened. Then it turned and slipped away through the shadows as the sound drew closer.

Like a force of nature, Elora found him. Her wise old eyes immediately found his hiding place. He had seen Elora's contempt for rats that invaded the stores of food at the ancient place where they lived, and thought better of seeking her sympathy for his meager, transformed size.

Without the distractions of being under attack by a more wily opponent, he quickly transformed back into his human form with an expression of fear and the added effect of a few mortal tears in the desperate hope she might have sympathy for his predicament.

He was sadly mistaken.

Over the years he had sorely tested the patience of the kindly old priestess. Perhaps it was age that finally caught up with her or some genuine fear on her part of retribution from those more powerful than she if she failed in her appointed mission—to see him raised to mortal manhood.

She grabbed him by the scruff of the neck and rather than whisking him back to their home as she might have, she dragged him all the way back through the forest, barking his shins and scraping his knees along the way.

For though Elora was a small creature, no larger than he at the age of eight, she seemed to grow in proportion to her anger at him that day, until it seemed that she loomed ten feet tall over him and with the strength of a giant.

Upon returning to their home, she had sat him down upon a stool and demanded that he tell her the lesson he had learned from his little adventure.

Lessons were always twofold—with the obvious thing one learned and the greater truth that lay beneath the obvious. Elora was one for demanding that he always understand both.

He was an apathetic, dirt-smudged, bruised little mutt. First he'd imagined different ways he could get himself out of his predicament, for he sensed even then that Elora was not about to let him go with a mere lesson.

"Do not even think it," she warned him with a knowing smile having sensed his thought before it was even fully formed.

"Now, tell me, my little student, what have you learned this fine day?"

He gave in to the fact that at age eight, in mortal terms, he had not quite yet reached the level of development, or discovery of the full potential of his powers, that he could possibly outthink or outwit the old woman. However, he thought long and hard about his answer, sensing that he should come up with the right one.

"I learned that one must not make hasty decisions. I must think things through more carefully for often there are consequences that cannot be foreseen."

She had nodded, obviously satisfied as far as it went, then added that small word that always vexed him, *"And?"*

"The rat was a poor choice?" he had suggested, hoping he had guessed correctly. She nodded again.

"Why is that?"

"Because though they are small and wily, and great in number, they are easily preyed upon."

That answer seemed to please her, and he began to think that he might escape punishment.

"What else?"

What else, indeed. He gave it much thought and said the only other thing he could think of, grinning foolishly, certain that she would see the humor of it.

"Next time, I won't get caught."

She had not seen the humor, and for the first and only time gave in to the purely human failing of emotions that she was not supposed to possess.

She invoked several curses, some of which he had heard before, but many of which he had not, with much rolling of the eyes, and pleaded for the intervention of the powers of the Ancient Ones, with something that he remembered sounded very much like, *"Please stop me if what I am about to do is wrong."*

They had not.

She pulled him across her knee and proceeded to wail the living daylights out of him. Truan was completely stunned. It was such a pitiful, senseless, completely inane human response. And yet because it was, because he sensed that he had transgressed in a way that he should not have, it had the normal desired mortal effect of bringing him up short.

Gone was all his bravado, all his reckless daring and thoughtless experimentation. In one completely human, some might consider it abusive, act, Elora, that small mini-tower of wisdom and strength had gotten his attention when all other attempts at reason, logic, and wise counseling had failed.

She had been as undone as he by the episode, reduced to another very human condition—tears. At the age of eight, he'd learned a very valuable lesson that was never forgotten. He had foolishly put himself at risk in a situation he was ill-prepared to handle, acting on the emotion of the moment rather than using the extraordinary intelligence he'd been given. And in doing so, he had caused unbearable pain and anguish to someone who loved him deeply.

He grew up that day, and afterward it was he who comforted the old priestess. Ever afterward, he remembered the lesson and the wolf.

"No offense," he told his present companion who sat in the corner of the chamber regarding him with avid curiosity. "But there are wiser choices, much higher on the food chain." He turned back to his other options.

There were at least several dozen feet of stone masonry, rock, and earthworks overhead between his present location and the main hall of Camelot, passed through on that long descent through the darkness guided by torches. Not an insurmountable obstacle, but a time-consuming means of escape.

The side walls were common walls of the chambers on either side, where he risked being seen by his fellow prisoners. Again, not insurmountable, but once he was in another chamber he was then presented with the task of escaping from that chamber. Again, it was time-consuming. That brought his attention back to the door, and the passage beyond, which afforded the most accessible means of escape.

It required no great skill to simply concentrate his energy and physically ease the iron bolt out of the lock. But the sound of iron grating against iron would alert his guards, whom he knew had been posted in the passage beyond. And that was not something he wished to deal with. That meant he must find an alternative means of escape.

He flattened both hands against the wall to the side of the door. Applying a light pressure as he leaned forward, turning his thoughts inward.

He sought the light, that inner place where the power dwelled within him, a candle flame that never rested but burned continuously. He concentrated on it, expanding his thoughts until the flame expanded, reaching out, surrounding him with the powers of the Light, until it moved through his blood, burned along each nerve ending and pulsed at his fingertips.

He envisioned the wall as nothing more than a wall of mist, disappearing beneath his hand, closing over him, pulling him within, surrounding him until he stepped through the mist, and stepped through the wall.

When first attempted, all those years ago, stepping through solid mass had been a disconcerting experience. Trying to impress a young changeling girl he'd discovered intense human emotions with, he'd launched himself right through a tree and misjudged what lay on the other side.

He'd been ill-prepared for the much denser mass of the rock behind the tree and found himself soundly stuck. Elora had not rescued him that day. He'd been forced to think his way out of that dilemma. He'd carefully concentrated his fluctuating, humanly hormonal powers, and eventually extricated himself.

Learning of it afterward, Elora had been horrified at the danger he'd risked, all because of normal human feelings and emotions, which at the age of fourteen in human terms, caught him soundly between boyhood and manhood.

She did not attempt to punish him that day, nor would he have allowed it if she had. Instead she spent the next several days deep in thought, which was even more disconcerting. One day she seemed to have come to some confusion.

She disappeared for several hours and said nothing of where she'd been upon her return. He did not learn for several more days where she had gone. But one particular morning when they would normally have begun his lessons in the usual manner, she instead insisted that they take a walk together.

As they walked she explained that there were many things she simply was not prepared to teach him about—the more humanly aspects of his existence of which she had no experience.

She had been uncertain to what extent the mortal blood that flowed through him might affect his life, leaving that unknown and uncharted territory more to chance and the guidance of the Ancient Ones. But clearly his experience with the tree had changed her mind.

It had been decided that the area of human experience that was also a necessary part of his existence must be confronted not ignored.

He had listened to much of this as he had since he was eight, with both his human sense of sound and his inner sense of perceiving that which was left unsaid but articulated in unspoken thought. As she quit speaking and they arrived before a small dwelling in the community, he sensed the conclusion that had been reached.

The dwelling belonged to a young changeling woman several years older than he. She was called Mara.

She had been raised in the mortal world by her father, born of his relationship with a half-mortal who had died when she was born. Upon the death of her father, she had returned to her mother's home.

Mara was skilled in the healing arts, and he had often passed her cottage and wondered at the scent of fragrant concoctions that drifted through the open window. He had spoken to her several times, procuring remedies for the various injuries he'd suffered in the normal process of growing up.

She was slender and pretty with gentle eyes, a soft smile, and an equally gentle hand as she applied healing salves to various cuts and scrapes.

He had turned to the old priestess that day, certain of her meaning, uncertain of himself.

"You are immortal," she said prophetically. "But human blood flows through your veins as well, along with human needs. You are a child no longer. Neither yet are you the man you must become to fulfill your destiny."

She had gently touched his arm then, in love and tenderness, and with a measure of sadness as though bidding farewell to the boy.

"Go, my son. It is time you became that man."

He did not argue, nor did he act the foolish adolescent as he turned toward the cottage. He understood, with the first stirring of greater understanding of that man he must become. When he turned at the doorway to glance back, Elora was gone, and so too he sensed was his childhood. The door had opened then, and he took that step toward manhood as he took the hand Mara extended to him.

She was gentle and tender, telling him in equally gentle words the way that a man and woman came together in a physical joining of their bodies. Then she showed him.

Her body was as slender as her breasts full and lush as she came to him completely naked.

She had taken him into her cottage and into her body and shown him a mortal passion and desire he had never imagined existed. When he spent himself too quickly in embarrassed eagerness, she lovingly washed him and then showed him with her mouth and hands how quickly his mortal flesh restored itself.

She let him explore her body with youthful enthusiasm and wonder, and then afterward, lay spent beneath him with equal wonder and unexpected wistfulness.

"You will lay with others," she prophesied. "They will pleasure you greatly, until the day you lose your heart."

"Never. You have my heart," he said as he drew the taut peak of her breast into his mouth and felt it harden as his flesh within her slender hands once more hardened.

"Not I," she whispered almost sadly between deep shuddering sighs. "It will be another."

He had looked at her then over the swollen peak of her breasts, wet with his loving of them.

"If not you, then who? For I could not imagine feeling more than I feel now."

"It will happen as it must for all creatures of mortal blood. And you will know it for at that moment you would gladly give your life for the one who claims your heart."

"Impossible," he vowed as he rolled her beneath him and plunged inside of her, losing himself in the wet heat of her body closing around his. Impossible, he had thought, with that lesson still to be learned.

But he had learned well enough that day, afterward returning often to her cottage. Not entirely naive in the ways of things human, he had voiced the hope that Mara might conceive his child for he truly believed that he loved her. He had even begun to think that he might not possess that ability.

She had shown him then the reason she had not gotten with child. Skilled in medicines, she was also skilled in the ways of preventing a child.

Afterward, when he recovered from his surprise and no small amount of hurt pride, he realized the wisdom of the choice she had made without his knowledge. But when she first told him of it, he had been angry, thinking that it was because she did not want to bear his child.

She had taught him then a deeper lesson of the destiny that awaited him, that she had played a small part in, but could not share in his future.

"You possess great powers which you have only just begun to realize. Your destiny will take you far from this place and me. It will require much of you and you must not be turned from it. Somewhere within that destiny another waits for you."

She gently laid her fingers against his lips when he would have continued to argue with her. "I am your first. That was my destiny. It is not my destiny to bear your sons. That lies in your future with another."

He accepted it because he knew the futility of fighting it, and though it saddened him, he had stayed with her until he left on his journey to the middle empires where his knowledge of mortal man grew and expanded. As she predicted, he lay with other women, and with them he found much pleasure.

When he returned to that place of his childhood that last time, he had found her there still beautiful, still desirable. They had lain together again. But this time, he sensed it was the final farewell. When they parted last, it was as friends, as he left to join the struggle against the forces of Darkness that gathered once more at Camelot.

That was all a long time ago. In human terms he was a man of a full score and eight. He doubted he would ever see her again. The thought did not bring him sadness but gratitude for what she had taught him, and that she had accepted her destiny and not born his child.

It was only now that he had accepted exactly what he was, that he realized it must never happen.

Silently, like the mist he had envisioned, he moved down the passage. The first guard sensed nothing as he stole up behind him. A light pressure at the base of the neck and the guard slumped. Truan eased him back against the wall. When he awakened, he would have no sense that anything was amiss but continue guarding a chamber that was empty.

The second guard turned. "Eh?" he called out, coming away from the wall where he'd taken his position. "Is that you?" He slowly approached down the passage. At the sight of Truan, his eyes widened. Then he saw his fellow guard leaning against the wall, eyes wide open, yet unseeing.

"What is this!" he brought up his weapon.

"This won't hurt at all."

With lightning swiftness, Truan cut off any warning of alarm in the light pressure of his fingers against the man's throat. He too fell silent, eyes staring but unseeing.

Both guards remained at their posts. To any other guards who passed by the end of the passage it would seem as if they were standing duty as they'd been ordered and naught was amiss.

He slipped around the corner.

The stone steps that led to the upper levels of the fortress lay just ahead.

Guinevere watched the young girl's reflection in the metal plate at the table before her—the way she hurried through her usual evening routine, each chore performed efficiently and without flaw, but in silence as though her thoughts were elsewhere.

She guessed where her thoughts had strayed, a particular young warrior encountered in the forest who seemed to be of much interest to many, including the king.

"That is the third time you have folded that gown," Guinevere said gently, smiling as the girl finally looked up.

"Milady?" Amber asked, uncertain what had been asked of her.

"You are a dear friend and your service is beyond reproach," Guinevere complimented the girl who had so recently become her companion. She thought wistfully of the friendship shared with her companion now gone, Ninian, and felt once more that pang of loss and wished it could have been otherwise.

She closed her eyes briefly, and thought of other

things that might have been. Then she tucked them away, hidden with the pain in that corner of her heart.

"If you insist on folding and refolding each garment," she continued, "I fear they will fall apart from so much handling."

Amber smiled, her cheeks coloring as she hastily laid the garment on top of the others she had removed from the traveling trunk.

"Is there anything else you wish, mistress?" she hastily asked.

Anything else she wished? Guinevere thought. If it was only a matter of wishing.

She smoothed her hands down over her gown, thinking of all the things she had wished for—love, passion, tenderness, the freedom to choose her own destiny—all of which were not to be found by wishing. Not even the wishes of a queen. Especially not the wishes of a queen.

She stared into the mirror, as she had so many times over the past months. What did she see? A girl whose destiny it was to be born to a chieftain of great power who had loved with all the passion in her heart and soul; the woman whose greatest value in the world was in the alliance of power between her father and the king, faced an uncertain future that promised neither love nor passion.

She accepted that future because she had no choice in it. But what of the young woman who asked now, "Is there something I can get for you, milady?" but whose thoughts were elsewhere.

"Apples, I think," Guinevere replied.

"Apples?"

Guinevere smiled. "Are there not several in the basket?"

"Yes, did you care for one, milady?"

"I was thinking that an apple, or perhaps several apples, might be appreciated by our guest."

Amber's eyes widened. She had seen the guards surround him as Arthur retired for the evening. "Sir Bors had him taken to the dungeons below."

Guinevere sighed. "Yes, I know. Something that I will have remedied in the morning when I have the opportunity to speak privately with the king. But perhaps a few apples will prevent him starving before morning and give him strength for what I fear Sir Bors intends for him." She smiled secretively.

"If the guards trouble you, tell them that the queen sent you."

Amber's eyes widened with both measurable surprise and admiration. On the long journey from Guinevere's home to Camelot she had been aware of the young woman's sadness on what should have been a happy occasion. Of course, she heard it whispered that an alliance with Arthur was not the young woman's first choice. There were rumors that she had perhaps given her heart to another.

Yet Lady Guinevere stoically agreed to the union and resigned herself to it. But at the moment she was someone Amber had not glimpsed before, someone of strength, regal bearing, and an emerging certainty of the power she had acquired the day her betrothal to Arthur had been announced.

"Do not be late," Guinevere warned as Amber quickly donned her mantle and filled the hem with a half dozen gleaming apples.

"Deliver the apples then quickly return. Speak to no one along the way. And take this." She thrust a small pouch into Amber's hand.

Amber knew it contained camomile, a simple soothing

restorative she had packed into one of Lady Guinevere's trunks.

"If you are questioned by anyone, tell them that I sent you upon an errand for this sleeping powder and you lost your way. You can find your way safely back?"

"I have an excellent sense of direction," Amber assured her. "And I know a back way where I will not likely encounter anyone."

As she left the chamber, Guinevere again admonished, "Be careful."

Eleven

Head down, senses alert, drawing on the power that he'd been born with, Truan explored the passages and hallways of Camelot, searching for that elusive evil of Darkness that had brought him here.

Like an animal following the scent of its prey, he slipped silently past doorways where sleeping men lay, past closed chambers behind which slept the king's counselors, advisors, generals, past an alcove where he heard urgent whispers behind a heavy tapestry and felt the sexual tension that throbbed in the air like blood through a vein and reminded him of mortal needs, followed by the sound of clothing hastily pushed aside, the urgent joining of two bodies, and the aftermath of sighs.

In the main hall, all was quiet except for the sudden flare of the fire on the huge hearth in a stirring of the bond that connected him to the elements of nature as he passed by. When the hounds would have wakened, he reached out through his senses, calming them to deep slumber.

The cook snored on his pallet, his large hand closed over the breast of a young servant girl who lay curled beside him. Throughout the open passageways, past guards who stood at their posts, oblivious to the faint stirring of mist that swept along the stone floor, paused briefly at their feet, then moved on, slipping around corners and up the stairs to the second floor chambers.

He sensed her before he saw her in the urgent rhythm of her heart, felt before in that other time when he had held her with that animal awareness found in the wild; in the elusive stirring softness of her fragrance—that mixture of shy sweetness and subtle heat; in the light tread of her feet on the stones.

Then he saw that brief flash of gold as she passed very near him along the second-floor balcony which was open to the courtyard below, the moon catching the color of her hair, the pale gleam of skin above the bodice of her gown, and the stark contrast of dark green velvet—the queen's colors—that wrapped about her shoulders and slender body. He sensed too the dangerous discovery that waited, in the guard posted at the lower landing directly in her path.

He should let her pass by. He told himself she was only on an errand for Lady Guinevere, but in the urgency that thrummed through her like a powerful current, he sensed she was on no simple errand. And in the two guards who now joined the first, he sensed a reckless danger from which she might not be able to extricate herself.

He reached out from the shadows, grabbing her as she passed by. Her cry of alarm was smothered beneath his powerful hand.

Her fingers clawed at that smothering grip as her other hand instinctively came up against the chest of the man who had accosted her. In the process she lost her hold on the hem of her mantle and a half dozen apples thudded to the stone floor and rolled in a half dozen different directions.

"Did you hear something?" one of the guards called out to his companion.

Truan pulled Amber against him.

"Eh? What are you talking about?" a second guard asked in reply.

Amber struggled, her arms pinned between their bodies as she was held tight against her captor.

The first guard stepped up onto the landing.

The light from a nearby oil lamp on the wall pooled across her terrified features and across the features of her captor. Above the curve of his hand, her eyes widened as she finally recognized him. Pressing a finger against his lips, Truan motioned her to silence.

"I heard something," the guard said with certainty, starting across the balcony.

He walked directly toward them and Truan pulled her back into the shadows. When the guard drew his sword and approached closer, he turned with Amber in his arms, sheltering her against the wall, concealing them both as if they had disappeared.

An apple rolled across the stone floor, propelled by some unseen force. Then gravity took over as it sped past the incredulous guard who turned and followed it back toward the stairs. It fell down the steps like a ball, hitting with a bouncing thud as it rolled from one step to the next until it plopped onto the landing below and slowly rolled to a stop.

"Heard something, did you?" his companion remarked, picking up the apple and examining it. "Aye, dangerous it is, too. I knew a man once who was attacked by one of these."

He took a crunching bite from the apple through his laughter.

"You're fortunate my friend. It might have killed you!"

Chuckles greeted the first guard as he re-joined them, seized the apple, and finished it with slashing bites. Their laughter echoed after them as they returned to their post.

Truan slowly released his hand, the soft curve of her mouth felt there in a lingering heat long after he had removed it. His fingers slipped down her arm and around her wrist. He pulled her in the opposite direction, away from the landing and into the safety of one of those alcoves.

"What are you . . . ?" she whispered.

He laid his fingers against her lips until he was certain no more guards were near.

"What are you doing here?" she asked insistently.

"I felt the need for a walk."

A slender golden brow angled upward.

"After walking about the forest afoot? I'm certain you felt an excess of energy."

He laughed softly at this unexpected, spirited side of her that he'd never been allowed to know. In traveling through the portal, she'd not only apparently lost all memory of her life at Camelot, but had also been freed of the pain and anguish of her past as well.

"How did you escape? Are Sir Bors's men lying about with split heads?" she asked.

From between their bodies, squeezed tightly together into the shelter of the alcove, he produced an apple very much like the ones she'd carried to him hidden in the hem of her mantle.

"No worse than apples scattered to the floor. A bit bruised but none the worse for wear."

Slender brows knit together over blue-green eyes. For a moment he sensed that she struggled with some vague memory that peeked at her through whatever darkness lay over the past. She stared at the apple as if it were a gold coin he'd suddenly plucked from behind her ear. Her gaze met his in soft confusion.

Then just as suddenly as it had appeared, the memory was gone before she could grasp it, disappearing once more into the dark void. She laughed then, a soft musical sound filled with traces of smoke. Like rich velvet. Smooth and silken to the touch when stroked in one direction, softly stirring when stroked in the other.

In that other life, her laughter had been silenced. He had looked for it in her eyes, a small fleeting reward for the simple tricks he conjured.

"First you elude Sir Bors's guards, now the king's. You, Sir Wolf, are not trustworthy." She reached for the apple. Their fingertips brushed, and in that contact, as brief and light as the touch of a feather, he sensed another memory whispering to her.

She looked up at him, her face angled toward his, her mouth only inches from his. He sensed the sudden change in her heartbeat, then saw it in the pulse that beat wildly at the slender vein at her throat.

Her slender hands lay on his arms as though to push him away, but she did not. Instead he felt the gentle pressure as her fingers closed, instinctively reaching for that memory as she leaned toward him.

The brilliant blue-green of her eyes darkened. And in their depths he sensed the memory of something once shared, a brief encounter, a kiss, something that should never have happened.

"Perhaps," she whispered, lashes lowering as she reached for something lost in memory, something she should remember but could not, "I have reason to fear for my own safety."

Her breath was warm and sweet as it brushed his lips. Truan closed his eyes in agony. His hands trembled as he held her. He had only to pull her closer and then taste her. He sensed she would not resist.

"Amber." Her name was both a gentle sigh and the deepest agony.

For things that could not be.

The sound of her name seemed to whisper to her from some corner of her memory, *his* voice as if he'd whispered her name a hundred ways, and in that one sound the way she'd longed to hear it.

Amber slowly opened her eyes. And in that way of knowing that one has been in a certain place and experienced certain things before, she was certain that they had stood together just that way and touched before.

Truan saw it in her eyes. Not a question, but a certainty. He knew it was on the tip of her tongue to say it. He felt it in the sudden heat that flowed through her—that moment when memory and desire became one.

His hands closed over her arms and he gently held her away from him, severing the physical contact as well as the memory.

"I will take you back to your chamber."

He'd hurt her. He sensed it in her confused silence as she followed him. If it seemed odd that he knew exactly where her chamber was when he had never been there before, she said nothing of it.

Outside Lady Guinevere's chamber he reached for the latch. Her hand closed over his arm.

"Sir Bors is determined to prove you false to the king," she warned him.

He had anticipated it, and would have been surprised otherwise.

"He suspects you may have been sent by Malagaunt."

Arthur's foe in this time and place—a warrior chieftain from the northern regions where he amassed among the Saxons—if this part of history had been accurately recorded. But he knew well enough that the true danger had not come from Malagaunt but from within Camelot. Arthur had been betrayed, by someone close to him, leaving Camelot exposed and defenseless.

"And by what means does he seek to prove me false?"

In the light of the lamp at the wall, her face had become very pale.

"It will be called a contest, a show of skill and bravery with swords and other weapons. But you will be outnumbered and . . ."

"Killed?"

In that single word lay every fear within her heart. A fear that went beyond concern for a mere stranger she had met just that day, even if that stranger had saved her life.

"Why do you warn me?" Truan asked, wondering if she remembered something more, something that might put her in grave danger.

"I don't know." She looked away from him then, a frown drawing her brows together.

With his fingers beneath her chin he forced her to look at him. What did she remember?

"Why do you warn me?"

"Because of the way you're looking at me," she whispered. "The same way you looked at me in the forest." Her hand came up, her fingers closing around his.

"As if I know you somehow . . ."

It took all his strength to step away from her, when all he wanted was to pull her against him and feel her softness melting into him, to hear the soft startled sound in her throat, and then feel the warmth of her breath on his lips.

"Go," he said tightly. "Before you are discovered."

Again he saw the confusion and hurt in her eyes. Then it was hidden away.

"You'll remember what I said?"

He nodded and smiled then to hide his true feelings.

"I will try not to die," he assured her. He waited until she had slipped inside the chamber and heard her set the latch.

Amber leaned back against the door. The candles had been doused. The only light came from the fire in the brazier. Her mistress did not stir but seemed to sleep undisturbed.

She was silently grateful for the lack of light and the surrounding silence. She could not have trusted her voice, nor concealed the wild heat that flamed her skin and the frantic beating of her heart as in the forest that afternoon when for a moment she was certain she knew the man who stepped from the shadows as if he was part of them. And something within her, something lost that she could not even remember made her reach out to him.

She had remembered tonight, if only for a moment. Like a reflection in a looking plate, a glimpse of another place and time . . .

But now, try as she might, it slipped away from her.

Eventually she pushed away from the door. She undressed in the light of the brazier, carefully folding her gown and tunic. She slept in the soft muslin shift, slipping beneath the thick furs. And as her thoughts slipped into dreams, her fingers spread through the soft fur, stroking it, letting its warmth surround her, like the warmth of a wolf that lay down beside her.

Guinevere stared through the shadows. She continued to stare, long after she heard the deep, even breathing of the girl who slept at the pallet near hers. Her thoughts refused to sleep, tormented by what lay in her heart and the future that lay before her. Remembering. Thinking of what might have been. A single tear slipped down her cheek.

Merlin stood before the crystal sphere, shimmering silver and white one moment, then glowing blue the next. With eyes closed he slowly passed his hand across the surface, summoning the power of vision, attempting to draw back the veil across time.

It came to him as near as yesterday, five hundred years in the past, a lifetime in spinning, shifting images that moved across the surface of the crystal and then coalesced into a single point of light.

He saw time spinning out of itself, a journey, and a traveler. Himself, caught in a ripple of time, imprisoned, the power of the Light engulfed by the powers of Darkness, the passage of years little more than a heartbeat, an echo of voices past, present, lost, forgotten, then remembered. And then a single image within the crystal. Himself, but not him. A young man, the future of the Light, surrounded by Darkness, the father's past repeated by the son.

"No!" Merlin cried out, his hand clenching into a fist of rage. "You shall not have him, too. You shall not!"

His body was taut with anger and the power of the Light that burned within him. He was young still, filled with memories, regrets, ambitions, and dreams. The dreams shattered, a kingdom lost. And it was all happening again. The past was reaching out to destroy the future.

Without looking up, he sensed Vivian's presence. So like her mother, filled with life and the essence of fire that was her power, a healing power that had saved the life of another king in another time and place.

His firstborn daughter, but not his firstborn. Yet she in so many ways more than the others was a kindred spirit, more like him and yet unlike him in that unique way of the melding together of mortal blood and immortal powers, and temperament. Passionate about those she cared for, stubborn, willful—purely human traits that they were—she was also the child he had the most contact with through the years of her mortal life.

She was the one they had the most contact with until the danger became too great. That danger that reached down across the centuries so that now it touched them all. And now, he thought, she had come to try and heal the deep wound between himself and Ninian.

"Daughter," he said tenderly through the connection of their thoughts as he turned from the crystal.

"You're going back," she replied with certainty for there was no need to ask it. *"It will be dangerous. The way is not clearly marked."*

In the cool logic of her thoughts he still heard the whisper of fear, the need to persuade him against it, which he knew even as he sensed it that she would not do. For stronger than the fear, she knew with the sense of the powers she'd been born to that she must not ask it, just as he could not turn from it.

"His passage will guide the way that he has gone," Merlin replied.

And she knew he spoke of Truan.

"And when you get there? What will happen?"

"He is part of it now." For a moment his thoughts strayed from hers, returning to some distant memory. *"As he was from the beginning."* Then he looked back at Vivian. *"He must be warned. I will not let the powers of Darkness have him."*

"I will go with you!" she cried out passionately. *"Surely with both our powers . . ."*

"No, daughter!" he said with a fierceness she'd never heard before. *"I will not allow it!"*

He saw the stubbornness and defiance that leapt into her eyes, his own eyes that he saw looking back at him, along with a trace of his own fierceness.

He thought of Cassandra's son, Kaden, his grandson, and the child that Brianna now carried. They were the next, bright hope for the future. A legacy of the powers of the Light for whom there might be no future if he failed now. He reached out to Vivian with reason.

"You must not risk the child you carry. You will be needed here, you and your sisters. For I have great faith in your strength and power. And if I should fail . . ." he hesitated at the thought, too horrible to imagine, for even their combined powers would not be enough to stop the Darkness if he failed.

"If I should fail," he continued, *"you must use your powers to protect the children for they will be the only hope for the future."*

Because she knew it was pointless to argue Vivian reluctantly accepted his wisdom. And in her acceptance, he knew he had her solemn vow that she would carry out his wishes.

"Mother has gone," she said softly.

In the simple thought, he heard her heartfelt need for him to reassure her, as all children needed to be reassured, that all would be well between himself and Ninian once more.

"Yes," he replied, for he could give no such assurance.

"Will you say and do nothing to stop her?"

"She came to me of her free will. She leaves of her free will."

"She leaves because she believes you can never forgive what she has done. But how is it any different than keeping my sisters safe all these years?"

"It is different, Vivian."

"Would it have changed anything? Would anything have been different if you'd known?"

"I should have been told!"

"Just as mother should have known that you loved another before her?"

"She knew."

Vivian stared at him. She had assumed that Truan had been born of some fleeting affair before her father ever knew Ninian. It was often the way of things in the mortal world.

Her own husband had been born of a brief encounter between his father and a woman who was not his wife. But until that moment she had not truly considered that her father might have loved another before Ninian. Might still love her and might have chosen to remain with her if not for his exile.

"Leave it, daughter," Merlin said gently. *"It is between your mother and me."*

Merlin had known that Ninian would not, could not, remain with what was between them. The pain would be too great—the pain of the truth she had carried for all these years; the truth she had kept from him; and her certainty that he could never forgive her.

That which he possessed, as close to a mortal heart as it was possible to experience, clenched with sadness and pain for that loss. What they once shared had been taken from them with the truth, perhaps the hand of Darkness reaching across time to exact some final revenge against him. And now it reached for his son and threatened them all.

"But what if . . . ?"

What if he did not return? The question lay half-formed in her thoughts.

He sensed her torment. She was so like Ninian. They possessed that same red hair and heart-shaped face.

When he looked at her, he saw Ninian, as he had first seen her and loved her. He laid his hand against her cheek. But he could not say the words she needed to hear—that he forgave Ninian.

His hand dropped to his side and he turned from her. *"I must go. Already, I have delayed too long. Time grows short."*

Vivian flung her arms around his neck and hugged him, giving in to the purely human emotions that welled inside her. Whatever lay between him and Ninian, he was still her father. It was a bond that could not be broken—not by anger, pain, truths from the past, or even the uncertain future. This might be the last she would ever see him.

"Father!"

He held her tight, cradling her head against his shoulder as he had when she was a child and suffered some childhood injury or fear. He kissed her cheek.

"Tell your sisters . . ."

She nodded against his shoulder. Then, so like Ninian who was brave, and in so many ways stronger than he, she stepped away from him.

"We will be waiting for you."

There was no more time.

Merlin turned his thoughts inward, seeking the power, drawing on it, stepping through the portal that linked his world with the mortal world, bidding her farewell in a long, loving glance back, then beginning the journey back to Camelot.

When Merlin stepped through the portal, he stepped into the star-chamber. Not as it had been, but as it was now. Scarred, it bore the signs of an ancient struggle where brave knights had died in that final battle, the last stand to save a dream of what might have been.

Months ago, he had come here, freed at last from the world between the worlds that he had shared with Ninian. At the thought of her, his heart ached.

Ninian, the passion of his life. The one who had saved him from an existence worse than death with her gentle love, who had given him hope, passion, and beautiful children and shared his exile.

All those years she had kept that secret, never betraying it, never sharing it with the one who should have known.

He slowly approached the stone seal. Arthur's seal in that other time and place. They had commissioned the inscription together. The warrior king and his counselor. Friends. As close as brothers. Torn apart by the secrets that lay between them. And a kingdom lost.

He had thought never to go back. The past was written, there was no changing it. Arthur was dead. A memory that lived with him in exile, like so many other memories. And his memory of *her.* She would be there.

His presence would change things, might well change the order of the precious balance within which they now lived. But that balance had already been jeopardized when his son journeyed into the past.

His son. Lured into a trap meant to destroy the future. Just as he had caused the destruction of the kingdom all those centuries ago.

"The sins of the father."

He laid his hands against the ancient stone seal and turned his thoughts inward, seeking the power of the Light, beginning the journey into the past . . .

Twelve

"Here you! On your feet! You're to see the king," the guard called out. Iron grated against iron as the bolt at the chamber door was thrown back.

The guard looked at him with surprise as he came away from the wall with an easy grace and energy not usually found in prisoners who'd spent the night in the dungeons with nothing more than food and water to sustain them, and the possibility of execution awaiting them upon his arrival.

"Good morning," Truan greeted his jailer. He'd polished off the last apple and tossed the core into the corner where he knew the rat was.

He and his beady-eyed companion had finished off a lively conversation just after dawn upon his return with half a roast fowl, several hard-cooked eggs, and a thick crust of fresh bread. Whatever the king and Sir Bors had in mind for him, he wasn't about to face it on an empty stomach, even though it was a strictly mortal affliction.

After he'd left Amber his search had taken him into another part of the castle. From there he searched the armory, the barracks that housed the soldiers in residence at Camelot, and the king's apartments.

He found no trace of Gareth as he slipped like a silent

wraith over stone and step, beneath doors and through window openings. Then very near dawn, he'd slipped into the king's stables.

Horses were highly valued and well cared for. The invading Romans of several centuries earlier had brought them to Britain in great numbers. That influence could still be seen in the descendants of those first war horses whose ancestry was traced to the middle empires and the elegant fine-boned animals who raced the wind of the arid desert kingdoms Rome had first conquered.

He found many empty stalls and came to an obvious conclusion that needed no gift of insight. Many of Arthur's knights had been absent from the welcoming celebration the previous evening. They had obviously been called away and not yet returned to Camelot. But no doubt they were expected shortly. The wedding of the king to Lady Guinevere was to take place in five days.

And so, after paying a visit to the kitchens, he'd slipped back into his dungeon cell to await his jailers.

It was now midmorning, long past the hour when he'd expected his jailer in the unappealing event that he was to be hung, beheaded, or drawn and quartered. The jailer's announcement that he was to see the king assured him that his wait was not in vain. Arthur was curious about him. Curious enough at least to delay his death in favor of something more entertaining as Amber had warned. And he was curious about Arthur.

Arthur the boy-warrior, conqueror, politician, king. A man brilliant enough to build a kingdom that was to have lasted a thousand years for the dynasty of kings that was to follow—but hadn't.

For according to legend and fleeting accounts of history, written by those same scribes whose lives depended on the eloquence if not entirely the accuracy of those written accounts, it had all been lost through betrayal. Some said it was the queen's betrayal with one of Arthur's knights.

Some said that he had died, betrayed by his own son, a son conceived by his sister as a young man. Such, he knew, was frequently the case, when a blood line to a throne must be ensured. Whatever the cause that had set the wheels of destruction in motion, Camelot had fallen to the powers of Darkness, Arthur died without a rightful heir to the kingdom, and all was lost. That same darkness of evil had taken Amber and brought her here.

"Clean this place while I am gone," he said over his shoulder to the rat which watched from the corner where it had fled when the bolt was thrown back.

There was no response, nor had he expected one. His satisfaction came from the bewildered expression on his guard's face as he glanced about the small chamber to see who he had spoken to.

It had been after nightfall when they arrived at Camelot the previous evening. Torches along the walls and in the main rooms hinted at the grandeur that had been Camelot. Now in the light of day, he saw fully what had inspired both legend and myth, a hint of it left behind in the crumbling ruins he and Lord Stephen's men had found and taken refuge in.

It was much larger than the ruins they had found, a full half again as large, with vast wings expanding out from the main hall, linked by yet more colonnaded balconies.

These wings housed the living quarters for other members of the king's family, his advisors, accommodations for visiting personages of importance, no doubt including Guinevere's father, upon the conclusion of their negotiations for the marriage some months earlier. And the living quarters of the lord high counselor to the king, the one to whom the king once confided everything—Merlin.

The walls and stone floors gleamed with newness, the pale sandstone catching the light that poured through open balconies, doors, and windows, the Roman influence strong in the light that flooded the chambers and great hall and in stark contrast to the closed, dark chambers of the cold, forbidding towers and castles five hundred years in the future.

The king's blue and gold colors were now intermingled with Lady Guinevere's brilliant green colors in the bold tapestries that lined the walls and decorated the floors, and pennons that flew from the uppermost towers. Already her presence and influence was felt, even in the star-chamber.

It was there his guards escorted him. It was there, just outside the chamber, they had been instructed to wait until the king was ready for him.

He sensed those within the star-chamber, beyond those stout doors—Arthur and eleven of his knights including Sir Bors, his advisors, and two of his generals. Lady Guinevere in a position of honor as befitted her station. Amber was there as well. With that unwanted, heated, stirring of the blood, he sensed her—that which needed and wanted her reaching out, connecting with her in a way that had bound them from the moment he first laid eyes on her in another time, sensing a restlessness and uncertainty within her. That same restlessness of awakening desire in her eyes that had looked back at him from the shadows as they hid from Arthur's guards the night before; that moment when he could have kissed her and she would not have resisted.

But nowhere among those within the star-chamber

did he sense the one he needed to find; the one to whom he was connected in the blood that flowed through him, brilliant and wise, who had made a man king of Britain with the powers of the Light and whose fate had been sealed by events in this time and place, doomed to exile when Camelot was lost. His father. Merlin.

Then the massive doors of the star-chamber opened and he was escorted into the chamber by Sir Bors. In that great knight's eyes he saw nothing that would reveal what lay in store for him. In his thoughts, he sensed not death but challenge as Amber had said.

Arthur was not about to accept him at his word that he was a warrior. He would have to prove himself. And he cursed his short-sightedness that he had not possessed the foresight to acquire a horse.

Arthur had turned in conversation to Guinevere. Already history was being proven to be incorrectly written. Though she had come to him as the means to a marriage of power to strengthen his hold over the warring factions of Britain against outside invaders, it was clear by Arthur's expression that he respected her and valued her opinion in matters.

Whatever else was written about this legendary king and queen, Truan sensed that theirs was a true partnership of ambition and power, united by intelligence and duty. History had given them both a role to play and no matter what their other feelings might have been, they both accepted that duty.

Yet, from respect Truan knew that love might grow. A love that would have to be strong enough to withstand the accusations of infidelity and betrayal that lay in the future.

As before when they had first met in the forest, Truan was aware of Guinevere's thoughtful expression and the sudden intensity of emotion that moved through her as she watched him—that sudden certainty of recognition, of having known someone before. But only he sensed it. She gave nothing away to anyone else. Already she had become very skilled at concealing her emotions from others.

Amber sat beside her, in a position of one who is allowed to accompany her mistress, at least until Guinevere became queen of Camelot. It was Amber's hand, not the king's, that Lady Guinevere reached for, betraying her apprehension at the fate that awaited him. An apprehension that seemed unwarranted for he had only met her the day before.

"Join us, warrior," Arthur bid him, the more important affairs of state obviously concluded.

"I trust you slept well."

Truan's gaze met Amber's briefly, and in their blue-green depths he saw a flash of mischief.

"Very well," Truan replied, restraining his desire to smile back at her. It would not improve his position to be caught grinning like a jackanapes before the king.

"And you have eaten?"

He heard a soft strangled sound, and glanced at Amber once more. Color crept across her cheeks and sparkled in her eyes with the effort of maintaining her composure.

"Very well indeed, milord. You are to be commended on the apples from Camelot's orchards. A rare, fine crop."

This time it was Sir Bors who choked and then tried to cover it with a sudden cough behind his gloved hand. Over the top of that glove he glared at his men in a sweeping, furious look that included Truan and promised punishment.

"Now, sir warrior," Arthur continued, sitting back in

his chair with the confidence of one who is assured of his power. "Perhaps you can tell us what is to be done with you?"

That caught Truan by surprise. He had sensed Arthur's intelligence and cunning, but he had not known the form it might take. He looked at Arthur with new appreciation, a mortal to be certain, which made him vulnerable to mortal failings, but one to be admired. The legend grew. Truan sharpened his wits.

"Most would feel the need to see me thrown in a dungeon," he cut a glance to Sir Bors, "or perhaps hung from the gates, drawn-and-quartered," he added a few more well-known tortures to the list, usually applied in the present century.

"But you suggest otherwise?" Arthur concluded, resting his chin upon his hand, a look of amusement glinting in his blue eyes. Beside him, Guinevere's apprehension seemed to increase although she too watched him with growing interest. Amber had grown decidedly pale, her soft lips parted in silent warning at what she considered his foolishness before the king. Her thoughts connected with his.

What are you doing! Arthur is no fool! But treat him like one and you will *find yourself hanging from the gate!*

And would you regret my death, sweet Amber? his thoughts moved like silken heat through hers.

He saw her startled expression at the tender invasion and the reply that came before she could call it back.

I could not bear it!

The force of it, as if it came from her soul, stunned him. He had been aware of her infatuation in that other time and place that they had shared. He had kept from her the depth of his own feelings, thinking her but a girl who reached out to him with the feelings of a child that came from that wounded place within her.

But the emotions he sensed stirring within her were not the feelings of a child, nor were they the feelings of one who has been deeply wounded and seeks comforting. They were the fierce, passionate feelings of a woman, in the sudden heating of her blood, the quickening of her pulse, and a sweet longing of physical need that quickened deep inside her.

He forced his thoughts back to Arthur. "I suggest," he told the king, "that you make the best use of what you have before you."

Arthur sat up with greater interest. This brazen young warrior reminded him of someone. The memory brought with it both fondness for the camaraderie found only in manhood, in the sharing of a quest, and sadness for the loss of it.

"And what might that be?" he asked with growing curiosity.

"I am a warrior," Truan explained. He angled a glance at Sir Bors, the older warrior's confident expression measuring him, waiting for him to slip the noose around his own neck.

"A warrior," he continued, "who might be of service to you. A king has need of his warriors. Why squander such useful skills to the hangman when they might be put to good use?"

"Why indeed?" The question was asked, drawing the attention of all to those large doors through which he'd entered moments before.

The doors of the star-chamber had opened. The young warrior slowly entered, followed by his men.

Like the rest of Arthur's knights, he was dressed in royal blue tunic and leggings, with a silver breastplate over. He was tall, and walked with the assurance of one who has proven himself in battle beside his king. Not a young knight-in-training who had once called himself Gareth of Montrose.

"Welcome home, nephew."

And in Arthur's greeting, Truan discovered a great deal he had not known. Gareth was the king's nephew! He met Gareth's gaze evenly as the young knight slowly circled the round table, greeted in turn by each of his fellow knights. He was one of Arthur's trusted inner circle, the king's flesh and blood, and a traitor who had traveled into the future.

It was not the meeting he would have chosen. The advantage clearly was against him. Here, Gareth was trusted as a loyal warrior. The deadly game that had begun five hundred years in the future had now been taken to another level. At least now his adversary was out in the open.

"Milady," Gareth greeted Guinevere, going down on his knee before her.

In the polite greeting Truan sensed a sibilant threat. Did Guinevere perhaps scnsc it as wcll? Or did something more lay between them? Ambition perhaps, in the simplest mortal terms? Arthur's forthcoming marriage to Guinevere and any heirs born of that marriage would preclude any claim Gareth or Gaheris might hope to make to the crown.

As far as history was written, Guinevere had borne no children to Arthur, though it was widely speculated that she had borne a child, conceived of an adulterous affair before Arthur's death on the battlefield at Camlann. By recorded history, an event that would not take place for another year.

Guinevere maintained her composure, but her slender hands were white-knuckled where she clasped the arms of her chair, as Gareth turned his gaze to Amber in silent greeting.

His eyes glowed with a possessive lust as he bowed his head to her, his gaze never leaving hers, forcing her attention when she would have looked away, glimpsing something in her thoughts that made him angle a look at Truan.

"I have heard of this warrior in the streets, milord," Gareth told the king. "All of Camelot is abuzz with tales of his daring rescue of Lady Guinevere. Methinks he hardly has the look of a warrior, but more the look of . . . the barnyard."

"He has suggested the offer of his services," Arthur pointed out, much amused by his nephew's participation in the conversation.

Gareth nodded as he rested a foot casually upon the raised dais where Arthur and Lady Guinevere sat apart from the knights at the round table, resting his weight upon an arm braced at the back of Amber's chair.

"Ah, the keeper of the pigsty, no doubt, for surely he has the look of a pigsty about him."

Like a cat toying with a mouse, he took Amber's hand in his, lightly playing with her slender fingers. When she attempted to jerk her hand away, his fingers tightened.

Truan sensed her inner turmoil and pain, as Gareth increased the pressure of his fingers, capable of snapping slender bones, deliberately trying to force her into submission.

She grew pale. Her eyes filled with tears. But she stubbornly refused to yield in his childish game of brutality, until Truan feared Gareth would break every bone in her hand. Even then she did not cry out, did not plead for help either in look or thought, instead closing her eyes and attempting to close out the pain, making him wonder if this was perhaps how she had survived another far more brutal encounter in that other time and place.

"If you continue, nephew," Arthur intervened, "you will injure the poor girl, and she will be of little use either to her mistress, or as your wife."

Gareth's grip loosened but he did not release Amber's hand, but instead stroked it, a kindness offered to soothe the abusive bruises. She endured it in wounded silence. But what of Arthur's last pronouncement? Truan looked at Amber, his gaze burning through her. Was she to be wed to Gareth?

"She has not said that she will have me, uncle," Gareth confessed. He looked down at Amber possessively. "But I intend to persuade her."

"There are matters of far more importance than this," Amber said softly, but clearly enough for all, including Truan to hear. "The king's wedding is only days away." She tucked her bruised hand inside her other hand at her lap.

"And then you will have no more excuses, fair Amber." He seized her hand, insisting when she would have resisted.

Truan sensed her bracing for the pain that was familiar in small and subtle ways. But Gareth did not hurt her this time as he forced her hand to his lips, his gaze angling toward Truan as he kissed it.

"But what is to be done with the pig-keeper?" Gareth asked, his attention once more focused on Truan. "Perhaps he may entertain us. But alas, I fear we may have a shortage of pigs, so many have been prepared for the feast on the occasion of your wedding, milord."

"I see no shortage of pigs," Truan replied, drawing a stunned silence in the hidden meaning that was hidden to none except the deaf and idiots.

"But pigs provide no appeal except upon a roasting spit. I propose an entertainment that might appeal far more to Sir Gareth, a competition of skill at weapons. What better way," he said with an engaging smile, "to prove my claim?"

Arthur studied both men with a thoughtful expression. He had no desire to see the young stranger's blood spilled. Still, if he was a skilled warrior he might have use of those skills. If he was not, then he had no use of him whatsoever. Although he liked him very much. Very few, beyond Sir Bors and Merlin, had stood up to Gareth's youthful hot-headedness.

"What say you, nephew?" Arthur asked. "You have just returned from the northern borders. Shall we postpone this competition until you are rested?"

"I see no reason to delay," Gareth replied. He smiled through his hatred. "I shall prove you false, warrior, and have you upon my sword squealing, like a pig on the spit!"

"Why are you doing this?" Guinevere demanded as Truan entered the small private garden where she had summoned him. Amber stood nearby, her face pale.

"The king doubts my abilities. A fair competition is a means of proving my ability."

"But this is not necessary!"

"It is if I do not wish to be thought of as a swineherd," Truan replied, smiling with good-humor as he tried to ease her fears.

Guinevere frowned. "Gareth is not to be taken lightly. He is a skilled warrior who has bested several of Arthur's knights. And . . ."

"And?"

She had only been at Camelot three days. Soon she

would be its queen. She was not without some awareness of the life that stretched before her—a life that would be filled with intrigues. She glanced about as if she thought the walls might have ears and spoke softly and urgently.

"He is very ambitious. There are times that ambition overrules compassion.

"I do not trust him."

Truan smiled as he leaned forward and whispered. "Neither do I."

Guinevere looked at him with surprise. "You are a stranger here, you know nothing of him. You cannot possibly know what he is capable of."

"Then it is safe to assume he is capable of anything."

She threw up her hands. "I give up. You are the most stubborn, foolish, intractable man I have ever known . . ."

There was something in her voice, a hesitation, as if in saying it, she had been reminded of something. Her expression changed then, softened, as she reached out and laid a hand at his arm.

"Promise me you will be careful," she smiled softly, some of the humor returning to her eyes. "I would not wish to lose such a gallant warrior who faces down wolves without his sword."

He laid his hand over hers and assured her, "You will find that I am not easily lost, milady."

Amber started to say something, but then apparently thought better of it. Yet, he sensed it within her thoughts. Perversely, perhaps unwisely, he wanted to hear it from her lips.

"What is it, sweet Amber?" he asked, taking her hand gently in his. It was the same hand Gareth had forcibly held two days earlier upon their first encounter in the star-chamber. Bruises marred the pale, silken flesh. He sensed the pain in the bruised muscles and bones, yet her grasp was strong and sure.

"Gareth has much to lose," she added her warning to Lady Guinevere's.

"Aye, he *does,*" Truan replied, tenderly rubbing his thumb back and forth across the back of her hand. His gaze never left hers as he felt the pain within those bruised muscles, taking it away and replacing it with the warmth that flowed between them.

He heard her surprise, then saw it in her eyes, as the pain disappeared. She looked up at him then as an image slipped through the darkness that imprisoned her memory.

"What is it?"

Her delicate brows knit together. "I don't know how to explain it, but it is as if . . ."

He sensed the beginning of a memory, a memory that might endanger her. He gently released her hand and the connection to her thoughts as he turned to Lady Guinevere.

"Will you think of me on the morrow, milady?" he asked, mentally and emotionally distancing himself from the look in Amber's eyes. "I shall need all the help I can get."

"I will do far more than that, sir warrior, for I would like nothing better than to see a new champion at Camelot." She removed a length of brilliant green ribbon from the length of braid that lay over her shoulder.

"Our chance encounter in the forest brought you to Camelot. The least I can do is offer you my support. Will you wear my colors, sir warrior?"

Truan accepted the ribbon. "I would be honored, fair lady."

"And you shall have the return of your sword as well," she assured him. "I persuaded the king. He appreciates fine weapons and suspects that unless you are also a thief, there may be more competition than Gareth has bargained for. I pray 'tis so," she added wistfully.

"If I should fall, will you see my body properly mourned," he asked Amber, using humor at her expense. Her face lost all its color, then flooded crimson with anger.

"You are a fool! It would serve you right if Sir Bors or one of his men does run you through." Then, completely abandoning all sense of protocol, she fled the garden without waiting for permission from Guinevere amid a fluster of swirling skirts and flaming cheeks.

"You seem to have the ability to anger her as none other," Guinevere commented after Amber had gone.

"Better her anger," Truan replied softly as he turned and bid her farewell. There was much to be done before the morrow.

Guinevere watched him leave, a part of her heart following him for he reminded her of someone else, someone with as much pride, anger, and sense of duty. And that terrified her.

Merlin walked through silent gardens, along the colonnaded balcony, and past chamber doors. He stopped at one, sensing a presence he had not felt in a very long time, a presence of life, gone from his other life, passed away five hundred years earlier.

Friend. The word moved through his thoughts, part supplication, part apology for what had been lost between them out of blindness.

"I turned my back on you because of a great wrong. Two wrongs did not make a right. I should have stayed. Perhaps if I had . . ."

Regret was deep for the loss of Arthur's friendship,

too blinded had he been by the lesser wrong he thought he had committed in loving *her* too much. It could not be changed now.

He moved on, quickly finding that other chamber. His steps slowing in spite of his resolve not to linger. He reached out, lightly touching the wood at the portal of her chamber, no longer a man of three score years, but a young warrior who had walked these same halls and passageways, who had felt the fire of ambition and the promise of the future, and the stirring passion of love rising in his blood. A forbidden love.

His fingers clenched into a fist, closing over air, knowing he dare not pass beyond that portal to where she lay. That his choices—however misguided—had already been made and could not now be undone. Not for her sake, not for the sake of their son.

He lingered but a moment longer, drawing her essence within him once more, feeling that stirring of youth, remembering the passion and desire that had leapt between them like a fire out of control and threatened to burn everything in its path to cinders. And then, as he had five centuries before, loving her no less than then, he moved on, seeking the one whose life mattered above all else—the son born of their passion, in whom the powers of the Light carried the hope of the future.

Merlin found him sleeping in the knight's quarters, safe enough among them whose loyalty to Arthur was assured. Only one was missing, Arthur's nephew, who by his station had his own chamber within the main hall.

Gareth whose treachery was now known. If he had known then . . . But he had not, and he had left Arthur in grave danger that had slowly closed around him until all was lost.

There was still hope. It lay with his son. He knelt beside the sleeping man, keeping his presence from him as he touched his shoulder, the cheek with the growth of beard, then gently lay his hand over the heart that lay within mortal flesh, but that held the power of the universe within its pulsing beat, and he felt the power within. The power that he had unknowingly passed on when he and Guinevere lay together knowing that it was the last time. That her destiny was with Arthur, not with him.

If he had known that she carried his child, could he have left her? Even now, he did not know the answer. Except that he knew what would never have been if he had *not* left her. And neither could he have made that choice.

In the man who was his child, he saw himself and the hope for what might have been and might still be.

"Truan," he whispered his son's name as he laid his hand at his forehead and let the power flow between them.

"Dream, my son, of things you must know, and remember that I love you."

"Remember . . ."

"You are the destiny, my son," the voice whispered through Truan's dreams.

"I was turned from my destiny. You must not be. For within you lies the hope for the future of mankind. Beware the choice that must be made, or all will be lost. You possess the wisdom of the ages. Do not stray from that truth, and all that you seek shall be yours."

The child of his dreams returned, looking back at him. And then he was the child. Then no longer a child, but a man looking back at himself.

"I don't understand. You must tell me what it is that waits for me."

"Do not stray from the truth, my son. Believe in what lies within your heart. Do not abandon yourself."

"You must tell me! Do not leave me! Father?"

Truan jerked awake. He was bathed in sweat, the dream still real within his senses. So real that he leapt to his feet, certain that someone had been standing over him.

He sensed something in the air, a powerful presence that seemed to touch him, like that of a comforting hand upon his shoulder. But when he whirled around there was no one there.

An encounter with the Darkness? He knew it had not been, for that powerful presence was familiar to him. This was something else. Something that had reached into his very soul and touched him. A single word leapt into his thoughts.

Father.

Thirteen

The day was warm, the sun beating down overhead, a light breeze stirring the sides of the pavilion, billowing panels of brilliant green and snapping the pennons overhead in that same color. Lady Guinevere's colors, where Truan now prepared for competition.

A deadly competition, Truan had no doubt, if Gareth was able to determine the outcome. An outcome he had no intention of fulfilling.

Beyond the gates of Camelot the greensward was dotted with tents and pavilions of other bright colors, including Arthur's blue and gold. Guests had been arriving for days for the celebration of his marriage to Lady Guinevere, and their excitement over the competition added to a festive atmosphere through which ran an undercurrent of nervous expectation.

History had never seen the likes of it before, except perhaps in the grandeur that was once Rome, or perhaps in the far empires where Alexander the Great had once ruled. Nor was it likely that it would see it again.

There was a pageantry of hope and destiny, as if the future somehow began here and now, on the occasion of this wedding and the dreams that it might have fulfilled. If not for treachery and betrayal.

It was that destiny that Truan now stepped into as he

closed his eyes and turned his thoughts inward, summoning the power and the wisdom within, letting it flow through him in the blood that pulsed through his veins with every beat of his heart.

The dream washed back over him.

You are the destiny, my son, the voice whispered once more. *I was turned from my destiny. You must not be.*

For within you lies the hope for the future. You possess the wisdom of the ages. Beware the choice that must be made. Do not stray from that truth, and all that you seek shall be yours.

I don't understand. You must tell me what it is that waits for me.

In his thoughts he heard again the voice of his dream, the voice of the child . . . himself.

You must tell me!

Do not stray from the truth, my son. Believe in what lies within your soul. Do not abandon yourself!

You must tell me! Do not leave me! Father?

And as if he had suddenly broken the surface of water, he surfaced from the dream, gasping at the realness of it. Like the night before when he had awakened, certain that someone had been there.

He wore only breeches and his boots, his tunic and shirt set aside for practice earlier that morning. A fine sheen beaded his skin and dampened the palms of his hands. The dream had seemed so real.

The breeze stirred through the pavilion as the flap was lifted and he turned, half expecting to find the embodiment of that dream standing before him.

"I'm sorry," Amber said, realizing that she had startled him.

He slowly released the air he had been holding in his lungs, and lowered the tip of the unfamiliar sword he'd been given to practice with, unaware until that moment that he had been holding it before him, slicing the air as he turned his thoughts inward, relying on his senses.

It reminded him of another time when he had looked at her down the length of a blade that had almost cut through her gown and the tender flesh beneath. In her eyes he saw a fragment of that same memory that stirred in a fleeting look of fear that was gone the moment he lowered the blade.

She took a deep breath. "I called out . . ."

"But I did not reply."

She gave him an odd look. "You replied. It sounded as if you said . . . *father.*"

Truan smiled. "Perhaps I was praying for divine intervention."

Her face paled then. In the soft, stricken expression he saw all her fear and far more that came from the fear, something glimpsed when she would have preferred broken bones rather than yield to Gareth the knowledge that he'd hurt her. Strength and passion.

"Were you praying to God?"

The question caught him off guard. How to answer? That he did not believe in God as she had been raised to believe in such things. That for him *God* meant other things. Those things that defined his existence were far different from hers. But was it any different in matters of faith? Different only in what each chose or needed to believe?

"Yes, I suppose I was." He smiled then, because she seemed so very serious. "It certainly couldn't hurt to pray."

Her eyes darkened, catching and holding the color of the panels around them, green like leaves stirring at the trees in the forest.

She suddenly approached closer, clasping her slender hands over his where they rested on the sword with a fierce strength as if she would force him to understand what he must.

"You mustn't make a joke of this. Gareth is deadly serious. He believes you have insulted the king and Lady Guinevere, and . . ."

"And you?" He turned his hand, cradling hers, lacing his fingers through hers. "Have I?"

"You know you have not."

"Then where is the insult?"

"It lies in what he believes . . ." she hesitated, suddenly uncertain. Her fingers would have slipped through his if he had not gently closed his hand over hers, stopping her retreat.

Small and firm, her breasts pressed against the fabric of her tunic with each breath, as if she suddenly found it difficult to breathe.

Truan raised her hand to his lips, knowing that he dare not, but needing to feel the softness of her skin, to taste it, if only in a kiss on her fingertips.

"What does he believe?"

Her gaze met his then, the same yet different, not shy or frightened, not hidden, but open, filled with emotions she no longer bothered to hide, and the vague, illusive memory that she had touched and been touched just this way, in some other time and place.

Her voice caught on a softly drawn breath. "He believes there is something between us."

The sound of her voice, that startled sound as though she remembered something and could not clearly see it but felt it, the fragile strength of her hand, reaching inside him, inside his heart, tearing apart every reason he'd vowed he must not feel anything for her.

Death or destiny waited beyond the fluttering green panels of the pavilion. He willed it back.

"What do you believe?" he whispered, daring to slip into her thoughts, her heart, her soul.

"I . . ."

It was on the tip of her tongue to deny it—that moment that hung suspended between them in the forest when it seemed they both saw into a shared past that was the future; in that sheltered alcove when he had held her in his arms; outside her chamber door when he tasted desire at her lips and ached for more.

But she could not.

She reached up, her breasts soft against him through the layers of her clothes as she pulled him down for her kiss, an intense fiery explosion of the senses that burst between them like an inferno.

Her lips parted beneath his, a soft, yielding sweetness that burned through him as he deepened the kiss, his arms closing around her with a fierce, possessive need, a hunger too-long denied, as if he could pull her inside him.

He stroked the length of her back, memorizing the feel of her, each slender bone, the strength in each muscle, the way the slender ridge of her spine curved down to the softness of her as she seemed to become part of him. Then, the sound at the back of her throat as her fingers stroked down his back, clinging to him, the sweetness of her mouth as she opened herself to him, the warmth of her breath filling his lungs, burning through his blood in the surrender of that kiss.

She suddenly backed away from him. The expression on her face was stunned. She'd wanted to prove them both wrong. He saw it in the confusion amid the desire that burned in the depths of her eyes. May the gods help them both, she had.

She ran past Sir Bors at the entrance to the pavilion. The knight thoughtfully glanced after her, then dropped the panel across the opening back into place as he stepped inside the pavilion. He handed Truan his sword.

Truan looked at him questioningly as he took the weapon, testing its balance, refamiliarizing himself with the feel of it, heavy and sure in his hands.

"I serve the king," Sir Bors explained, "*and* our new queen. She said you were to have it." He nodded. "A man should have his own sword when he is about to go into battle."

"Even if it is a 'mock' battle," Truan suggested. After Amber's warning he knew there would be nothing "mock" about the fighting he would encounter.

Sir Bors grinned and in his smile confirmed Amber's warning. "Aye, anything can happen on the battlefield as any warrior knows." He gestured to the green pennon and said with surprise, "You wear the queen's colors."

"Either that, or the colors of the swineherd," Truan suggested. The knight grinned again. Then the grin flattened.

"Sir Gareth is young," he explained. "He has much to learn of men and battles. He often acts before he thinks."

Truan arched a brow at this unexpected breech in loyalty. "A warning, Sir Bors?"

The knight shook his head. "Make no mistake. My first loyalty is to the king. If I think that you play him false I will be the first to run you through with my own sword. But I believe in fairness. There is neither fairness nor honor in condemning a man *before* he has proven himself."

"But hang him afterward, if he fails," Truan suggested, liking the older knight very much in spite of the fact that he'd spent his first night in the dungeons at Sir Bors's orders—at least insofar as the knight assumed.

The knight laughed, slapping him on the back. "Of course!" He winked at Truan. "But I think you do not intend to fail."

"I do not," Truan replied.

Beyond the pavilion the trumpetfare announced the call to competition. The contest was to begin soon. As Sir Bors turned to leave, Truan sensed that something bothered him as he paused at the entrance to the pavilion. Then having made his decision, he said, "Though it is not allowed, take care of those who may strike at your back," he offered by way of advice. "I have never considered such actions to be fair in competition."

"But fair in war?" Truan suggested.

Sir Bors grinned. "*All* is fair in war. That is why it is called *war.*"

Truan nodded. "My thanks for the warning."

As Sir Bors left, Truan had no doubt whom the knight had warned him against.

The competition that had been planned as part of the celebration of the royal marriage was made up of two teams of twenty men each. Truan was to stand in for Lochiel on his team. He was relieved not to have to face that giant on the battlefield.

A mock battlefield had been formed by lines cut into the greensward before the row of pavilions with a line marking the middle. On each side of the field were three points of defense—a mound of earth like the ancient hill forts; a barrier of rocks where opponents could easily hide and lay in wait to attack; and a "forest" made up of trees, logs, and brush that had been hacked down, dragged to the site behind horses, and reconstructed to simulate a forest.

The rules for the mock battle were clearly called out by Arthur's seneschal. Each team was to plan a battle strategy, for taking the other team's defenses. One team was represented by Arthur's royal blue colors, the other team represented by gold. Truan carried two colors; royal gold and Lady Guinevere's green. Each warrior carried a pennon in his team color.

Conquests were made and points earned when a defender's pennon was claimed. Once taken by an opponent it could not be reclaimed. The team claiming the most pennons after all defenses had been taken, was declared the winner and honored as champion of the day.

Swords were allowed, as well as the mace, shield, and helm. Arthur's knights all wore helms. Truan declined. He preferred a full field of vision unencumbered by the heavy headpiece.

Injuries were common, but no man was allowed to strike a man when he was down and his pennon claimed, nor was he allowed to strike a crippling blow.

Excitement ran high. It was palpable among the king's knights and guests who watched from the pavilions. Wagers had been made throughout the morning on the outcome.

Truan accepted a shield but declined the mace, preferring to concentrate on the precision of one weapon. The horns sounded the king's fanfare. Arthur rode out to the battlefield amidst his knights.

He was impressive astride his mount, a warrior king who had fought many battles for much more than pennons and the thrill of victory. He dismounted, speaking to all about honor, courage, and fairness. Making them all laugh when he reminded them of the ladies who watched.

"It is most disconcerting to find oneself flat on one's backside in the mud," he reminded them. "I know well enough. I ask that you leave your opponent's clothes intact. At least his breeches. I would not have the ladies of Camelot discovering that the stories my knights have been boasting as to the length of their 'swords,' are in fact lies."

This met with much laughter among his men.

"Fight fairly and well. I have need of all my knights."

"Will you give me your own pennon, sire?" Gareth asked. "To carry for family honors."

Arthur nodded and gave one of his own blue pennons with the royal seal embossed upon it, to his nephew.

"Good hunting!" Arthur bid them all as he swung astride his horse once more and galloped to the edge of the field. The teams took their positions far afield, behind rock and mound.

Arthur's seneschal handed him a bow. The tip of an arrow had been wrapped with cloth and soaked in oil. The king notched the arrow. His seneschal lit the oil soaked tip and Arthur released the arrow, sending it aloft in a signal that the contest had begun.

The strategy of Truan's team was simple. They were to divide into two forces, sweep inward from the sides of the battlefield, then rejoin in a penetrating thrust at the edge of the forest.

Their own pennons were the lure to draw the enemy after them. Once inside the forest, they would take individual conquests. The wisdom and brilliance lay in not wasting foolish time on the taking of individual landmarks as their opponents were clearly intent upon doing. Once the enemy had been conquered by the loss of their pennons, the landmarks were automatically theirs as spoils of war.

The simplicity of it was not anticipated by their opponents who were left to defend rock and hill against an enemy that swept past them rather than fought. They followed the lure right into the trap that waited at the edge of the forest.

Among his teammates were Gaheris and four of the king's younger knights. Sir Bors and Lochiel watched with the king, having participated in their share of competitions over the years. Along with Arthur, they were to be the judges of the contest.

The forests that had been built were elaborate mazes of thick underbrush, gorse thickets, trees, and fallen logs. The contest began in earnest once they entered the forest. An opponent attacked Gaheris, a glancing blow that he sidestepped at the last moment as he saw the gleam of his opponent's sword in the sunlight. He countered with a bruising blow, seized the man's pennon, and secured it to his belt.

Through the forest they saw other opponents and took up positions to cut them off, their tunics clearly visible against the colors of the forest.

Truan stripped off his tunic, laying it across a bush the same height of a man. Seeing his strategy, Gaheris shed both helm and tunic, grinning at the deception as they slipped away through the trees.

Within moments they heard wild battle cries as their tunics were attacked. The cries quickly turned to exclamations of surprise then curses as their opponents realized the deception too late and then found themselves under attack. He and Gaheris claimed two more pennons from the skirmish, then retreated to the edge of the small forest where they were to rejoin their team.

A flash of gold drew their attention. Gaheris grinned as he signaled to those he thought to be his teammates and started through the underbrush to join them. Truan saw the flash of the blade too late to warn him.

Their opponents had used confiscated pennons from their teammates to lure Gaheris into a trap.

The young knight was down but not bleeding badly. "I should have been more cautious," he groaned more with frustration and anger, than pain. "He claimed my pennon."

"Did you see who it was?"

"He wore a helm." He grinned. "But I recognized his crest. It was Sir Malcolm. He will not let me forget this."

Truan grinned cunningly. "Then I shall have to claim his. Return to the field so that your wound may be tended."

Already it had ceased bleeding. Gaheris nodded and they parted, Truan setting off through the trees in search of Sir Malcolm. He found him at the edge of the greensward, making his way back to the hill fort. He attacked high, aiming for the man's helm.

It was a glancing blow that rolled the helm from Sir Malcolm's shoulders. The knight grunted and reeled, going down on one knee. Then he pushed to his feet with raised sword. He was a fierce warrior, wielding the battle sword with great strength and stamina. But Truan had the advantage of the powers he'd been born with and sensed each move before the knight made it.

After a half dozen strikes, he deftly wielded the tip of his sword, swept Sir Malcolm from his feet, and plucked the pennon from his tunic as he went down.

"You learn quickly," the knight grunted, grinning through the sweat and grime that streamed his face as he pushed back his helm.

Truan saluted with his sword and quickly moved on, edging the rock promontory he had passed earlier in his charge into the forest.

He climbed to a high point surveying the field before

him. Several teammates from both teams had left the
field, their pennons surrendered. But an equal number
were unaccounted for. He saw Gaheris among those
who sought aid among the ladies of Camelot.

The warning cry came from Sir Malcolm, whom he
left at the edge of the forest. He turned and rolled to
his left as the blade was brought down where his head
had been only moments before. Each strike was a vicious, slashing blow, meant to maim, or kill. Through
the heat of battle, he glimpsed Gareth's crest on the
helm. He rolled away from the next blow, vaulted to his
feet and brought his own sword up to meet the next
blow.

They fought to the top of the hill fort, slashing, blocking, defending, slashing again in a contest that clearly
was for far more than a mere pennon. This he realized
was what Sir Bors had warned him of.

To his left and right he saw other teammates as well
as opponents. They were engaged in fierce competition
with no idea of the deadly battle that went on in their
midst.

A war cry went up as an opponent yielded and a pennon was seized. Truan escaped the center of the battle,
his left side momentarily exposed as well as his right,
which he defended against Gareth.

He sensed the young warrior's power, the flow of fury
and rage that wielded the sword with relentless strength.
He anticipated each blow, meeting it. But Gareth anticipated as well as they fought past the middle of the field
very near the pavilions.

In the blur of colors and faces, he heard a woman's
cry of alarm and recognized the vivid green colors as
Lady Guinevere suddenly stood. His blade shuddered
beneath another blow as he tried to defend himself

amid cries of outrage among Arthur's knights who watched from the pavilions.

He feinted left, sidestepped, then brought his own sword down, blade flattened in a numbing blow. Gareth staggered back, regained his balance, then turned and sought refuge behind the second hill fort. When Truan pursued him, he discovered him gone, then saw this retreat into the nearby forest of his opponents. Truan went after him.

At the edge of the forest, he saw the blue gleam of the pennon Arthur had given his nephew beneath the glare of the midday sun. As he entered the forest, he passed a wounded teammate. Truan dropped to the ground beside him.

The knight's name was Rohan. He'd been badly wounded, a gash opened the length of his thigh. The blade had nicked the large vein. The wound bled profusely.

The young knight shook violently, teeth tightly clamped together against the pain and the loss of blood, even as he warned Truan, "Watch your back! He attacked even though I have already lost my pennon to another."

He extended the handle of his short-bladed knife, all he had left toward Truan. "Take this."

Truan nodded his gratitude and accepted the blade. He seized a pennon from his belt and folded it into a thick square of cloth. He pressed it against the wound, temporarily stanching the flow of blood.

"Rest easy," he told the young knight as he pushed to his feet. "I will find him."

A cold rage twisted low inside Truan. Competition among fellow warriors was one thing but this had become much more than a game.

He slipped into the blind of trees, letting his senses

expand and become one with the earth and wind. Listening, feeling, sensing that which could not be seen by the human eye.

Then he felt a dangerous presence in the sudden raising of the hair at the back of his neck, that warning tingle of some subtle change in the air, a shimmer of movement felt but not seen.

He was struck from behind, the force of the blow glancing the trunk of a young sapling beside Truan's head as he ducked and countered with a return blow that caught his attacker at the shoulder. It momentarily stunned his opponent, who wore a full helm and breastplate. Then both recovered.

They fought through the trees and into a small clearing, the blades of their swords flashing beneath the midday sun, leaves, twigs, and pieces of bark flying as they hacked at each other, missed in the dense foliage, then struck again.

Truan struck, right and left, striking a blow to his opponent's helm. It staggered his attacker, driving him to one knee. He fought back, to his feet, but Truan sensed his strength waning.

The warrior's moves slowed and his steps became less certain. Each strike quivered with growing weakness. Still Truan relentlessly drove him back, thinking of Sir Rohan who'd been ruthlessly attacked, even though he'd already surrendered his pennon, in spite of Arthur's insistence that they strike no lethal wounds.

When he took a slashing wound at his side, he didn't even feel the pain, but struck back, fierce words screaming through his thoughts, driving the next, and the next blow, as if some demon had taken control of his thoughts.

Strike! Kill before you are killed! the words whispered through his thoughts.

He drove his opponent back, consumed by hatred, and swung at him until he went down again, this time with barely enough strength to lift his sword. Then, as Truan brought the sword up for another blow, another voice whispered through his thoughts, urgent and low, moving through his blood. A voice that was familiar from his dreams.

Do not! Your rage has blinded you!

Eventually the warning permeated the fog of his rage. Truan slowly lowered his sword. His opponent lowered his sword as well, then reached for his helm, and pushed it back.

Truan's blood ran cold as ice in his veins as he stared in horror—not at Gareth, but at the bloodied, sweated face of the king!

Sweat and grime caked Arthur's features. His chest rose and fell with the effort of each breath beneath the heavy breastplate. He had a gash on the forehead where he'd taken a blow to the helm, the creased metal cutting deep. His hair was matted with blood and sweat, molding his head. He smiled grimly, the look in his eyes keen and appraising.

"For a moment I thought I might be in real danger."

Their gazes met. "I thought it as well," Truan admitted. "You fought as if you intended to kill me."

He held his hand out to the king. Eventually, Arthur accepted it, and rose slowly to his feet.

"I forgot to protect myself. You are a formidable opponent."

"This is not your helm," Truan said, kicking it aside.

Arthur nodded.

"I lost mine against another opponent and Gareth gave me his."

"Gareth," Truan muttered, driving the tip of his sword into the earth, another kind of rage moving through his blood at the deception that had almost lured him into killing Arthur.

"Aye," the king said, speaking proudly. "The only one on my team who was not forced to surrender his pennon."

"I was not aware that you planned to join the competition," Truan commented still struggling with the horrible mistake he'd almost made.

"I often join one team or the other. It is a way to keep my skills sharp." Arthur wiped his brow with a green pennon Lady Guinevere had given him. He glanced thoughtfully at Truan as though trying to see more.

"I wish my knights had half your skill with a sword." He handed over his pennon. "You have earned a new title this day, I think. For I have never seen a swineherd wield a pig stick with such skill. I think there is much you have not told me."

Nor was there time for him to tell it then, as Arthur's knights approached through the forest and surrounded them, the competition over.

Gareth was among them, slowly striding toward his uncle; his own pennon intact—the same pennon he had carried for family honor. Arthur smiled as he greeted him.

"My thanks, nephew. If not for the use of your helm," he lifted the battered headpiece, "I might have lost my head."

Truan's gaze swept past the king, to Gareth. The young knight smiled at him.

"You have only two pennons, swineherd." He also held two aloft. "The same number I have claimed." He was smug and arrogant.

"It seems we do not yet have a winner."

"He has claimed three pennons this day," someone

called out. Several of Arthur's men stepped aside as Sir Rohan hobbled forward, assisted on either side by two companions. The bloodied pennon Truan had given him was tied about his leg.

"He gave me one of his claimed pennons to bind my wound after I was set upon at the edge of the forest." Sir Rohan handed the pennon to the king. "I would have died had he not given aid. He has claimed *three* pennons," he declared loud enough for all to hear, "he is clearly the winner of the day's contest."

A muscle spasmed at Gareth's cheek, but he gave no other outward sign of the rage that burned through him at the humiliation of the obvious loss to Truan. He dared not before the king, nor could he claim another pennon unless he plucked it from the air.

"It seems, *swineherd,*" he said scathingly, "that your team has claimed the day. You were fortunate to have such skilled teammates. Next time you may not be so fortunate."

Arthur wrapped an arm about his nephew's shoulders.

"Accept that you have been beaten, as I have," Arthur reminded him. Then he smiled companionably at Truan.

"There is much we can learn from his skills, and there will be other competitions," he promised, suggesting that the outcome next time might not be the same.

"Come," he said, pounding Truan on the back with enthusiasm that clearly was not shared by his nephew. "Let us celebrate. You have proven yourself this day, warrior. I think we shall have to come up with a new name for you."

Fourteen

Amber looked for Truan among the knights in the king's pavilion. She had seen him earlier only briefly as Arthur toasted the victorious team, bestowing upon them the much-coveted garland of woven blue and green ribbons, the first garland won under the reign of King Arthur and Lady Guinevere, who was soon to become his queen.

Truan had been injured in the competition. She glimpsed the dried blood at his side beneath the mantle Sir Bors has thrown over his shoulders. But she could not reach him to inquire about the seriousness of his wound.

Then there had been several more rounds of congratulatory toasts among the knights and warriors, each participant recounting his version of the contest, the fierce fighting, good-natured criticism made of those who had become perhaps over zealous during the contest, and many jests made about wounds received in embarrassing places. For the most part, Arthur's knights maintained their humor, their dignity, and most of their clothing in the mock battle.

Except for Gareth.

There was an edge to his jests and the recounting of his conquests, as if he now attempted to salvage some of his wounded pride with boastful remarks about his conquests of the afternoon. But she heard the whispers that some warriors had not fought fairly and wondered if he perhaps boasted too loudly. Eventually, he retreated to the corner of the pavilion surrounded by his companions and ample wine.

When he tried to draw her into their conversation, she escaped with the excuse of an errand for Lady Guinevere. She searched for Truan again among the other warriors who celebrated, but she could not find him.

She grew restless and fidgeted, already weary of the celebrations that would last long into the night and continue with the culmination of the wedding ceremony three days hence.

Guinevere saw her gaze wander again to the entrance of the pavilion, sensed her longing to escape, and the cause of it as well.

She too longed to escape but could not. The hours dwindled toward morning. Soon another day would be gone. In a few days she would wed Arthur and take her place at his side.

The thought brought a pang of longing for things lost that could never be, her fingers curling over the fabric of her gown, taut across her slim waist, a memory stirring like life stirring in a mother's womb. Then, as she learned to do, she willed her hand to relax and the memory back into the past where it must remain.

"He has escaped," she said, smiling gently as Amber turned to her with a look of surprise. Oh, to feel those things once more which she saw so clearly reflected in Amber's eyes; longing and anticipation along with that first stirring of desire. "Sir Bors saw him leave after he returned my colors," she went on to explain.

They exchanged a look. In the girl she saw what she

had once felt, an innocence of passion and longing in the shimmering depths of her eyes.

"He was injured," Amber explained, trying and failing to hide her true feelings.

Guinevere nodded. "Go quickly," she said, "before any see you leave."

As Amber rose to leave, her thoughts already far beyond the pavilion, Guinevere asked, "Do you love him?"

Without thought, as instinctive as breathing, it was on the tip of Amber's tongue to say yes. But that was impossible. They had met only days before. She did not know him. And yet . . . She stared down at her clasped hands, uncertain how to answer.

"I don't know."

"What do you feel in your heart?" Guinevere asked.

Amber looked up at her then. Their gazes met. Not as future queen and subject, but as two women. "I feel as though I have known him always. As though we must have met before. Is that the way of it, milady?" Amber asked. "Something you can neither understand nor explain, but somehow feel deep within you? As if it is part of your soul?"

Guinevere was stunned by the passion of her words, a passion she had once felt and that echoed deep inside her. Something perhaps only to be understood once it had been felt.

"I think it must be," Guinevere answered softly. "And we are powerless to deny it no matter the consequences." Understanding flowed between them, a bond of something both had felt and experienced.

She looked away from Amber, her gaze distant, her voice filled with longing. "Take this time and hold it within you," she told Amber almost fiercely. "A moment, an hour, a day, however long or short. For it may have to last you a lifetime."

"What if he will not have me?"

Guinevere smiled at her once more. She had seen the expression in the warrior's eyes. Once she had seen that same passion looking back at her from a lover's eyes. With the certainty of that remembered passion, she said, "Go to him."

He had not returned to the main hall, nor the knight's quarters where she knew he had slept the night before. Eventually Amber found a young squire who had seen him near the king's stables. With pain like a fist around her heart, it occurred to her that he might have decided to leave Camelot.

She called out as she entered the stables, small dust clouds exploding beneath her slippered feet amid the pungence of hay, leather, harness, and horses. But there was no response, only the sound of the horses restlessly moving in their stalls as they picked up her scent.

With a sinking heart she realized that no one was there. But as she turned to leave, she saw a movement at the shadows along the wall of the stables. A fleeting movement as if some creature lurked there, watching her.

"Sir Wolf?" she called out again, using the name she had given him after their first encounter in the forest, a name she had also heard passed among the knights after his team had been victorious. They had called him that partly in jest at the story of his encounter with the wolf that day in the forest, but with a measure of growing respect after he had won the competition for his team. For a wolf was to be both feared and respected.

Again she saw that shadowy movement as though someone or something was there. The horses seemed to sense it as well, the ones in the stalls closest to the wall lunging against stall gates, snorting as if they had caught a new scent. Amber forced back her uneasiness as she approached closer.

Truan sensed her presence as he stood in the shadows. Her sweet scent as familiar as breathing. Through the haze of his own clouded senses, filled with pain, the stench of his own blood, and the power of the spell cast, he felt the instinctive warning when she approached closer.

Like a wounded animal, he had retreated into the shadows, drawing on the power, mending the wounded flesh beneath his fingertips as he clenched his teeth against the searing pain that healed.

Then, panting heavily, nauseated by the pain and the smell of blood, he leaned back, eyes closed, against the stable wall. When he opened them again, he saw her as she entered the stable. The uncertainty in the tension of her slender body; the way the late afternoon sunlight slanted through the opening behind her, slipping through her golden hair like fingers of fire, framing her in light.

He sensed her sudden apprehension as the horses grew restless, and saw her hesitation. He felt the sudden wild beating of her heart as though he had touched her. Then she walked farther into the stables, refusing to be afraid as she called out to him.

It wasn't his name she called out, but the name toasted by Arthur's knights as they celebrated their victory. *Sir Wolf.* A name she'd innocently given him after their encounter in the forest, unaware how close she came to the truth.

He would have laughed at the cruel irony of the name she'd given him but he was afraid the sound would terrify her. For it would not be the laugh of a mortal man, but the wild, fierce snarl of an immortal creature transformed.

But even as he moved through the shadows moving toward her, stalking her, allowing her a glimpse of the creature he had become and that she should fear, she did not turn and flee, but instead bravely approached closer.

He pushed away from the wall, the painful wound at his side all but forgotten for it was already healed. His expression was bittersweet at the wonderful powers he possessed as he rose out of the shadows. Powers that could give him everything, *except* mortality.

Amber saw the sudden movement in the shadows. Too late, she saw the creature that moved along the wall toward her with a terrifying swiftness, as if it stalked her. As if it hunted her. Then the creature was upon her.

She was thrown against the wall of the stables. She instinctively braced for the attack, and those powerful fangs tearing her apart. But instead of some creature's powerful claws tearing her apart, she felt strong hands at her back preventing her fall, and the length of a lean, powerful body molding against hers. Her terrified scream was muffled against the curve of straining muscle at a heavily corded shoulder.

Instead of pain, she felt a sudden, fierce heat everywhere those hands touched. At her shoulders and down the length of her back, as they closed around her with a wild, possessive strength that could have torn her apart.

Heat spread across her skin like a lover's caress, a seduction of the senses so complete, so fierce, so primal and passionate, that it stole the air from her lungs.

"You should not have come here." His voice was harsh, a snarl torn from somewhere deep inside.

"I had to," she said, struggling between fear and desire. "I was afraid . . ."

"You should be afraid." His hands framed her face, fingers pressing against sleek bones, bruising her. "You should be terrified. You should run, as far away from me as you possibly can."

"I cannot!" she whispered. "I wish I could, but I cannot!"

"Then I will make you leave!"

He forced her back against the wall, his hands plunging back through her hair, fingers pressing into her skull as if he would tear her head from her shoulders.

He did not, but instead kissed her, forcing her mouth open, bruising her lips, then plundering her mouth until she cried out.

In that tender, surrendering sound that slipped through his senses, in that moment when he realized she would endure anything but leaving him, including a violation every bit as wounding as the one she'd suffered in that other place and time, he knew he could not send her away.

He breathed her strength and passion, tasted it in the soft swollen bruises at her lips, then still cradling her head, fingers stroking through her hair, he leaned his forehead against hers. His voice was raw with agony.

"You do not know what you say. You do not know me . . . what I am."

She laid her hands over his, unbelievably small, slender bones that could so easily be broken within his powerful hands, yet with a fierce strength and stubbornness that matched his own.

"I know that I cannot bear to let you go. I know there is something inside me that comes alive when you touch me." She took a deep breath that trembled at her lips as she spoke from her heart.

"I know that I love you. That I have always loved you."

His head went back, eyes closed in silent agony, as he held her, the helplessness of rage leaving him like a great bone-deep weariness, something that he had fought too long and couldn't fight any longer.

"There are things you must know."

But he did not know how he could tell her. Of the other life that had brought her so much pain; of the journey through the portal and things he did not yet fully understand; of the powers of Darkness and his fear—that uniquely mortal emotion—that he might not be able to protect her; that by loving her, he might destroy her love for him.

"Take me away from here," she said and in those softly whispered words accepted everything that he must tell her. His hand closed around hers.

Truan held her against him as they rode bareback through the late afternoon shadows, sheltering her in his arms as she curled soft and small into the curve of his body, sleeping, dreaming, waking as the horse's pace slowed, the coolness of low-hanging branches brushing softly against her gown as they entered the forest, the soft sound of the birds oddly familiar.

Had she been there before, or had she dreamed it?

They finally stopped and Truan slipped to the ground. He reached for her then easing her down beside him. Then he freed the horse to graze untethered.

Wordlessly, he crossed the small clearing, familiar in every rock, tree and bush, as if she had been in that same exact place before.

She ran her hand over the faintly stirring fronds of deep forest ferns, light as air against her fingers, the lush green moss that wrapped the trunk of a tree, springy to the touch, the rich dark loam soft beneath her feet.

She closed her eyes. The air within the forest moved lightly against her cheek, a caress of warmth, sunlight, and deep forest fragrance that brought with it the memory of other things experienced in another time and place, and an encounter that had been both terrifying and soul-stirring. Then she felt his nearness, the warmth of him reaching out to her. Amber slowly turned toward him and opened her eyes.

Dark hair, tangled by the wind on their ride from Camelot, fell wildly about his shoulders and framed his lean, intense features. His eyes were deepest blue, almost black and gleamed with a strange golden light. He wore the rich blue mantle Sir Bors had given him. On the ride from Camelot, he had dropped it about her, sheltering her in the warm cocoon of his body. Now the mantle fell open, revealing that he wore only breeches and leather boots.

Incredibly, the wound at his side was almost healed. All that remained was a pale, pink scar. She touched him there, drawing back at the sound he made, fearing she had caused him pain. But the expression in his eyes was a different sort of pain and another memory whispered to her. She touched his cheek, tracing the strong bones, the shadow of beard on his jaw grazing her skin; a muscle flexing beneath the skin; the curve of dark brows over blue eyes that darkened with each touch as she memorized each feature.

His gaze held hers and in their shimmery blue depths she saw and felt the stirring of another memory. His memories as they reached out to her, like a gentle breeze that stirred the tapestry drawn over a window and allowed a fleeting glimpse beyond. He reached out to her, willing her to remember, with glimpses of the memories of her other life, at the same time protecting her from the pain of those memories.

Amber's gaze never left his as she reached up and slowly untied the laces at the bodice of her gown until it hung loose about her shoulders. Then, still held within the memory of what had begun between them long ago in another time and place she eased the gown from her shoulders and let it fall to the ground at her feet.

Truan tenderly picked her up and carried her to the shelter of a nearby tree. There he spread his mantle on the soft, spongy ground and lay her upon it.

Desire raged through him, powerful, dark, and possessive, as he gentled his hands at her shoulders, then forced himself not to touch her, tortured by the knowledge of what she had suffered in that other time and the need to be joined with her.

"Amber . . ." he whispered her name, as if he would tell her then, but she silenced him with her fingers against his lips. Then she took his hand in hers and brought it to her breast.

He felt the sudden tautness as her nipple beaded beneath his fingers, heard her sudden drawn breath at the heat that leapt between them, and the sudden fierce pounding of her heart beneath his hand.

Her breasts were small and high, sculpted in pale satin skin that gleamed at the rest of her body, then darker where the skin pebbled and thrust against his hand in awakening desire.

Her hands trembled as she pulled him toward her. His trembled as he bent over her and kissed her, and in the kiss giving her a memory of a first kiss stolen long ago in the halls at Camelot in that other time and place.

When the kiss ended she looked up at him with that

memory, and it expanded, drifting into other memories of laughter and friendship, magic, trust, and the tenderness with which he'd always loved her.

When she kissed him again, she gave back that laughter and magic, tenderness and trust, in the first stirrings of her body reaching for his.

She was silken every place he touched, tenderness and joy, warmth and passion. At first he let her remember only that, then entwined it with what they now shared as he removed his clothes and then lay beside her. With each touch, each caress, each kiss, each new experience he gave her, he built the fire within her, burning her with the memory of what they now shared and nothing else.

Her legs moved restlessly against his. Her back arched as her head went back, her hair spilling through his fingers. He stroked her tenderly, watching the changes in her skin, the quiver of flesh, the spasm of a slender muscle in response, then heard her frustrated sounds as he drew his hand away and began again, tracing every curve, each tender hollow; the swell of her breast, the slope at her side, gently squeezed the fullness of her bottom, then gliding over the bone at her hip and the smooth hollow of her flat belly, teasing lower before retreating.

The sounds she made became wordless sobs of yearning she had only begun to discover as her eyes opened, wide, dark, filled with sweet torment as he lightly brushed his lips at her shoulder then lower in the valley, between her breasts, then circling over a taut beaded nipple.

Her breath shuddered in her lungs, her hand clasped his shoulder then feverishly slipped behind his neck even as he forced himself to go more slowly.

"Please . . ." she whispered.

"Soon, little one," he whispered, forcing back all doubt as his words rippled the skin at her breast and his lips brushed her nipple.

She gasped softly, part agony, all pleasure, as her hands slipped through his hair and she pulled him to her. When his tongue brushed her nipple she shivered, when he drew it into the wet heat of his mouth, she cried out.

She tasted of earth, wind, and fire, her body convulsing with pleasure with each tug of his lips. When he grazed her with his teeth her body spasmed violently. He stilled her with his hands at the same time he slowly fanned the fire of passion inside her.

When he stroked her hips, her body arched in that instinctive, primal need to be joined; when he stroked her breasts and belly with his tongue eager to taste all of her, her legs stilled their restless movement and trembled in anticipation. When he pierced those soft golden curls and flicked his tongue over damp, heated flesh, she opened to him on a tiny sob. And when he finally tasted her, making love to her for the first time as no one ever had in this life or any other, he branded her as his own.

Her hands clasped his shoulders as her body arched beneath him, then spasmed as she climaxed, breathing in small, jerky sounds of discovery as if every part of her was aflame, spiraling from that place where his tongue thrust inside her, refusing to release her, tenderly forcing her to endure what she was certain she could not endure, until she lay sobbing in his arms, clinging to him, crying his name over and over as he held her.

Fifteen

Eventually the wild, fierce beating of her heart slowed, her breathing eased, and her skin cooled. Truan gently brushed damp tendrils of hair back from her forehead.

Her eyes slowly opened, staring back at him with ghosts of old memory that disappeared at the new memory of what they had just shared and the wildness of the passion that lay merely resting within her.

He sensed the question, unanswerable at least for now—*Who are you?*—because it would have endangered her to know, and instead silenced her with a kiss as he gathered her in his arms and carried her through the woods to a sheltered pool.

There was no wind, only a whisper of something that seemed to murmur across the surface of the water as it spilled over rocks at a waterfall into the pool, plunging to the bottom, then exploding in bubbles that returned to the surface in soft, sighing sounds.

The water was neither cool nor warm, but a silken wetness that enveloped them in shades of blues and greens, that shimmered brilliant one moment, dark as velvet the next, sparkling with millions of tiny lights as though the bubbles were stars.

Nor was it daylight or night, but a place in between.

Twilight gilded the surface of the water and her skin as if the light of the sun and the moon streaked her body, pale where it touched, then dusky shadow where he touched.

She was buoyant in his arms and at the same time slippery as a water reed, gliding against him, then away from him, as he laid her back over his arm and then gently cast her adrift, his fingers gliding over her hips, then down the length of thigh, knee, and slender calf, like a ship adrift in a water world, until he brought her back, his fingers closing around an ankle, reconnecting them in a tender, gentle tug that glided her back to him.

In the safety of his arms, connected by touch, she relaxed, her muscles stretching, drifting, like the streamers of moss at the edges of the pool that stroked her hips and the sides of her breasts with green water fingers, until it seemed as if she might float right out of her body, no longer confined within simple flesh and bone, but a bubble bobbing gently, like the bubble of desire that moved just beneath the surface of her skin in those unexpected places, bringing back in gently stirring waves of memory the passion he'd given her, and teasing at other passions that waited to be discovered.

Water sprite, goddess, sorceress. All of those images sprang to mind as he gently navigated her through the water, watching the undulating currents of water lap at her sides and gently stir the golden curls where he'd tasted her, the folds of flesh parted, offering up that pale, glistening pearl.

She was completely oblivious, lulled by the water, as his hands glided past her knee to her thigh, his thoughts slipping into hers with images of his hands touching her, stroking her, as he slowly drew her back through the water, letting the current touch where he longed to touch, her nipples thick and smooth with the luxuriance of the water, then beading taut and hard at the thoughts he gave her, until he brought her slowly against him, guiding her legs about his waist, until those soft curls lay against his belly and all that separated them was the pulsing current of the water.

Her eyes opened then and she stared up at him from her watery bed, floating, adrift with the desire that built once more within her.

"Not yet," he whispered to her through the connection of their thoughts, pulling her to him and with him, deeper into the middle of the pool until the water lapped at their shoulders and her breasts were flattened against him as she held onto him.

Within the connection of their thoughts, he sensed that she could not swim, then he took away any fear when he tenderly kissed her, pulling her thoughts toward the passion that waited as he slowly pulled her beneath the surface in a gliding descent, her body entwined with his.

He sensed her holding onto the fear, resisting, her hair streaming overhead like the fronds of shimmering gold water ferns as they slipped deeper beneath the surface.

He blew bubbles against her closed eyes and she opened them, staring back with surprise, the air still held in her lungs. Finally, she could hold her breath no longer. He felt the instinctive struggle to return to the surface. When that instinct became panic he gently pulled her against him.

He held her face between his hands, angled his mouth over hers, and kissed her. In that kiss, he breathed for her, gently filling her lungs with air, letting her release it as she had before, then breathing with her again in the connection of that kiss.

He felt the panic subside, then the moment she let it go, trusting him completely, putting her life in his hands as they slowly drifted together in that underwater world, safe, where no one might find them, like a womb that sheltered and protected them.

They slowly rose to the surface, connected by the air that flowed between them, the currents of water that flowed about them, and the current of passion that built within.

They broke the surface of the water like one of those bubbles, sighing softly, cradling each other, her body gliding against his, stirring the current of desire.

Her eyes were closed as she floated once more, drifting against him, then away. His hands glided down her sides, thumbs stroking her breasts as he steadied her, then lower over her hips as he slowly brought her back to him.

He watched her eyes and her thoughts, feeling her, sensing the changes in her that leapt like bubbles beneath her skin, color skimming across the surface as desire expanded with each stroke of his hands, steadying her, rousing her, gentling, then arousing once more, in a succession of waves that washed over her then receded, her breasts bobbing, nipples breaking the surface as he brought her to him once more and let her feel him.

That first penetrating glide, the length of him brushing her, nuzzling at that glistening pearl, floating her away then gliding her back once more, letting her learn him, replacing those old memories with memories of him.

Her breathing changed, trapped in her lungs as he brought her to him once more, then shivering past her lips as he let her feel him. He stroked her, opening her, letting the water stroke her glistening flesh, bubbles tickling past his fingers as he stroked inside her.

Still he watched her eyes. Heated, shimmering, blue-green pools in a blue-green world, giving herself over to that naked desire as surely as she had given her life over to him as they slid beneath the surface of the water. Trusting him, giving herself completely to him as she opened her body to him and let him touch her as he'd tasted her.

She arched her back, as he slipped his fingers inside her, her hair floating about her like a golden nimbus, fingers clenching over his arm, holding onto him as her body held onto the sensations of his fingers stroking inside her.

His thoughts moved through hers, capturing each image as he watched her, then showing her what he saw in the connection of their thoughts, letting her feel what he felt as he stroked inside her again. In her eyes he saw those images reflected back as he replaced his fingers with the flesh that ached to be part of her.

Hypnotic, dreaming, seeing, feeling.

The images slowly rolled one after the other, one replacing another, her body adrift in the water, moving toward him, emotions and sensations washing over her with each stroke of water, each stroke of his hands.

Those startling images wouldn't release her. She saw exactly what he saw—the way her body reached for his, her legs wrapped around his hips, the center of her pressed against his belly, his gleaming flesh pressed against the tangle of golden curls, the pale pink folds of her flesh as he tenderly stroked her. Then the slow glide of his flesh, moving deep inside her as her body opened to him.

She was made for him, flesh, and heat, and passion, her slender body clasping his, then reaching for him as he lifted her from the water and held her against him, his fingers gently bruising as he held her hips and thrust high inside her.

He felt the instinctive resistance of her body, that moment when she tensed at the fierce invasion of his body, then the moment that followed on a slow deep sigh when another tension shivered through her and her body eased him into the hot liquid center of her.

Amber clasped her arms tight about his neck, her face buried against his throat as those images moved through her thoughts. Startling, erotic images in a joining so complete that she saw as well as felt his body within her, the taut, straining muscles that fought to take him deeper even as she was certain she could not, then the length of him buried deep inside her, touching her womb, touching her soul.

She raised her head from his chest, and in her eyes he saw a fragile, fierce wildness of passion. *His* passion, deep within her. She continued to stare back at him as he began to move within her in a current of desire as old as time. Until he felt that current move within her and saw it at her eyes, her flesh moving against his. Then those first waves of passion that welled inside her as if from some eternal spring.

He saw her climax begin in the dark fathomless blue of her eyes in that expression that was both fear and wonder, heard it in the startled sound of his name on her lips, then felt it in the pulsing spasms of her flesh that gripped his flesh, like submerging underwater, then that moment when he joined her, breathing his life into her, pouring his life into her.

Afterward they slept for hours, wrapped in his mantle, safe, sheltered within each other's arms, within each other's bodies. Or was it days? It didn't matter.

When they awakened, Truan carried her back to the pool and bathed her, his hands gentle in tender places, gliding through her hair and over her breasts with the same care, banking the passion, until she thought she would die from it, then carrying her back and drying her with the edges of the mantle. Tender and caring until she no longer wished him to be tender and caring, and pulled him down to her, and then inside her, until she lay wanting and needy beneath him, crying his name at that moment that was both life and death.

"What is this place?" she asked as they lay together, uncertain whether she spoke it or thought it.

He heard her thoughts and answered simply in the connection of their thoughts, *"A place apart."*

"How long will we stay?"

"Until it is time."

Time. Hiding from the outside world, the past, the future that waited. He fought it back, holding onto each precious moment, holding onto her.

He fought the dream back when it came, unlike those other times when he had reached for it, wanting the knowledge, needing it. But now it came to him, more than a dream, that wakened him with an urgency that built along every nerve ending, and burned through his blood. That ancient call of immortal power that he'd been born with, that set him forever apart from mortal human beings. From her.

He left her there, safe, sleeping, and slipped into the forest, feeling the power move through him, becoming one, transforming him as he stepped through the mist, a creature once more, sensing the nearness of the Darkness, hunting for it.

Amber dreamed that he had gone. When she reached

for him, he was not there, an immortal lover, a dream within a dream. Someone she knew. Someone she had always known.

And then she dreamed that he returned to her through sunlight and mist, a creature of mortal flesh and blood, and immortal soul. A dark wolf, loping through the forest, leaping through the mist, the leaves whispering as he passed by.

He stepped through the light, a mortal man, an immortal creature, rousing her from sleep with a new urgency in his touch. He peeled the mantle from her body and stroked her back, his hands trembling at her flesh.

Not a dream.

He moved low over her, hands gliding through her hair, fingers wrapping around the silken strands, then stroking low over her belly as he lifted her hips. Her body answered as she arched her back, her head going back on a startled, passionate sound, taking all of him in one fierce stroke as he suddenly thrust inside her.

In that age-old way of all things wild, he claimed her, marking her as he gently sunk his teeth into the skin at her shoulder, loving her as he sunk his flesh deep inside her, pouring his seed into her womb, joining his soul with hers.

He wanted to stay there with her forever, in a world apart, safe. But they were not safe.

The Darkness closed in, even there, reaching out in the shifting shadows of the forest, like the dark creature he had stalked, illusive, growing more powerful, and dangerous.

PART THREE

DESTINY

Sixteen

It was dusk when they returned, riding through the deep purple shadows at the hills that surrounded Camelot like ancient guardians.

Had they only been gone for a few hours? It seemed longer and she wanted to hold onto it. She didn't want to go back.

He felt it in the rigid muscles of her body as she rode before him, curled into the curve of his body, her slender hand closed over the edges of his mantle as if it was a shield she held tightly before her. And he sensed it in her thoughts as she clung to the images of what they'd shared, holding onto them even as images of what waited for them at Camelot closed in like waiting shadows.

All of Camelot was ablaze with light. Bonfires dotted the greensward. Torches rimmed the battlements and glowed at the towers like fiery, golden jewels set in a brilliant crown. Guests who had come for the king's wedding had abandoned the tents and pavilions for the castle as celebrations following the day's events continued into the night.

But as they approached the gates of Camelot, Truan sensed a far different tension of excitement, something that ran through the blood in silent warning. The glow of lights within the walls of Camelot were not the torches of celebration, but the torches of Arthur's knights as they gathered in full battle armor—the glow of flames gleaming from their breastplates and the blades of their swords as they sat astride their war horses.

He felt her sudden alarm in the tension of her body, her hand tightening over the folds of his mantle.

"Something's happened."

He sensed it as well in the chaos of tension that came to him from inside the castle walls—the fierce, impassioned thoughts of warriors who prepared not for a night's celebrations with lurid images in their thoughts of the women who would share their beds, but the thoughts of warriors who prepared for battle.

They entered through the smaller postern gate beside the large double gates that in times of siege sealed Camelot into an impregnable fortress. Truan dismounted. Amber slipped to the ground beside him.

"Halt!" a guard called out.

Truan pulled Amber behind him, concealing her for her own protection in the shadows at his back as the guard approached. In this time and place she was a young lady of some position and betrothed to the king's nephew.

It would put her at risk to be seen returning with him. Although he'd improved his position at Camelot with the day's events, Truan had no doubt he was still looked upon with suspicion by many. Especially Gareth.

"Show yourself!" the guard snapped, the light of a torch gleaming at his sword as he approached closer, the sword held before him.

Truan rounded the horse, holding the bridle firm in his hand at the bit. With the touch of a hand he calmed the animal lest the beast sidestep and harm Amber where she stood beside it in the shadows. To all outward appearances, he seemed to merely adjust the bridle while calming the animal with gentle words. At the same time, he cut a glance to those shadows and with a single thought, warned Amber to stay where she was.

If he could not see her there, pressed against the wall, then the guard could not. But he sensed her there. The rise and fall of her breasts beneath her wool gown, the wildness of the blood just beneath her skin, and the soft, sweet essence of her stirred by the fear of discovery. But it stunned him to realize her fear was not for herself, but for him. It brought back again the remembered taste and scent of her, thick and hot in his blood.

Then he sensed another presence. He had sensed this presence among the gathered knights, and it was much stronger now. He felt it in his blood, causing every muscle to tense, coiling anger deep in the pit of his stomach.

He also sensed Amber's panic, that deeper, instinctive fear which he was certain she wasn't even aware of as being different from her fear of the guard. But it was.

It was a fear that came from that memory of her other life in that other time, cloaked in the same darkness that prevented her memory of him and what they had shared in that other life.

It was a memory of instinct, soul-deep, of the man who now slowly rode toward them, the man she was betrothed to in this time and place.

"Well, well, what do we have here? A thief at the gate?"

He would have recognized Gareth's voice even if he had not sensed him.

The young knight wore a gleaming breastplate and helm over a tunic and leggings in Arthur's blue and

gold colors, his battlesword glinting as he held it before
him with self-assurance.

"You know what we do with thieves at Camelot." This
directed at the guard who had first approached them
with a hint of a smile that held no hint of humor.

He had bested Gareth's team on the tournament field
and set in motion a deadly game. Both knew the treachery that had been exposed, a treachery in the simple
switch of steel helms that might have meant Arthur's
death if Truan had not pulled back on the final death
blow.

"Stand away, guard," Gareth ordered. "I will deal
with this thief, myself." He leveled his sword at Truan's
heart.

From the shadows, Truan sensed the fear and knew
Amber would have revealed herself if he had not willed
her back into the safety of the shadows with a single
powerful thought as he closed his fingers as though
encircling her wrist and gently but firmly restraining
her. And in the connection of that thought, he actually
felt her wrist within his grasp, the rapid beating of her
pulse beneath his thumb, the warmth of her skin as if
he touched her.

"Do not, little one!" he whispered to her in the connection of their thoughts. Like a caress, he assuaged
the fear, letting his strength flow through and around
her, protecting her.

"Where have you been all afternoon, champion?"
Gareth demanded, his voice dripping with resentment
and hatred. "I would have thought you would have
been eager to claim the favors of all the young ladies
who waited to greet the hero of the day. Perhaps," he
suggested, "you were plotting some treachery against
Camelot. We know so little about you. Perhaps, I have
just caught you, stealing back inside Camelot after meet-

ing with Malagaunt, for 'tis reported he now rides across the northern borders."

He sensed the young knight's thoughts, the barely controlled rage and the dark ambition that lay within his soul, which would betray a king and destroy a kingdom in the future time that awaited them all. He sensed too Amber's sudden panic—that soul-deep fear that welled inside her.

It would have been so easy to destroy Gareth, to simply crush him and tear out his heart. The need burned through his blood, that powerful, all-consuming instinct to protect what was his.

But the part of him that was logical warned against it and steadied his hands as he reached up and clasped the blade of the young knight's sword. If he'd been mortal, he would have severed his hand. But he held on, his gaze steady as the blade heated beneath his touch.

"Be careful," he warned. "You might get hurt."

Tension pulsed in the air, like a living, breathing creature that lurked there, coiled, waiting to strike. A silken thread of light glowed at the edges of the blade, white-hot as it moved up the blade toward the hilt and the hand that held it.

"Hold, Sir Gareth!"

Sir Bors's deep voice snapped like thunder as he strode toward them.

"What is this?" the older knight demanded as he reached them and immediately recognized Truan. He glanced between the two men, sensed the cold edge of fury that quivered the air, and saw Gareth's drawn sword. He stepped between them.

"You have duties elsewhere," Sir Bors reminded the young knight. "See to them."

"Ask him where he has been," Gareth challenged.

"He returns less than an hour after we have received word that Malagaunt rides across our borders."

"Stand away, lad," Sir Bors warned with the authority of one who had long served the king and felt no threat from the bond of blood between king and nephew.

"This man has earned the king's favor this day. It would not bode well to slay him at the very gates. If you have charges to make and can support them with more than an ill-temper at being bested in the contest today, then make a formal complaint and it will be heard before the tribunal in good time. If you cannot, then I suggest you see to your men."

Eventually, Gareth lowered his sword, but made no attempt to disguise his contempt as he turned his horse about.

"Another time," he vowed, then rode off to join his men.

Truan felt Sir Bors's speculative gaze and sensed the older knight's thoughts. He too had questions, but they were tempered by wisdom and caution, and he sensed, a hint of respect.

The knight laid a hand against the sweat-stained neck of the horse, his expression thoughtful as though he guessed far more.

"You've ridden far this afternoon, my young friend."

"Aye," Truan replied.

Within his thoughts, he sensed Amber as she hid in the shadows. He sensed too Sir Bors's speculation, saw him glance toward the shadows, and knew he guessed at the truth. He said nothing, but finally nodded, accepting that no further explanation was forthcoming.

"You've returned in time," the knight said instead. "We've received word that Malagaunt has crossed the northern border." Sir Bors watched him intently. "You'll have need of a fresh horse. The king intends a very special welcome for him. He has asked that you ride beside him." Sir Bors handed him his sword.

It had been cleaned and polished, light from the torches at the top of the walls gleaming blue death at the steel blade.

"Take care, warrior," Sir Bors told him. "I ride at the king's other side." He made no attempt to disguise the warning.

"Then he shall be well protected," Truan replied.

Sir Bors nodded. "See that you are ready when the king arrives."

The knight turned and crossed the yard, calling orders to his men, until he could no longer be seen among the warriors, knights, and warhorses that filled the yard. But when Truan turned, Amber was gone.

He sensed her movement as she slipped through the shadows along the wall, behind the tanner's shop, then across the yard to the door of the small chapel that adjoined the main hall.

The chapel was cool and dimly lit with only the glow of the altar candles to light the way. She had been there earlier that morning with Lady Guinevere before the competition to pray that there would be no injuries to any of the brave knights. But she had sensed a deeper need, revealed in gently whispered words she knew Lady Guinevere thought no one had heard.

"Heavenly father, forgive my sins, help me accept what I must and guide me down the path I must follow."

Words filled with sadness and desperation, that she might have mistaken had she not glanced at her mistress and seen the tear that slipped down her cheek as she bent her head over hands clasped so tightly before

her that the skin was drawn tight across slender bones
so that they showed through.

She had wanted desperately to go to her then, and offer
comfort for whatever it was that tormented her mistress
so. But she dare not, for in doing so would have revealed
that she had heard those intensely private prayers, and so
she had held back, kneeling that small distance behind
her mistress, hearing the young woman's torment and
anguish, and wondering at the cause of it.

Now her slippers made soft whispering sounds as she
made her way across the stones. The chapel was small,
the meager light from the candles flickering across the
faces of the saints and the holy mother. As she hastily
approached the altar and the small door that connected
it to the main hall, she discovered she was not alone.

A figure knelt there in prayer. At the sound of her
approach, a head lifted, and the light from the candles
at the altar fell across the startled features of her mistress.

She had been praying again. Perhaps for the depart-
ing warriors, perhaps for the king, perhaps for another.
It was written on her face as color drained from her
lovely features, her eyes wide and filled with dark shadows of sadness, as well as a look of understanding.

It was Lady Guinevere who had sent her from the
pavilion earlier that day, who seemed to understand
the deep, compelling need that she must go and so
had released her, with a hastily whispered warning—*Be
careful*—but had not tried to stop her. As if she understood too well the things that Amber barely understood.

A sound at the chapel door she had just entered
through startled them both. Lady Guinevere hastily
grabbed her hand and pulled Amber down beside her,
with a single, hastily whispered word, "Pray!"

They knelt there with bowed heads, side by side, hands clasped before them, hearts beating fiercely as the door closed followed by the sound of heavy, booted footsteps that slowly approached the altar.

With each approaching step, panic built along Amber's every nerve ending. Had she been seen crossing the yard? Had something happened to Truan? Was he perhaps even now being dragged below to that chamber where he was first imprisoned?

Who was it that approached? Truan? Gareth? Or perhaps one of the king's other knights, who had seen them return and would surely report it to the king?

A shadow slowly appeared within her field of vision. It took all her concentration of will not to give in to the panic, not to reveal it by either word or gesture, but to remain calmly staring ahead as if she concentrated on those prayers she so fervently whispered.

"I hear your prayers, mistress."

Fear constricted around her heart as she recognized Gareth's voice, and for a moment she almost believed it was possible, so completely did he seem to control her life.

Once she had thought him kind and gentle, when first she had met him, when she first went to be companion to Lady Guinevere.

Was it months ago? Weeks? Or only days, as it seemed? For truly the memory she had of it did not seem clear to her. As if it was something she had dreamed, but had not been part of. Yet it all seemed so real. As real as Gareth, standing beside her, watching her, waiting for her to betray the slightest emotion, the smallest lie.

"Then, you know I pray for the safe return of all," she replied, fixing her gaze straight ahead on the image of the holy mother at the altar.

"Indeed, Amber? Or the safe return of one among those who ride to face Malagaunt."

Guinevere hastily stood, her expression cool, hidden, regal even now though she was not yet queen.

"If you wish to pray, Sir Gareth, then we will leave you to your prayers. We do not wish to disturb you."

Amber stood also, and Guinevere's hand closed around her arm. But Gareth stopped them before they could leave.

"And how long have you been praying?" he asked, his gaze intense.

"We have been here since this afternoon, when word was first received of Malagaunt's treachery," Guinevere replied, lying straight through her teeth, her expression never wavering, never betraying the lie.

But Gareth was not satisfied. "Is that your answer as well, Amber?"

"Yes, of course."

He reached out, plucking the tip of a withered fern frond from her hair.

"And you have been here the entire afternoon?" he asked, crushing the delicate leaves between his fingers.

"I have said it is so," Guinevere replied, though the question was not directed at her. "Do you doubt my word? If so, perhaps you wish to take it up with the king."

Gareth's eyes narrowed, his expression one of hatred as he looked at Lady Guinevere. But it was not a challenge he was prepared to take up now. Not yet.

The doors were thrown open, startling them all as a young knight strode into them.

"The king asks for you! We ride!"

This time when he reached out Amber was certain he intended to strike her. Instead his fingers slipped beneath her chin, gliding back to her throat, closing with a bruising power.

His hand shook as though he fought to close his hand tighter and could not, as though prevented by some greater strength that denied him the pleasure of hurting her. Finally, he jerked his hand away.

"There must be no secrets between us, Amber." The silken words hid a sibilant threat. "We will speak of this again when I return."

When he had finally gone, Amber released the breath she had been holding, a quivering sound very much like a sob.

Lady Guinevere wrapped an arm around her shoulders, trying to offer comfort, yet knowing there was nothing she could say that would ease the pain the girl now felt—the pain of loving someone when she was betrothed to another.

Truan watched the chapel, knew the moment when Amber was in danger, then slowly released his hand around the image he had focused upon, and continued to watch until Gareth and one of his men finally left the chapel.

"*Yes,*" he silently vowed to the knight. "*We will speak of this again.*"

They found the village just before the next midday, near the borders of the ancient kingdom of Gwynedd, long ago claimed by the Celts, now protected by Arthur.

The smoldering ruins and charred bodies left behind by Malagaunt were a grim reminder of the battles that had been fought in the past in the name of peace, and the destiny that awaited Camelot in that future time Truan had traveled from.

Arthur considered splitting his force to search for

Malagaunt. Truan rose from those tracks embedded in the soft earth.

"At least three score men, they travel light and to the east. If you split your force," he subtly suggested to Arthur as he remounted his horse, "you will be outnumbered with no time for the rest of your men to join the fight."

"What would you suggest, warrior?" Sir Bors asked, his eyes narrowing thoughtfully.

"Follow these tracks for no others lead from the encampment. They ride ahead no less than a day's ride and to the east."

"How do you know this?" the king asked. "Do you perhaps possess some special gift of knowledge?"

Their gazes met. In the king's even gaze Truan sensed a memory of a friendship of many years and dearly held, that between the boy-warrior and the mentor-counselor who was rumored to have made the boy into a king, and in the king's thoughts he also sensed a flash of recognition—that brief moment that was part memory, part hope, when Arthur wondered fleetingly about his old friend and perhaps recognized something of the sorcerer in the young man who sat astride his warhorse before him.

Truan smiled. "It takes no gift of magic to see the direction they have fled."

"And the means by which you divine the exact number of hours that have passed since their departure?" Gareth demanded, standing beside his horse, his expression challenging and arrogant.

Truan's smile deepened. "You are stepping in it."

Sir Bors was suddenly beset by a fit of coughing to hide his laughter, while Arthur's other knights were not so adept at hiding their own reactions. Even Arthur was hard pressed not to smile.

Truan said nothing as he swung astride his horse once more, while Arthur gave the order, over his nephew's protestations, that aside from a small force left to see to the needs of the survivors of the village, they were all to ride east.

"How can you be certain it is not a trap?" Gareth asked his uncle.

"Do you wish to make an accusation, nephew?"

Gareth glanced at the warriors and knights surrounding him, saw them struggle to maintain their composure and knew they laughed at him. He swung his horse about and rode far ahead. To the east.

Just after nightfall they reached a place of encampment. Both men and horses were weary, their tunics and shields mud-caked and splattered from the long ride following tracks that seemed to disappear altogether across the rugged terrain.

Truan sat unmoving, his thoughts reaching far afield. Malagaunt and his men were close, perhaps only a few hundred yards away, perhaps watching even now.

"We will make our camp here," Arthur announced. And when Truan did not immediately dismount, but urged his horse beyond the site to a small hillock to stare out into the darkness, Arthur joined him.

"You disapprove," he said with some bemusement.

"It is not for me to disapprove," Truan answered carefully, reminding himself that he was on tenuous ground here, a stranger among them who had proved himself adequate with a sword, but hardly with his loyalty. That remained to be proven.

"By God, you remind me of someone . . ." Arthur said, his voice lowering with a memory. "Someone I miss very much. Someone I once called friend."

Truan sensed the king's thoughts, the wistfulness over

a comradeship lost, a friendship stronger than the tie of brothers.

"He had your way of turning a phrase." Arthur snorted at the memory. "Of making a suggestion that I could either follow or not, but with the certainty that if I did not, I was doomed to failure." He shifted in the saddle as though he did not wear the mantle of loneliness well.

"And then he was gone, without a word as to the cause. I became angry with him over it, then regretted the anger for he had a way of knowing such things." He looked over at Truan, his gaze thoughtful.

"As you sometimes seem to know things. Three score riders among so many hoofprints that it would take a wizard to divine the truth of the number."

Truan shrugged. "A lucky guess, which has yet to be proven. I could be wrong."

"Men do not gamble lightly with their lives."

"I might be a fool."

"I think not," Arthur concluded, then asked, "What is it that bothers you?"

"This place is not safe. At least not for soldiers who might be caught sleeping in their bedrolls in the wee hours before dawn. It would be easy to sweep in on them from all directions."

They sat in companionable silence for several moments, Arthur thoughtfully considering his suggestion.

"There might be some merit in what you say."

When Arthur gave his orders, Sir Bors looked at him questioningly.

"Trust me, old friend," the king told him.

They built their campfires high against the night chill. Bedrolls were laid out before them, the shapes of sleeping soldiers dotting the campsite. Horses were tethered nearby, while guards stood their post.

That is what Malagaunt and his men saw as they surrounded the encampment and struck in those waning moments before dawn, when gray streaked the sky, and guards stood hunched against the cold at their posts.

Sleeping soldiers, stationary guards, the king asleep in his field tent. Ghosts all. An illusion of the trap that awaited.

Just as he had sensed the king's plan, Truan also sensed when the enemy approached, still several hundred yards from the encampment.

There was still time to withdraw. Truan knew the dangerous chance he took interfering even in this insignificant moment in history. How much, he wondered, might he change things simply by his presence here in this battle? How might things change if he did not act?

He silently motioned to Arthur whose gaze sharpened in the lifting darkness beside him. Word was passed along, silently, from man to man by gesture, swords eased from their scabbards, arrows notched at bowstrings.

Several moments passed as they sat astride their restless horses, sheltered in a copse of trees. Then a sudden movement, quickly followed by another, followed by a shrill war cry as several score men swept down upon the king's encampment.

"Not yet," Arthur ordered, his gloved hand raised, his men awaiting his command, while before them, the encampment stirred to life like a beehive suddenly rattled on a tree branch.

Warriors swarmed the camp, thrusting swords into those motionless bedrolls, sweeping into the king's tent, charging the few horses tethered there. Guards were silently struck down. But no blood flowed or soaked the ground.

Instead, empty bedrolls were kicked aside. The king's

tent was sliced to shreds only to reveal it too was empty. And the guards who died at their posts, fell before the enemies blows, to reveal not bloodied bodies, but empty breastplates, helms, and tunics. At that moment, when Malagaunt's men began to suspect they had been duped, Arthur gave the command to attack.

A single torch flared to life as the signal was given to all his men. They charged down the hill and swept in on the encampment.

The fighting was brutal and bloody, Malagaunt's men were near a full three score and heavily armed. Their first surprise quickly gave way to blood lust and their own battle cry went up.

Warrior met warrior, swords flashed in the light of the campfires, horses screamed amid the war cries of both sides.

Truan sent his own horse into the thick of battle, protecting the king's left side. Sir Bors rode to the right of the king, with Gareth riding at his back. They formed an impregnable wedge that drove into the heart of the battle, swords swinging and hacking at those on the ground around them.

Once in the thick of battle, he sensed a moment of danger as the protective wedge that surrounded the king faltered. He glanced and saw Gareth step too far to the right, almost knocking Sir Bors off balance. The young knight lost his sword.

Was it one of the common hazards of battle or intentional?

The stumble would have left Arthur protected only on one side, completely vulnerable on the other. Truan scooped a fallen sword from the ground with the tip of his boot and tossed it to the young knight.

"Take it! And defend your king!"

Gareth stared at him. Whatever he considered, he

decided against it, seized the sword, and turned to meet a new enemy assault.

Twice the enemy sliced through the protective wedge and drew close to the king, intent on cutting Arthur down, his blue and gold crest easily marking him among his men. And each time, Truan sensed the danger, deftly turning to meet it, shoving one warrior away as he ran another through with his sword, then kicking the body from the end of his sword. Then he sensed the moment when the battle waned, followed by the enemy's cry of retreat.

As quickly as it began, it ended, with Malagaunt's warriors fleeing for their lives. A few of Arthur's men gave chase, until the call was given to return to camp.

Truan retrieved his sword from the body of an enemy warrior. During the battle he'd abandoned his horse and taken up the battle on the ground, preferring the solid earth beneath his feet. He spat onto the ground, ridding himself of the taste of death. But like the others he was coated with it—that grime of sweat, dirt, and blood, the smell of battle one could never truly rid oneself of.

Arthur was hardly recognizable for the grime, filth, and blood that caked his breastplate. But he grinned broadly as one of his men reported to him. He clapped Sir Bors on the back in the way of brotherhood among warriors who have come through a battle and survived as victors.

"What say you of this young warrior now, old friend?" Arthur asked of the older warrior who leaned heavily upon the hilt of his sword.

"I am told there are at least two score dead, and another score have flown. By my account that makes three score of Malagaunt's men."

Sir Bors merely grunted as he gingerly shoved his

helm back from his head. He'd taken a blow that dented the armor and creased his forehead.

"A lucky guess?" he suggested.

"Aye," the king said, his gaze narrowing thoughtfully as he looked at Truan. "As lucky as the one that we would be attacked in our bedrolls." The king nodded at Truan.

"I give you thanks for your insight, warrior. Malagaunt will not soon return to our borders, but when he does it will be with the assurance that he will not find us sleeping at our posts. And when we return to Camelot, you must accept a place at the round table. You have earned it this day."

Truan was stunned by this turn of events that he had not foreseen, but he was no more stunned than Gareth. He saw the young warrior's furious glare and knew that the time drew near when they must face each other once and for all. He prayed he would be able to protect Amber.

They began the journey home that day, confident at least for the moment that Malagaunt was far across the northern borders where he'd retreated to lick his wounds. But Truan knew that another day would come in the not too distant future, with a far different outcome.

They made their encampment that last night before returning to Camelot in a protected place. Here, they warmed their hands over campfires and cooked rabbits and squirrels hunted in the forest.

A double perimeter of guards encircled the encampment, one visible if one took the time to look for them, the other concealed as they watched from their hiding places. Arthur was a warrior who learned from every mistake, both his and those of his enemies. He would not be caught as Malagaunt had been caught.

The king sat nearby with four of his knights, their voices heard in the retelling of the attack. Gareth had been silent the entire ride from the northern borders and now was nowhere to be seen.

But Truan sensed his anger, and the darkness of evil that clung to him.

"How did you know Malagaunt's men would be found in that place?" Sir Bors asked as he thoughtfully chewed on a piece of meat taken from a skewer at the fire.

"And do not placate me with *'perhaps'* answers," he added.

In Bors, Truan sensed wisdom born of much experience. He was older than Arthur, a warrior who had been the first of Arthur's chosen inner circle of knights to the legendary round table. A mentor who had made a warrior of the boy, just as another mentor had wisely counseled him in the strategies of taking and holding a kingdom. What did he know or believe of Merlin?

"There are those," Truan began, choosing his words carefully, "whom it is said possess a special knowledge, a gift of insight that others do not possess. They see things others cannot see. A change in the wind, a vision in a dream." He spread his hands before the fire, letting the warmth steal through him until it found that inner fire he'd been born to.

He parted his hands and the flames parted marginally, allowing a glimpse deep within the heart of the fire. Of shifting light—yellow, orange, red, blue—constantly changing, and of shadows that dwelled there at the edges of the flames. The shadowy images of faces of those who had gone before, and faces of the future.

He brought his hands back together, clasping them before him.

"I have heard of this," Sir Bors said thoughtfully. "Such men are called conjurors, or sorcerers. 'Tis said they are not of mortal blood." He stripped another piece of meat from the skewer and popped it into his mouth.

"I know such a man," he said, chewing thoughtfully. "A man with much knowledge and wisdom. 'Tis said he sees the future in visions of flames." He frowned over a thought. "Perhaps you know of him. To some he is known as Merlin."

Truan curled his fingers over his palms at the sound of that name, then slowly flexed them again.

"I have heard of him. His name is mentioned with that of the king."

"Once their friendship was deep," Sir Bors said, his frown deepening. "Deeper than that of brothers. Together they built Camelot."

"But no more?" Truan asked, for Merlin had not told him of leaving Camelot, nor his reasons. He had thought perhaps to encounter him there. But he had not.

"He left Camelot more than a year ago. He gave no reasons, neither to the king nor to anyone else. He said only that he could not stay. Some say that he went on a pilgrimage to the holy lands. Others say that he is dead." He glanced at Truan. "Still others believe that he will return when Arthur needs him."

And Truan knew that this last was what the knight believed.

Sir Bors gestured toward the fire that lay between them. "What do you see in the flames, warrior."

How much to reveal? Dare he say anything and risk

altering the future more than it might already have been altered by his presence there?

"Malagaunt will return," he finally said. "And he will not be satisfied with stealing away into the night with his tail tucked between his legs."

Sir Bors nodded. "*If* you were able to see into the future, when might this be?"

Their gazes met across the fire. It was only conjecture, of course.

"If I were able to see into the future, I might say that it will come in the year that follows," he said solemnly of the history he knew would play out if history in the present time survived the Darkness.

"And if this were to happen," Sir Bors continued their verbal game of what-if, his gaze intense, "is it possible for the kingdom to survive?"

Truan sensed the turmoil within the knight, the need to know, and the reluctance. For with knowledge, as Truan was all too well aware, came an awesome responsibility.

He thought of the legend of Camelot that had endured to his own time in spite of the efforts of the Darkness to destroy it. Nothing more than a pile of ruins in a deserted valley, but the legend had survived and grown with tales of Arthur and Merlin.

"Camelot will live as long as there is hope in men's hearts."

Sir Bors nodded. He seemed to accept that. He sought his bedroll then, spreading it before the fire.

"And what of the king?"

Truan did not immediately answer for he could not lie to the knight. He searched for the best way in which to answer.

"Will he be remembered?" Sir Bors persisted.

"Aye," Truan replied, "he will be long remembered."

All about the encampment, voices grew faint as others sought their bedrolls. Arthur slept among his men, wearing the armor of a warrior. If they were attacked, he would not easily be found among them.

Sir Bors slept, his snoring rumbling amid the snap and hiss of the fire. But sleep was long in coming for Truan. He sat long hours before the fire, as though dreaming, but awake with visions of the past stirring the flames—when a young sorcerer and a warrior king built a kingdom that would endure for a thousand years. And he heard ancient voices that stirred in his blood and whispered through his senses. Voices of the past and the future.

As he continued staring into the flames he saw a vision of a great battle, and blood that soaked the ground—the blood of the past and future coming together. And in the midst of battle, a great king, the sorcerer who had helped him forge a legendary kingdom, and the gleam of a brilliant sword—Excalibur.

He tried to hold on to the vision, but it faded, as though seen across a very great distance, glimpsed from afar, and knew it was the future that waited.

"There is great danger."

It was as if a hand had touched his shoulder, rousing him from sleep. Then he heard it, more than the dying whisper of the fire, a voice that whispered through his thoughts, warning him.

It was that time that hung suspended between night and day, when the first light of dawn appeared at the horizon and stars still glittered in the night sky overhead. As if night reluctantly surrendered the sky.

Embers glowed among the ashes of the campfires. Streamers of mist clung to the trees and slipped like silent wraiths across the ground, curling over the warriors who continued to sleep undisturbed.

Guards still stood at their posts, their watchful gazes scanning the perimeter. Nothing, either by act or deed revealed they had felt it, or heard the voice that whispered an urgent warning through his senses.

There was danger in Camelot.

He stole among the sleeping warriors, silent as mist, like a creature of the night, his senses reaching afar, listening, feeling. He tried but could not shake off that prescience of danger, of something dark and malevolent, a force of evil so powerful that he knew he had encountered it before.

They were all there, either rolled in their blankets or standing at their posts, unaware as he stole among them. Except one warrior, Gareth. His blood ran cold in his veins.

He cast his thoughts afar, seeking the vision, but it was as if a veil of darkness had closed around all of Camelot, including Amber. In that void of Darkness, he sensed the trap, the Darkness reaching out to him, knowing as he knew that he must follow.

But not alone.

He roused Sir Bors from sleep. With the instinct that was blood deep in all warriors, the knight's hand closed over the hilt of his sword as he swiftly came to his feet. He was immediately awake and alert, his gaze meeting Truan's over the dying glow of the fire.

"What is it?"

"There is danger at Camelot."

As he had the night before when they talked across the campfire of things that might be, Truan sensed the knight's simple acceptance.

Sir Bors nodded grimly. "Then we ride for Camelot." He moved quickly among the other knights and warriors, rousing them from sleep. But before they rolled from their blankets, Truan was already gone.

He began running, guided by instinct. A man running into the light, streamers of mist clinging to him—a black wolf emerging from the light, mist glistening on its thick dark coat.

Seventeen

"I have never seen anything finer, milady," the young servant girl complimented Lady Guinevere. "You look like a queen already."

"I do not feel like a queen," Guinevere replied. "I feel like a sieve, all poked through with holes from your jabbing and poking at me with that needle." She glanced over at the young girl who stood so still and silent at the window of the chamber.

"What do you think? Will it please the king, mistress Amber?"

At the sound of her name, Amber turned from the window opening, a frown curving her lovely mouth.

"Did you wish something, milady?"

"What I wish," Guinevere replied, "is to be free of this cumbersome gown. 'Tis like being rolled in a tapestry, then stood upright and expected to walk about. It will be a miracle if I do not split every seam before the good bishop."

She motioned for the seamstress to remove the gown, which required loosening several lengths of stitches at the arms and bodice. So form-fitting was the shimmering, pale blue gown, trimmed in gold to match the king's colors, that it could only be worn by being stitched into it.

"You have been staring out that window all afternoon," she commented as she was at last relieved of the shimmering gown and the heavy train that fell from her shoulders. It was a gown to be worn only once—upon her marriage to the king.

Her voice softened, for she knew for whom the girl watched. "Surely they have not returned yet."

Amber shook her head. "There is a strange stillness to the afternoon and the sky has grown dark since midday."

"Perhaps it will rain," Guinevere suggested.

Amber rubbed her hands down the length of her arms to warm herself against the sudden chill that seemed to grip the chamber in spite of the fire in the brazier.

"It seems almost like night. I cannot even see beyond the walls."

The darkness of the afternoon seemed unnatural, almost as if night had fallen instead of a gathering storm. No clouds could be seen upon the horizon, yet it grew steadily darker and colder. Perhaps it was later than she thought. Her gaze swept the battlements and the towers. Her frown deepened.

"I do not recall hearing the afternoon watch," she thought aloud, wondering where the tower guards had gone. Every day at eventide, the guards changed and torches were lit in the towers. But no light shown in the towers, nor across the battlements.

Guinevere joined her at the window. Once again she wore a gown and tunic in shades of her own brilliant green colors.

"It *has* grown cold," she said, clasping her arms about her as the wind came up and gusted into the chamber. The fire in the brazier smothered and ash scattered about the room. Several candles were blown out and the flames of the oil lamps guttered. She too shivered.

"Close the shutters."

One of the servants swept up the ash. Wood was added to the fire in the brazier. Flames quivered as unseen drafts of wind seeped beneath the door and around the window opening, making it seem more like winter than early summer.

After supper Amber sat once more at the small tapestry she had begun, attempting to concentrate on the intricate design. Lady Guinevere sat before the brazier, reading aloud from an ancient Latin text, her two small dogs sleeping at her feet.

The two terriers were gold and white with fringes of hair that brushed the stones as they walked, their tails curled over their backs. Their snub-nosed faces made them look as if they'd run into a door that had been suddenly closed.

They were intelligent little creatures who liked nothing better than setting upon the occasional rat that dared to make an appearance, then depositing the limp carcass at Lady Guinevere's feet for her approval.

In the short time they'd been at Camelot the rat population had been all but eliminated and the terriers had gained favor with everyone, particularly the cook in the kitchen who had an intense dislike for discovering a beady-eyed rat glaring back at her from the depths of her pantry.

Even the king's massive hunting hounds learned to respect the small beasts, steering a wide berth around them for fear of being nipped about the ankles. What the dogs lacked in size, they more than made up for in temperament.

They were unfailingly loyal to Lady Guinevere, but they seemed to sense that where matters of the king were concerned, they must be on their best behavior. Otherwise they had the run of Camelot.

Any time of the day might find them scampering about, thick fringes hanging over their eyes and making one wonder that they could see at all. Like four-footed beggars they made the rounds of pantry, kitchens, and gardens, accepting handouts with great enthusiasm, or letting one know of their displeasure when handouts were not offered with a nip at hand or ankle.

Amber had quickly made friends with them, for she loved animals. When her mistress was occupied elsewhere they followed her about, always ready to play and get into some mischief. Guinevere called them her little scamps and they seemed to ease her loneliness at being so far from her home.

One of the dogs pawed at the door. Amber let it out, relieved for the brief respite from the tedious stitchery. The terrier bounded out the door, barking as it charged down the hallway toward the landing.

His companion was not similarly inclined, but laid his head back down upon his paws and dozed, satisfied to let his friend charge into the night chasing gusts of wind, leaves, and the occasional stray cat.

Amber returned to her stitchery, making slow progress, constantly distracted by the storm that rattled the shutters at the windows.

Guinevere saw the frustrated stab of the needle and heard the accompanying sigh as another row of stitches required removal.

"At this rate, you may finish that panel by the time you are an old woman, *if* the fabric survives with all the holes you're punching in it."

Amber sat back in frustration. "I have made the same mistake four times."

Guinevere looked at the panel and saw the difficult

design of the wolf stitched at the fabric. "You have said little since your return yestereve," she commented and asked tentatively, "Is all well?"

For a moment there was only the sound of the fire in the brazier, the soft hiss of the flame as it met golden amber in the wood, like centuries-old words that whispered down through time from the flames.

"I wish to be released from my betrothal," Amber finally spoke what was in her heart. Then almost defiantly, "I cannot wed Gareth. 'Tis not right. I do not love him."

The girl's defiance masked a deep unhappiness. It brought back memories of Guinevere's desperate wish asked of her guardian, and the only answer he could give.

You know your duty, child. Your future is not of your own choosing.

With those words in her thoughts, Guinevere asked, "Has your warrior asked you to wed with him? Nay, nor will he," she answered her own question before Amber could reply. She already knew all the lies. She had spoken them all to herself.

" 'Tis impossible," she said and saw the pain that flashed in the girl's eyes—pain that echoed deep inside her, and she bent over the thick Latin text so that Amber could not see her face.

Guinevere closed her eyes as she recalled that other conversation as if it was only yesterday, perhaps only hours or moments ago, so deep was the pain, and so intense the feelings that lay behind the words.

Her fingers dug into her palm, nails cutting into the flesh. Slowly she uncurled them, smoothing the fabric of her gown over the flatness of her belly where she had once felt the child moving inside her. A child conceived in passion. The same passion she saw burning in the girl's eyes.

Not the passion of a child bursting with infatuation, but the passion of a woman who knew what it was to lay with a man, to share that physical joining of body and soul, then afterward to lay alone in her bed with the memory of it aching deep inside her, so painful it could only be assuaged by joining in that way again.

Her fingers trembled at the page of the text, her hand unsteady. She knew what it was to love in such a way, to give oneself completely, to surrender to the pleasure found in that joining, to lie in a man's arms and convince herself that she might somehow escape the duty that awaited her . . . the duty that awaited them both.

Those thoughts opened a door always kept tightly shut—the door on the past and the memory of the child she had felt stirring inside her. A child that had grown within her with a fierce strength; for whom she had gladly borne the pain of childbirth to bring into the world, then tearfully placed into the arms of another woman, never to see the child again.

Even now she ached, as if the child was still part of her, perhaps forever part of her, a memory of that lost love.

"I know what I speak of," she said gently, trying to comfort the girl. "He can offer you nothing. Only his sword, and therein lies both his honor and his duty. But not to you."

Duty. Honor. Ties that had bound a young man more than her love.

"But I love him," Amber said softly, speaking aloud what she had felt the first moment she saw Truan in the forest. A feeling that came from deep inside, like a lost memory that suddenly returned. "I have always loved him."

"But does he love you? Has he spoken of it?" Guinevere asked. "Nay, nor will he. Because he cannot. He will lay with you and then he will leave you. Because he must. And you will be alone with the memories of what you shared, and you will ache for it with every fiber of your being until the day you die."

Amber was stunned by the depth of sadness in the softly whispered words.

"You must have loved him very much."

Guinevere looked up, her eyes glistening with tears. "With all my heart and soul."

And Amber knew she did not speak of the king.

The fire burned low in the brazier and it grew cold in the chamber. Earlier Amber had asked one of the servants to bring more wood for the fire but the man had not returned. Now the basket was empty. With a look of disgust at the uneven row of stitches she'd just labored over, Amber gladly set aside her stitchery.

"We need more wood for the fire," she said, retrieving the basket near the brazier, her thoughts filled with Guinevere's earlier words. Whom, she wondered, had Lady Guinevere loved?

The hall was dimly lit by oil lamps on the walls. They struggled feebly, guttering as the wind swirled over the edge of the balcony.

In the winter months when there was snow on the ground, wood was stored in a large chamber at the bottom of the stairs for ease in replenishing the supply of wood in the king's private apartments.

She refilled the basket and was about to return to the chamber when lightning arced across the sky like the gleam of a sword slashing the darkness, for a moment illuminating everything with brilliant light.

She called for the terrier but there was no response. Then the courtyard was once more plunged into darkness with only the light of the torch whipping in the wind. Even the watchtowers were dark.

No torches were lit along the battlements nor at the towers. When lightning flashed again, it briefly lit the courtyard once more, and Amber saw something near the fountain. She took the torch from the wall. Gathering her mantle about her, she crossed the yard toward the fountain.

The light from the torch provided meager light at best which was whipped about and threatened to extinguish at any moment. As she reached the fountain she held the torch before her, trying to see what it was that lay there.

Then lightning flashed yet again and in the sudden explosion of light overhead, she saw what it was on the ground at the base of the fountain. It was Lady Guinevere's terrier.

The wee dog lay on its side, head back at an awkward angle, the neck savagely broken. But whatever it encountered was not satisfied with merely killing the small dog. Its white and gold coat was blood-stained, a horrible wound gaping open at the throat. Whatever had attacked it had tried to tear it apart.

Her hand trembled as she touched the still-warm little body, and a thought surfaced, like emerging from deep waters, and with it came the certainty that this had all happened before—a cold, storm-filled day, the courtyard garden of Camelot, and the loss of a beloved little friend.

She jerked her hand back, with the certainty that it came from memory—her memory of another time and place, but very like this one. Yet different. And Truan had been there. Reaching out to her, taking her in his arms, comforting her over the loss. And she had felt safe. As safe as she had felt that day in the forest, certain that he would not let anything happen to her.

Pippen. Suddenly, the name came to her as if someone had whispered it, and with it a memory of the creature who bore that name.

Lightning again flashed across the battlements and for a moment the walls were illuminated. The gates of Camelot were open! And at the gates, she saw the bodies of the guards, struck down where they stood!

Amber pushed to her feet, the torch forgotten as she turned and ran back to the stairs that led to the second-floor chambers. As she entered the chamber, Lady Guinevere looked up from her text. The other terrier sensed Amber's alarm and began to bark.

"What is it?" Guinevere asked. "Has something happened? Have the king and his men returned?"

Amber did not tell her what she had found in the courtyard. There was no point in it. There would be time enough for that later.

The little terrier darted past her, barking fiercely. When Guinevere would have gone after it, Amber gently seized her by the arm.

"There is no time."

She looked wildly about the chamber for something that might be used as a weapon, saw the slender knife they had used to slice an apple after dinner, and seized it.

"You must tell me what has happened," Guinevere demanded.

"We cannot stay here," Amber replied. "Someone has opened the gates! Camelot has been attacked!"

arms, comforting him, even as Lancelot held the wars that
still rose at night, his wife reaching out, just as he had
reached out to comfort something beyond . . .

A woman whose love had slowly, yet surely slipped away,
one who cried out, and yet who reached out to fill an emptiness that had been . . .

It was there in Lancelot's anguish, even those stolen
moments that he knew . . .

Eighteen

"You are the destiny. Within you lies the hope for the future."

The wind was bitter cold, the storm lashing at Truan
as he ran, as though trying to drive him back, to keep
him from Camelot.

*"I was turned from my destiny. You must not be. Beware
the choice which must be made, or all will be lost."*

The words whispered through his thoughts and
burned through his blood, a legacy of the past that
awaited him.

He cast his thoughts into the storm, across the distance of miles they'd traveled from Camelot in pursuit
of Malagaunt, as near as thinking of her.

Beware the choice that must be made . . .

The choice to go back in time to Camelot as it had
been in Arthur's time.

The choice to give in to his love for Amber, as he
could not in their own time, fearing she might learn
the truth about what he was—a creature born of mortal
flesh and blood, an immortal soul that transformed at
will into a creature she had every right to fear.

The choice to share a friendship with Arthur, a king
whom some believed was only a myth, yet a flesh and
blood man who had built a magnificent kingdom that
had endured in the hearts of men for five hundred

years, and would endure five hundred more if *he* made the right choice.

Those things he thought of on the journey back to Camelot across wild, storm-ravaged moors and wind-swept hills, the ground passing away beneath a relentless pace, his thoughts focused on her; the pale gleam of her body beaded with water from the pool as she lay beneath him free of the memories of the past and gave herself to him with a passion that took his breath away; the deep gold of her hair, dark as amber, spread across his mantle; the color of her eyes, shimmering green as the shallows of the pool when he kissed her, then blue as the depths of the pool as his body joined with hers.

In another time and place, she had captured his heart with her gentle ways and wounded silence. In this time and place she had claimed his heart forever with sweet laughter, gentleness, and the courage to face a wolf alone in the forest.

He had not been free to love her in that lifetime, she was not free to love him in this lifetime.

It all came back to that shining dream that had become both legend and myth in the hearts of mankind. In that other time and place, he'd been drawn to Camelot swearing his allegiance to Lord Stephen, as his father had once sworn his allegiance to Arthur. But Merlin had failed. He had abandoned Camelot when Arthur needed him most. And the kingdom had been lost. What might have happened if Merlin had not abandoned Arthur?

You must choose . . . the dream whispered over and over through his thoughts, and he knew the choice that must be made waited for him at Camelot.

It lay dark and silent before him, a shining dream, the hope for the future of all mankind, wrapped in the Darkness. He felt that oppressive presence in the wind that whipped at him and the cold that cut like a knife, the same as when he'd first encountered it in a blinding snowstorm. A pervasiveness of evil reaching out through time to claim the future.

The battlements were dark and abandoned. No guards appeared at the watch towers, and a cold ribbon of fear knotted tight in his belly that he was too late. He transformed once more, a warrior with sword drawn, the animal instinct of the wolf still burning through his blood as hair raised at the back of his neck.

He did not approach the main gates, but instead went to the south wall. There, he turned his thoughts inward, summoning the power, transforming once more, his body disappearing as he leaned forward, hands flattened against the stones at the wall, then passed through the wall, stepping through to the other side.

He emerged beyond the main gate near the stables, and quickly dropped down low, the sword shielded against his body so that it would not be easily seen.

An oppressiveness enveloped Camelot. He'd experienced it before, once when Cassandra traveled through the portal of time into the past in search of the Oracle, and again when they'd followed Margeaux into the forest. With the same animal instinct as then, he smelled death.

He found the guard at the gate brutally slain as he had opened the gates to someone he had recognized. Gareth.

Three other guards were also dead, slain before they could sound the alarm of attack or draw their weapons. The guards at the watchtowers had suffered the same fate as Gareth's men had swarmed inside and cut them down.

He had followed a half dozen riders from Arthur's encampment, Gareth among them. But those tracks had been joined by nearly four and twenty riders who had waited in the hills that lay between the northern borders and Camelot—Malagaunt's men.

This then was the trap that Malagaunt had really intended. Not an attack on a remote northern village too small and poor to be of any strategic importance or significance, but an attack on the very heart of the kingdom while the king and his men were away and with only a handful of warriors remaining to defend Camelot.

Gareth and his men had moved swiftly. He found many more dead inside, the people of Camelot had wakened slowly to the sounds of fierce fighting within the walls of the castle.

Arthur's warriors had been brutally slain, many in their beds, others left to die in their own blood as Gareth and his men closed in on the prize they sought, the future queen. For Truan had no doubt that was what Gareth intended.

Arthur had finally decided to take a queen and ensure the future of Camelot. His marriage to Guinevere created an alliance with the powerful chieftains of the western lands, and promised an heir to the kingdom, and any sons born to Guinevere would thwart any claim Gareth had to the throne.

When Truan had left the northern encampment, Sir Bors had sounded the alarm and spread the word among Arthur's men. They could not be far behind, but Truan could not wait for them.

As he crossed the inner yard to the private courtyard that surrounded the main hall he sensed the extent of Gareth's treachery.

When he'd gained entry at the gates, Gareth had his men open those gates to Malagaunt's men. There was little then that any could do to stop them.

The king's personal guards at the entrance to the private courtyard had also been slain. Inside the courtyard, near the fountain, he found one of Lady Guinevere's small terriers. The little dog had probably been slain when it sounded the alarm.

In the little pet's death he sensed a cold cruelty, the same cruelty he'd sensed in the death of Pippen. And his thoughts sharpened. There was a pattern to it, of things repeating themselves. Of events happening all over again as they had happened before.

He heard sounds of fighting within the king's residence and pushed to his feet, running to the steps that led to the second-floor chambers. There he found the terrier's mate at the top landing, also dead. Just beyond the landing, the door to Lady Guinevere's chamber gaped open.

Inside the chamber he felt Amber's presence, a tangible thing that he could almost reach out and take hold of, it was so clear and strong in the lingering trace of her scent, her warmth still felt in the fabric panel that he knew she had touched it only a short while before, and in the fear that clung to the air.

And from that essence he could sense what her thoughts had been. Aware of the danger, she and Guinevere had fled together, hoping to find safety in another part of the castle.

He cast his thoughts beyond the chamber, searching for her and Lady Guinevere. He followed where they had gone, guided by that essence of her, as much a part of him as his breath. From another part of the castle he heard screams . . . or did he feel them in the fear that clung to the air.

He ran down the hallway where he had pulled Amber into the shadows shielding her with his power, longing to touch her, to love her, tormented in that other life by the fear that she would turn away from him when she learned the truth of what he was, tormented in this life by the destiny that reached out to them both with unseen dangers, afraid he could not protect her.

The main hall below was in chaos as the fighting reached there, more of Arthur's private guards fighting side-by-side with servants against Malagaunt's mercenaries. Desperate to cross the hall and to follow the path Amber had taken, he joined the fight, cutting down one man, then turning to fight another who charged at his back.

Truan blocked the blow, sensing the warrior's moves, swinging his sword in powerful strikes. Another blow quivered down the length of his sword. The warrior struck again. But instead of bringing his sword up to meet the blow as the warrior anticipated, Truan deflected the blow, dropped to one knee, and brought his blade up in a savage thrust.

The blade caught the warrior high under the ribs. With both hands clasped around the hilt, Truan drove the sword deep, slicing through the sheath of thick muscle and vulnerable organs protected within, and then he felt the scrape of steel blade against bone.

The warrior's expression was one of stunned surprise, then shock as his blood ran down the length of the blade. When he slumped forward, Truan shoved his body away, stepped over him, and quickly moved on.

He flew up the opposite stairs that led to the king's counsel rooms and the star-chamber, still following where Amber and Guinevere had fled. Shouts went up as he was seen. Two of Gareth's men charged him.

The first died quickly. The second fell to the floor in agony as Truan slashed his legs from under him. He stepped past both and kicked open the doors of the star-chamber. The flames of the oil lamps quivered wildly as he burst through the doors.

He sensed Gareth's presence immediately, a familiar presence first experienced all those months ago during a snow storm when he and Cassandra had followed Margeaux into the forest and found her dead, her unborn child torn from her womb.

That day the storm had closed around them as if it was a live thing, determined to destroy them. The creature he saw through the blinding snow was a child of the Darkness who had lived in the past during Arthur's time, born in the future as the Powers of the Light grew powerful once more.

As he entered the star-chamber, he confronted that creature that had been born into his own time, a spawn of the Darkness, sent to destroy the future.

Gareth whirled around. He held Amber before him, one arm closed over hers, holding her against him. In his other hand he held a knife, the tip thrust against her throat. One of Malagaunt's men held Lady Guinevere prisoner.

"Come no closer, warrior, or they both die!" Gareth threatened, holding Amber before him like a shield. In his eyes, Truan saw the Darkness that gleamed from his soul, the Darkness that had created him, born of mortal flesh and blood, but with the powers of the Darkness.

"Your powers are great," Truan told him, slowly advancing, his gaze fastened on the hand that held the knife at the same time he was aware of the threat to Guinevere.

"Use your powers against *me,* not mere mortals," he challenged, using the powers of his thoughts to manipulate the thoughts of Malagaunt's warrior. He felt resistance as Gareth sensed his game.

"Take up your sword against me, Gareth. Let me see

the powers of Darkness, not the coward who hides behind helpless mortal women." He saw the flash of anger in the depths of Gareth's cold eyes.

"Fight me," he pressed his advantage, seeing the calculation that gleamed in those eyes.

"No! Do not!" Amber cried out, wincing as Gareth pressed the blade deeper against her throat. The look in her eyes was pleading. "You must not," she whispered.

He closed his thoughts to her, closed off his own emotions and the fierce protective part of him that wanted only to charge Gareth, pull her out of his arms, and tear him to pieces.

"Choose whatever weapon you wish," he told Gareth, ignoring her. "Whatever means you wish to challenge me. The power of the Darkness against the power of the Light. Here and now, Gareth. Once and for all.

"Or are you afraid?"

"I am afraid of nothing!" Gareth replied, jerking Amber against him.

"Then perhaps my powers are greater than yours," Truan suggested, smiling.

Gareth too smiled, an evil smile as he accepted the terms of the challenge. "The choice of weapons is *mine.*"

"You must first release Amber and Lady Guinevere."

Gareth nodded, and in the acceptance of his terms, Truan sensed that perhaps this was what Gareth had sought all along. He released Amber and with a nod commanded Malagaunt's man to release Guinevere.

When Amber hesitated and he sensed that she would have run to him, he fiercely shook his head, ignoring the emotions he sensed in her. She went to Lady Guinevere, pulling her away from Malagaunt's man.

"Send him away," he told Gareth. "I do not trust a man with a weapon at my back."

Gareth nodded and cut a glance to the warrior who turned and left the chamber.

"If you lose, they will still die," Gareth assured him.

Truan smiled, keeping his thoughts from Amber's, refusing to give in to mortal emotions, and with only one thought, one purpose.

"I do not intend to lose."

Nineteen

"What is it to be then?" Truan asked, every thought, every sense focused on Gareth, refusing to let anything else interfere, aware with the knowledge of a kindred spirit that it was dangerous to do so. For other than the masters they served, they were very much alike. "What weapon do you chose?"

Gareth's eyes gleamed. "You have agreed to the terms," he reminded Truan. "You are bound by your word to keep the agreement."

A warning whispered through Truan's senses and ran cold through his blood, a voice from his dreams.

Beware, my son! The power of the Darkness lies in deception, trickery, and betrayal. It will use your own weaknesses against you!

"I have said it is so," Truan replied, eyes narrowed, senses sharply focused, watching Gareth's every move, searching his thoughts for any betrayal.

Gareth laid the knife on the round table and spread his hands wide, palms up. "You suspect me of some deception."

Truan snorted. "I grow weary of your tricks and games. You chose the means of the challenge. I have accepted. Now name your weapon, or concede."

A cold smile curved Gareth's lips. He was the embodiment of ruthlessness and cunning. "I will never concede."

Truan leaned forward, hands braced on the edge of the table. His expression was that of a predator, intense, deadly, eager for blood, following every move Gareth made as if he stalked him.

"Then name the weapons and let it begin!"

"Aye," Gareth said, also leaning forward, with hands braced at the opposite side of the table. They were like two deadly creatures, every muscle tensed, gazes fixed on the other, braced for battle.

"But there is no reason to call for weapons. We already have them. You and I."

Truan felt that warning move through his blood again, as if Merlin stood at his side and whispered it. A foreboding that the bargain he had made would be a costly one. Gareth's eyes gleamed at the depth of his ingeniousness.

"I chose the power of transformation. A formidable weapon. Do you not agree? It shall be interesting to see which is the more powerful."

Truan felt as if he'd taken a physical blow. Gareth was no fool. Far from it. He possessed many of the same powers Truan possessed and he had cunningly drawn him into a trap as surely as he had lured him five hundred years into the past to save Amber. Gareth had exposed his worst fear, like a knife thrust deep, cutting away the flesh to leave a mortal wound.

In that other life, the life he had shared with Amber in the future, he could not bear for her to know the truth of what he was, a creature that was both mortal and immortal, both human and creature of the mist. He was afraid if she discovered what he was, she would turn away from him in fear and loathing.

And so he had hidden himself from her, concealing

his powers with foolish conjurements and slights of hand—a coin or flower plucked from behind her ear; the sudden appearance of a small white dove sheltered in the palm of his hand; the sudden appearance of flame; silly pranks and foolish rhymes.

All of it was a magnificent disguise that brought laughter to her eyes and a gentle smile to her lips, where before there had been only wounded silence and haunted memories because of what she had suffered before.

And slowly, like a flower in spring she had gradually emerged from the sadness of the past. The expression in her eyes had changed from pain to infatuation, then love. Only then had he turned away from her, tormented by what he had come to feel—a deep stirring of mortal desire and passion that he must not feel. Because he could not bear for her to know the truth, because he feared the horror and revulsion he would see in her eyes when she did learn the truth, he had been deliberately cruel and closed off his feelings for her.

But in this world, this place five hundred years in the past, she remembered nothing of that other life, nothing of what they had shared. He had finally given in to those feelings and dared to love her.

He had lain with her as a mortal, giving her his body, heart, and soul. But in that joining of mortal flesh and blood he had also joined with her as an immortal creature, claiming her as a creature claimed its mate, willing to protect her with his life if necessary, tenderly marking her in that way of wild creatures, then joining his body with hers, planting his seed deep in that timeless way that connected him to her forever, and connected the past to the future.

Beware, my son! The power of the Darkness lies in deception, trickery, and betrayal. It will use your own weakness against you! His father's words echoed through his thoughts.

Gareth had been cunning. It was the cruelest irony that in getting him to agree to the power of transformation as the weapon of choice—the only means by which he might save Amber and Lady Guinevere—he risk losing her when she learned the truth of what he was.

Truan sensed her fear and confusion. He saw it in her eyes and heard the question that formed in her thoughts, drawing her slender brows together.

"No matter what happens, no matter what you see," he whispered in the connection of his thoughts to hers, *"you must trust me! Trust in what we have shared! Trust in my love for you."*

He heard the answer that came from her heart and whispered at her lips, of passion shared, of memories that lay hidden, glimpsed in the hours they'd shared in that sheltered place in the forest, surrendered to him in the depths of that shimmering pool when she had entrusted her life to him.

"I love you."

But when he turned back to face Gareth across that expanse of table, he was gone.

It had begun.

"Leave!" Truan told Amber. "Get out of here!"

His senses scanned the star-chamber. Gareth was there, but what form would he take?

"I will not leave you!"

For a moment he broke his concentration. "Leave this place! And do not look back!"

For even now, he sensed Arthur's men approaching the gates of Camelot. If she and Guinevere could reach the courtyard they would be safe.

When she still refused, he told Guinevere, "Take her and get out!"

Guinevere pulled her toward the stairs that led to the doors of the star-chamber. But when they reached them, they were unable to escape. They could see beyond the shattered doors but could not leave, prevented by some invisible barrier that imprisoned them.

Gareth's laughter rang out in the chamber, a coldness of cruelty and death that echoed from the walls and hissed like the warning of a serpent from the shadows.

Truan turned his entire focus back to the chamber and Gareth, opening his senses, drawing on the powerful gift he'd been born with, feeling it grow and expand within him, taking him beyond the boundaries of mortal flesh and blood, transforming—the weapon Gareth had chosen and the only means to keep her safe.

Amber turned from the broken doorway, shattered when Truan had come after them, yet still impregnable. In that moment as they had tried to flee the chamber, Gareth had disappeared, no doubt hiding somewhere within the chamber. Now, Truan was also gone. But she could still feel him.

If she closed her eyes, she knew he was still there, somewhere, moving through the shadows, like the dream in the forest. When she had awakened and first saw that creature coming toward her through the shadows and mist. Then Truan stepped through that prism of light, returning to her, holding her, protecting her. The same as that day in the forest when the wolf had leapt into the clearing, returning to her, protecting her . . .

She was terrified. She felt the danger, soft downy hairs

raising at her arms, an instinctive fear that came from some shadowy place within her memories coiling in her stomach and squeezing her lungs.

She pulled Guinevere into the shadows at the corner beside the broken threshold, terrified to watch as mist swirled angrily across the floor of the chamber, wrapped around each chair at the round table, then swept across the surface of the table with those ancient Latin words and the brilliant clear crystal that glowed like the heart of an eternal flame at the center.

Guinevere grabbed at her arm, pulling her deeper into the corner as a vague shape began to take form at the other side of the chamber. A long sinuous form with a long snaking tail and the head of a serpent. Then eyes formed at the head—they were dark and fathomless, like looking into death. As the creature continued to take form, that long neck angling forward as though searching for its prey, it hissed, a horrible sound like that of dying souls.

Amber turned from the sight of the horrible creature, refusing to look at it, blocking out all thought and the sound of it as it filled the star-chamber like the gathering of a storm. Terrified as she was, she forced herself to think of one thing and one thing only. Truan, and the words she had felt moving through her thoughts as surely as if he had spoken them.

Trust me.

The serpent slithered across the floor of the chamber as it searched for that illusive essence. Rage seethed within the creature as it swept beneath the table, shoving aside the chairs, an embodiment of evil that hissed its frustration and hatred, eyes glowing blood-red as it swept across the base of the royal seal, then slithered along the wall, searching, growing more agitated by the moment as it found nothing but the emptiness of the chamber and the swirling mist that constantly eluded it.

Its search was fruitless. Then it angled that large head toward the steps and the two mortals who crouched in the shadows. With a deadly sigh, it swerved toward those steps.

Amber saw the creature approach, pulling Guinevere with her along the top landing, past the shattered door through which they could not escape, hiding in the shadows, hoping the creature could not see them. But it seemed to sense where they went, angling toward them as it slithered up each step. Then she could no longer see it clearly as the mist gathered, then thickened and filled the chamber, making it impossible to see anything.

As surely as if he held her, the power wrapped around them both, encircling them in a foglike shroud that prevented the creature from seeing them—hiding them, protecting them.

Gradually the mist began to lighten. When it cleared enough for her to see, Amber realized they were no longer at the top of the stairs near the doorway, but across the chamber, hidden behind the large stone seal.

She heard the horrible hiss of the serpent. It raged like the wind, filling the chamber, sweeping the mist away in a stormy explosion of darkness and terrifying power. Then, she could no longer see the serpent. It was as if it had disappeared in the gathering storm.

Truan sensed the change in the powers of Darkness, that moment when it realized it could not find Amber or Guinevere in the blinding mist and transformed into a swirling darkness of evil that swept the mist away. He too transformed, drawing on the powers of the Light, seizing the power within to see what his mortal sense could not see—the form the Darkness would take next.

He had protected Amber and Lady Guinevere once. But the Darkness would continue to take new forms, for in that way the deadly game would go on, point and counterpoint. Eventually he had to strike back, to end this deadly game, and destroy the Darkness.

He sensed that gathering of evil once more, the coldness of betrayal, greed, and avarice that lived in all men's souls and at the edge of the known world.

Beware, my son! The power of the Darkness lies in deception, trickery, and betrayal. It will use your own weaknesses against you!

It filled the chamber once more, in the shadows that grew at the corners of the chamber, driving back the light of the oracle stone, slipping over the edges of the round table—the symbol of everything that was hope in men's hearts—as it took a new shape and form. That of a large gray wolf.

Amber saw the creature as it leapt to the top of the round table. A fierce, deadly creature, with bared fangs and death at its eyes—even more terrifying than the creature they'd encountered in the forest that long ago day when she and Lady Guinevere had journeyed to Camelot. It leapt to the floor of the star-chamber, gathering itself in great leaping strides as it crossed the chamber toward the seal stone where they hid, no longer safe.

Truan whirled around, transformed once more into his mortal body. It took precious moments for his senses to clear and his strength to return in order to meet Gareth's next challenge. Then he saw the gray wolf leaping across the chamber, closing in on the place where Amber and Lady Guinevere hid.

It will use your own weakness against you!

Those prophetic words rang with a warning alarm through his senses. Gareth had sensed his worst fear—

that Amber would discover what he really was—and now used it against him. But all that mattered was Amber. He could not bear the thought of her death, even if it meant she discovered the truth.

He transformed once more, feeling the power of the creature fill his senses and his soul, his mortal flesh and blood, disappearing, replaced with muscle, strength, and the killer instinct of the black wolf.

Amber watched with disbelief. When she first saw the serpent take form she knew that somehow they had entered a world where everything was somehow changed. The creature didn't come from her fear and imagination. It *was* real.

Just as the mist that blanketed everything and prevented the creature finding them had been real.

She felt it, not cold and terrifying, but warm like a caress against her skin, soft as a promise that whispered in her thoughts.

Trust in me.

She did not understand what was happening. She didn't begin to understand where Truan had gone— there one moment, gone the next. But she accepted there were things in this world that could not be explained.

Had not time stood still in that magical place where Truan had taken her? Days that passed as no more than a few hours as he loved her? Had she not seen the wolf in the forest one moment, and then Truan, coming to her through the sunlight and mist? Did he not seem to know her thoughts as clearly as she knew them?

Magic? Sorcery? Or something else?

She accepted it because she had to. If not, then she had to believe that Truan had somehow abandoned her to this hellish, terrifying nightmare. And that she could not believe.

She did not know what it was that bound them together any more than she'd understood the reasons she had to go to him the day of the tournament. Except that she must. That her future, her life, whatever it held, was joined with his. In this life, in another life, perhaps through eternity, if such a thing existed.

Trust in me, he had asked. She trusted, because she loved him with all her heart and soul. And as she watched the black wolf leap across the chamber, attacking the gray wolf, their savage snarls tearing at her soul, she knew she had nothing to fear of the black creature.

They slashed and clawed at one another, teeth sinking into heavy fur, angling down low at the throat or the vulnerable underbelly. Their growls and snarls filled the chamber until Amber couldn't bear the sound of it anymore. She pressed her hands over her ears trying to close out the sounds of tearing flesh and hide.

In the frenzy of battle, as teeth and nails slashed and tore, Truan sensed the transformation begin again. More slowly this time, the movements lethargic, hampered by the loss of power from those previous transformations and the wounds inflicted by their present transformation. Then gradually the form beneath him changed, shifted, and took another form—that of a man that slowly emerged, wounded, trying to protect himself against Truan's savage attack.

Blue tunic, torn and slashed, the hood was all that protected the face and head. Then that too was slashed and torn away by flashing teeth and claws. Hands came up to protect the exposed head, vulnerable without a weapon.

Truan experienced a powerful blood lust. It burned through his veins, pounded in his heart, and echoed through his thoughts from some long ago day.

Kill! Before you are killed!

Then he saw brilliant blue eyes and the features of the man's face. Features remembered from distant dreams, mortal dreams, a gentle hand laid at his shoulder, and a voice that whispered of love and tenderness.

Son. And then the voice that answered, tearing through the memories, trying to destroy them.

Kill before you are killed!

As the power of the Darkness and the power of the Light fought the battle within him, Truan stared down through the eyes of the creature he had become. But he saw with a mortal heart and soul. The man that lay beneath him, was his father. Merlin!

With a snarl of agony, Truan tore himself away from the man who lay prostrate beneath him. Sides heaving, the killer instinct still strong within him, he crouched several feet away, head down, struggling against the inner darkness that closed around his heart, staring at the man who lay there.

Amber watched as the gray wolf transformed once more, then continued to watch with disbelieving eyes as it took the form of a man. She felt a vague stirring of recognition though she could not recall when she had met the man.

"It cannot be," Lady Guinevere whispered beside her. She pulled free of Amber's hand as she left their hiding place behind the seal stone.

"No!" Amber warned, going after her.

"Is it you?" Guinevere said, crossing the chamber before Amber could stop her.

The man lifted his head. The hood had fallen back as he fought the black wolf, revealing strong aquiline features, the slope of strong jaw, the sensual curve of a mouth surrounded by a dark beard and mustache, stirring a memory of someone else Amber had known. Then he lifted his eyes and stared at Lady Guinevere.

They were intense blue, shimmering with light, love, and passion. Eyes that Amber had seen looking back at her! And she knew that she had met this man before. And as surely as she knew that she had met him, she knew who he was.

"Marcus Merlinus," Lady Guinevere said softly, her heart breaking at the beloved name she had spoken only in her prayers and dreams. "I thought I would never see you again."

"No! Do not!" Part snarl, part cry, the sound was torn from the depths of his soul as Truan slowly transformed once more and watched helplessly as Guinevere walked toward the man who lay on the floor of the star-chamber.

Only he saw the darkness that filled the man's eyes, overshadowing the blue; only he sensed the darkness in the creature's soul as it lured her from safety.

Beware the choice that must be made.

Amber heard the terrifying snarl, then watched in horror as the black wolf leapt at Guinevere, carrying her with it as it rolled across the floor. Then, continued to watch disbelieving as the creature slowly stood and shook itself off, expecting it to attack Lady Guinevere. But it did not. Instead it stood over her as if protecting her.

The transformation slowly began. Gradually the black wolf disappeared, powerful muscles and gleaming dark fur, replaced by the powerful muscles and dark shoulder-length hair of a man.

Amber's heart leapt at the sight of him as he slowly emerged from the form of the wolf. Deep in her heart she thought she must have always known from that first moment in the forest when he had come between her and danger, and then afterward when Truan had taken her to that special place, returning to her through the mist just before dawn, a wild, fierce creature, a fierce, impassioned lover who left his mark on her skin and on her soul.

She understood nothing of what had happened. She simply accepted it, because she loved him with all her heart.

He stood weak and shaking, his movements slow and filled with pain though he seemed not to be injured. Then she saw the movement on the floor as the man Guinevere had called out to pushed to his feet and lunged for the knife that lay forgotten on the round table until that moment.

She cried out a warning as the man seized the knife.

Truan sensed the danger, then heard it in the cry of his name. Hindered by a lingering weakness from the transformation he could not change again to save her, but warned her back with every ounce of strength he possessed.

He saw Gareth reach for the knife, saw too as it left his hand. Meant for him, a mortal blade capable of striking a mortal blow while he was not yet fully transformed, in that single moment when all creatures such as he were caught between the mortal and immortal worlds, and vulnerable.

It was less than a heartbeat, yet an agony of time as Amber ran between them to warn him.

"No!" Truan cried out.

He caught her, pulling her protectively into his arms, turning her away from Gareth, away from the deadly illusion, and the very real danger.

Her hair had come unbound from the long braid, spilling through his fingers at her back. The expression on her face was startled, her slender body taut as a bowstring. Then he sensed the shudder of pain that began deep inside even before he felt it in the fierce clasp of her hands at his shoulders or heard it in the gasp at her lips.

As he pulled her against him she suddenly seemed no more than a child, small, fragile, and helpless. A warm wetness spilled through his fingers, staining the soft gold silk of her hair. He carefully eased her to the floor. Her gaze was fastened on his, her expression filled with every emotion they had shared, and traces of old memories that now slowly returned.

He sensed those memories of her other life returning. He tried to hold them back but could not. He realized that she had been released from the darkness that had prevented her remembering and a coldness of dread moved through him.

In that way of all creatures, he sensed something moving beyond his ability to stop it.

"No!" he whispered fiercely. "Stay with me! Stay with me."

Amber felt the coldness that slowly moved through her, but she was not afraid. Her fingers trembled as she touched his face. She could not seem to see him anymore, but she felt his presence and knew that he was holding her. She heard the whisper of her name, felt the warmth of his breath against her cheek, then on her lips. She breathed in the sweet warmth of his kiss.

"I love you. I have always loved you," she whispered as she felt the cold disappear, replaced by a tender warmth that wrapped around her as her eyes slowly drifted shut.

Truan crushed her against him as the dying words whispered past her lips. He could not hold back death nor could he give life back where there was none. But what if she *gave* her life to him; what if he joined her mortal soul with his?

Through his rage and grief he saw the portal open and knew that Gareth escaped, saw the other side across the link between two worlds precariously opened, the past and the future. But all he cared about was held in his arms.

The sounds that filled the star-chamber were not mortal sounds, but the rage of helplessness of those things beyond his power—the wounded cry of a creature as it mourned its lost mate; the cry of a mortal man who feared he had lost the one thing that meant life to him, and felt as if his heart had been torn out.

Truan cradled Amber in his arms, and buried his face in her hair.

Twenty

Guinevere slowly stood as she saw two men walking toward them through that gaping opening at the stone seal. One was a young warrior, tall and lean. The crest he wore on his tunic was unfamiliar to her, but he wore blue and gold colors—Arthur's colors. And he had the bearing of a king. Or one who might one day be one.

The other man walked a ways apart from him, surrounded by clouds of swirling mist and the light that glowed behind them as if framed by a brilliant sun. She stared at him as he approached, his gait familiar in the long purposeful stride, the wide shoulders just as familiar, the length of his mantle whipping about him as if the very currents waited for his command.

She held her breath as he slowly came into view, the outline of his head, the aquiline features, cobalt blue eyes that had once looked back at her with a passion that took her breath away, the strong set of his jaw, the mouth wreathed by close-cropped dark beard that she remembered stirring against her mouth.

Except that the close-cropped hair on his head and the beard that framed his mouth was streaked with gray. And the eyes that looked back at her while filled with that same stirring of passion also held the look of time and sadness.

He was the same and yet different. The one she had loved with all her heart and soul, to whom she had given herself without reserve and had been willing to sacrifice all to be with. The man whose wisdom had helped create a wondrous kingdom built to last a thousand years, and whose friendship with the king had, in the end, taken him from her.

It *was* him. She sensed it in her heart with all the aching loneliness of the time since he'd been gone. Not some figment of her imagination, transformed from a hideous creature. *Him.*

Her cheeks were wet with tears. Her gown was torn and bloodstained, her dark hair streaming in tangles down her back. She looked like a refugee from some holocaust, and yet she had never looked more like a queen. Brave, radiantly beautiful, her strength and courage reflected in her soft eyes where he glimpsed memories of passion. For her, two years past. For him, half a lifetime—centuries, in the years that separated their worlds.

He had dared to love her and risked losing a kingdom. In the end, because he could not bear the pain their love would have caused the king, he had left her, never realizing that in doing so he left open the door to the betrayal that led to the end of Arthur's kingdom.

He saw the bewilderment along with the love in her eyes, the love that he knew would always be there no matter the choices or lifetimes that separated them. And he also saw the questions that seemed impossible to ask out of fear of the answers they would bring.

"Marcus?" she whispered.

Only she had ever called him that, the name given him when he became royal counselor to Arthur in those days before she was destined to be a queen, before her betrothal to Arthur, when he had served her father and watched a beautiful young girl grow to womanhood; when he had dared to love her intelligence, her beauty, and her rare spirit, finding with her that passion of youth that comes only once, flares into an inferno that bonds two people together for all time, no matter how briefly it lasts.

In that way he was bonded to her, and in the child he had left her with, never knowing until that day when Ninian finally revealed that Truan was not her son, that the young man at Camelot who played the fool with ridiculous tricks and conjurements was in fact the child of his and Guinevere's passion.

He wanted to reach out to her and take her in his arms, but he was bound by other loyalties, and a deep and equally passionate love for Ninian. In that other place and time that lay beyond the portal, while her future was here with Arthur.

"Is it really you?" She looked at him with both wonder and disbelief.

He nodded. "There is so much to say, dearest Gwen."

She nodded and he sensed her struggle to understand. She had known of the powers he'd been born to, but not of his immortality. He had known she would one day be queen, but not that she had borne him a son. But now the fate of the future lay in the hands of that son.

"In time, dearest love," he whispered in the bond of their thoughts, in that old way they had once known each other's thoughts without speaking them. *"We will have our time and we will speak of the things that must be said, but for now there is another whose need is greater than ours."*

He sensed her acceptance, for he had never lied to her, not even when he left her. He turned and crouched beside the young man who knelt, grief-stricken, cradling his lost love in his arms, and said a single word.

"Son."

Merlin felt the weight of Guinevere's stare, heard the startled breath she took as if she suddenly found it difficult to breathe, and realized she had not guessed the truth—that Truan was their own true son.

"Son," he repeated, laying his hand gently on Truan's shoulder and in the contact, allowed his strength to flow through the connection of his touch. He let the feelings of a lifetime pour through the words, in this son he had never held, whose eyes he had never looked into as a child, whose first fragile steps into the immortal world he'd never seen.

"You cannot hold onto mortal life when it is gone. It is the one power we do not possess."

Truan finally looked up. He understood, but he would not accept it. He lightly stroked his fingers across her features, her eyes, that remarkable blue-green color, once filled with such sadness, then filled with the passion they'd found in one another, now closed by death; the curve of her cheek, if he closed his eyes he could feel her as she had laid against his heart, her cheek pressed just there; her lips, warm with the passion he tasted there; her slender hand with each fragile bone gently curved beneath her skin, once lifted in shyness to take a foolish gift he offered, then lifted in fierce strength when she tried to protect him.

Protect him? The irony of it was like a bitter poison. With all his powers of the Light, the wondrous powers he'd been born to, the ability to transform, to summon the dawn and bring on the night, to move the stars in the heavens, it was she with her fragile mortal strength and fierce love who had tried to protect him.

"You are needed, my son," Merlin said gently. More

than ever, he understood how heavily the mantle of responsibility of the powers they possessed weighed.

"In your own time," he explained. "The Darkness grows powerful once more because of what has happened here. The enemy strikes from the north."

Truan slowly nodded. He looked up, his face a mask of anguish and pain, and looked at his friend, Lord Stephen, who ruled over Camelot in a different time and place. Stephen, who once traveled back through that same portal to reclaim his lost love.

Theirs was a bond of friendship as strong as Merlin's and Arthur's had been, forged in battle and blood, and across the years in the future time that awaited through the portal.

"I need you, my friend," Stephen said somberly, understanding his friend's loss.

Truan stood, cradling Amber gently in his arms.

"Son?" Guinevere said, tentatively laying a hand on his arm. It took all of her strength to grasp the impossible, that the young man she now looked at was in fact the child she had borne in her time and place, in her world. He was only a few years older than she—in his time and place.

There was such pain in his eyes, and with the instinct of every mother, she wanted only to take it away. But she knew she could not. And so she spoke from the heart of the things she knew to be true.

"You will always hold her in your heart. That is both the blessing and the burden of loving as we have loved."

He nodded. "I will leave her here, where we found one another, free of the pain of her past. If only things could have been different . . ."

If only . . .

Guinevere had wished it a thousand times. Prayed for

it. Tried to bend the future to her will. But she could not, not anymore than he could.

Behind them, the sounds of battle had ceased. Then they heard the sounds of warriors who swarmed through Camelot, reclaiming it. The debris at the doorway was kicked aside and Arthur entered the star-chamber. He slowly walked down the steps, surveying the destruction. As he reached the bottom of the steps, he spotted Stephen, and he quickly drew his sword. Then his gaze fell on Merlin.

He stared with disbelief. "Is it you, old friend?"

Merlin nodded. "Ayes. There is much to explain, and little time to explain it. Camelot is in danger." He gestured to the portal that lay behind him, through which he and Stephen had traveled.

Arthur walked forward, staring through the portal into the star-chamber that existed on the other side, trying to comprehend, remembering something Merlin had once told him of the worlds that lay beyond the known world. He turned suddenly, his gaze narrowed as he stared at Merlin.

"What is it that lays beyond?"

" 'Tis Camelot."

Arthur let out a low sound of incredulity. "When?"

" 'Tis the future you see."

"Just as you once spoke of it." Arthur nodded. "And Camelot has survived?"

Merlin nodded. "It has, though not as you wished it. And there is grave danger, which threatens us all."

Arthur turned and stared at the portal, the wildness of adventure burning through his blood as it had not in a very long time. They had spoken of such things when he was a boy. He knew Merlin possessed great power. He swung on his friend, words tinged with anger.

"You left without saying goodbye!"

"Would you have let me go, if I had?"

"I would not."

"I had to leave," Merlin told him in the connection of their thoughts. *"Trust that I had my reasons and that it was for the best."*

"I was angry with you," Arthur said. "I swore that if I found you, I would have you thrown into the darkest dungeon."

Merlin smiled faintly. "Do the charges still stand?"

"They do!" Arthur replied. Then his expression changed. He laid a hand on Merlin's shoulder.

"I have missed you, old friend."

Truan laid Amber gently on the mossy place in the shelter of the tree where they had first lain together. He carefully drew the edges of his mantle about her as if to protect her from the cold. But in this place there was no cold, nor time.

She looked as if she might only be sleeping, as if he had only to kiss her and she would waken, her eyes filled with love and passion as she reached for him and pulled him down to her. He bent over her and tenderly kissed her cheek.

"Sleep, dearest Amber," he whispered as he sent his thoughts to her, though there was no answer. *"Where no pain or sadness can touch you."*

Guinevere was waiting for him as he left the clearing. He was different now from the young warrior she had first encountered when the wolf attacked. He had been young, handsome, filled with passion, and that easy, feckless humor meant to disguise a more biting wit.

He was still young, handsome, and filled with passion, but overall was a sadness and sense of grim purpose.

Gone was the laughter from his eyes and it made her ache for his loss.

"I will stay with her until your return," she said, unable to find the words to say more. He took her hand in his and held it gently.

"I would have no other to watch over her, dear lady." Then he bent and kissed her hand.

She accepted that precious gift from the son she had despaired of ever seeing again. She had been given the chance to see him as he would be as a man, confident in the knowledge that he would grow to manhood and very like his father, whom she had loved so deeply.

"Go now," she said. "The others await you." Just as she had once bid farewell to Marcus Merlinus, not realizing it was for the last time. *Go now, Arthur awaits you.*

And she watched him leave, astride the warhorse, an immortal man, son of the Power of the Light. Merlin's son. Her son. And the ache she'd carried deep inside her since that day when she'd given him over to another for safekeeping, eased for the first time. Ninian, her dear friend, had kept her promise.

Truan rode through the mists of time, a short distance. Merely a few paces across the greensward that lay before Camelot, then across the wide, spreading valley, crossing five centuries as he joined his powers with Merlin's and opened a portal on that battlefield that linked their two worlds together.

His sword was secured at his saddle, a smaller knife secured at his belt. Across his saddle lay his battle shield with Lord Stephen's crest in blue and gold—the colors Arthur had carried when he faced an enemy on this very same battlefield.

They were waiting for him there. Lord Stephen,

Rorke FitzWarren, and Tarek al Sharif, astride their warhorses beneath a lowering sky as thunder rolled across the army that had amassed there. Three hundred strong, warriors, knights, archers, and infantry. While on the hillsides facing them massed an army of Saxons, mercenaries, and rebels from the northern borders, their battle armor glinting like black death beneath the cloud-laden sky.

"They crossed the northern borders a fortnight ago," Stephen said, his voice low, his expression grim. "Since then their numbers continue to grow. Every rebel and Saxon has thrown in with them."

They were outnumbered with no hope of reinforcements from London in time. And Gareth was among them. Truan sensed it.

"How many?" he asked, his gaze sweeping the strategic locations of the enemy army.

"Six hundred," Rorke FitzWarren replied. "By our last count from riders who returned just after dawn."

"We have faced worse odds," Tarek al Sharif noted. "In Syracusa, the enemy turned and ran."

They stared out across the small valley. The enemy had taken their positions. An expectant silence fell across the greensward. There was not even the stirring of air, nor the call of a bird. Only that heaviness of silence as if time somehow stood still and waited.

"Aye," Rorke concurred. "But they were not so well armed. And they fought for the promise of gold, not their own kingdom. A man will fight to the death if he fights for his home and family."

"As *we* fight for our home and families."

Truan turned with the others at the sound of the voice that came from behind them. The sound of steel being drawn shattered the silence as Stephen's guard and knights surrounded the lone warrior who sat astride his warhorse and slowly rode toward them. He had approached so quietly that none had heard or seen him.

Arthur was resplendent in his royal colors, with silver breastplate, helm, and shield, imposing, unafraid as he rode fearlessly ahead through the gauntlet of drawn swords, having passed through the same portal Truan had opened.

"Hold!" Stephen ordered as Arthur approached closer and finally reined in his warhorse.

Only now were the others who rode with him visible, emerging through the trailing clouds of mist, fanning out across the hillside as they emerged from that same opening in time. Gaheris, Sir Malcolm, Rohan, all of Arthur's knights, and a good portion of his vast army. Sir Bors was there as well, the lines at his face deepening with his grin as he approached Stephen.

"I am most pleased you did not run him through. We would have been forced to cut you down, then fight those cloddish Saxons as well," he said good naturedly.

"If I had not recognized him, we would have cut you all down," Stephen informed the knight.

Arthur chuckled. "Perhaps you are worthy, young warrior, of ruling over Camelot after all. We shall see."

Rorke FitzWarren rode forward, edging his warhorse beside Stephen's. His gray gaze scrutinized the man before him. He had served a great king in the conquest of Britain. This man's Britain. He saw not a fool, nor a coward, but a man not unlike William, a warrior who preferred battlefields where conflict was clearly revealed, not the subtleties of politics.

He took his sword from its sheath, a sword he had fought the darkness with. He laid it across his arm, extending it hilt-first toward Arthur.

"Your sword, milord."

In spite of the dull, ominous day, Excalibur gleamed with the promise of all who had gone before and those who now gathered on that battlefield, willing to fight and die for a dream.

Arthur had not brought Excalibur with him through the portal, for the sword—that shining symbol of hope—belonged to that time and place in the past until the events that had not yet taken place had come to pass. More than that, his friend would not tell him.

Merlin rode through the gathered knights. He nodded at Truan as Arthur closed his gloved hand around the hilt and took the sword, once more feeling its familiar weight solid and sure in his hand, as if it was part of him.

He raised the sword aloft and sounded the battle cry. The blade gleamed as the sun broke through the blanket of clouds.

"We fight for *our* kingdom," Arthur said, looking across at Stephen. "Let it begin."

As the armies gathered together to strike, Merlin laid a restraining hand on Truan's arm. "There is no need for you to fight this day. Lord Stephen will have need of his counselor if he is to be victorious."

Truan shook his head. "He already has a wise counselor," he replied looking at his father. Then he drew his sword.

"I fight at his side."

"Do you wish to die, my son?" Merlin asked, for the outcome of what lay ahead would not come to him in the vision he had summoned, but lay shrouded in the darkness of clouds and mist, like the clouds and mist that now blanketed the valley.

For a moment, the fierceness eased at Truan's expression. His voice broke softly. "I want to live."

And in the unspoken, lay the words both had spoken

in anguish as young men, in separate lifetimes that lay centuries apart.

I want only to live as a mortal man, to be with the woman I love.

And Merlin knew there was nothing he could do or say to stop him.

The history that was written of that day spoke only of a skirmish of Saxons against the Norman army of King William, one of many conflicts that arose after the conquest. It said nothing of the hundreds of warriors who met in battle, more than the number of William's entire army at Hastings as he met King Harold and fought for the throne of England.

Nor was anything written of the two warriors whose armies fought side-by-side against the enemy that tried to reclaim the throne of England. One dressed in royal battle armor of an ancient king whose name forever after was known in myth and legend, his battle sword raised high, the sun gleaming from the legendary stone in the hilt, the knights of the round table fighting beside him. The other, a warrior prince, who could never claim a throne, but who claimed Camelot and was willing to spill his blood for it.

And the bond between them, the past and the future of Camelot, was the warrior of the Light, whose sword struck as true as Excalibur that day as he called on the powers of the Ancient Ones and struck down the enemy one by one.

Truan fought his way through the enemy, cutting a path from atop the warhorse, then vaulting to the ground and taking up the battle there. He fought past the point of exhaustion, past the point where he felt the shudder of the blade as he struck down another enemy warrior, past feeling the blood that splattered his sword hand . . . past caring whether he lived or died that day.

The blow at his side stunned him back into that mortal world of pain. The blood he felt was his own, flowing freely down his side as the enemy blade sliced through his tunic and underlayers of padding that protected his ribs. He instinctively brought the sword up as he turned to face this new attack.

The air left his lungs in a deep sound that was a mixture of pain and grim satisfaction as he confronted Gareth.

He had hoped to find him with every blow he struck, each warrior he cut down, searching among the fallen enemy and those who still fought. Like a man possessed, knowing that he was among them, feeling it in his blood.

Twice before they had met like this. Once on the mock battlefield as they played a dangerous game of deception that had almost cost Arthur's life. Then again in the star-chamber.

"You will not escape this time," Truan vowed.

"Not if I kill you first," Gareth replied.

Truan's expression was stark, his eyes cold and bleak. "I am already dead," he answered softly. "As are you, since that moment when you took her life."

He struck then, horrible slashing blows with the rage and pain of Amber's death.

Gareth struck back, but soon his sword was raised in defense to prevent being cut down by each new attack that seemed to come with greater strength.

It seemed as if only they fought in this ultimate battle. The rest of the battle ceased to exist about them. The powers of the Light against the powers of Darkness, with each ringing blow of Truan's sword. Until Gareth's sword shuddered and faltered, raised next with less strength. Then the death blow, as Truan sunk his sword deep into Gareth's heart.

A great darkness rolled across the battlefield. As his mortal blood pumped from his chest, Gareth stared back at Truan with a mixture of surprise and rage. In that moment, the balance of the battle turned. All about them it seemed that Stephen and Arthur's men finally gained the advantage, driving the enemy back.

Truan shoved Gareth away from him. Gareth fell to his knees, his sword still clutched in his hands. But he could no longer find the strength to lift it.

He looked up at Truan and smiled cruelly. "You have still lost," he snarled.

Truan swung the sword one last time. The blade shuddered as it cut through skin, tissue, and then the connecting bones of the spine, separating head from body.

Light exploded all around them. It surrounded Truan and then seemed to move through him like a sword thrust deep, cutting away the darkness.

Then the battlefield lay silent around Arthur's army, the blood of the past and the future soaking the ground at their feet.

"You fought well."

Truan looked up from where he knelt, leaning heavily against the hilt of his sword, the blade embedded in the ground beside Gareth's body.

He welcomed the physical exhaustion that filled his mortal body, letting it sweep through him, leaving him unable to feel anything else. He didn't want to feel anything, because he knew the pain that waited. The pain of a wound far greater than the one at his side. A wound that could never heal until he was with her again.

Just as Truan had once extended a hand to him on that mock battlefield, Arthur now extended his hand.

"It is ended, my young friend."

* * *

Excalibur gleamed in the light of the setting sun, reflecting the gold rays of the promise it held both for the past and for the future. Then, Arthur turned the sword and extended it toward Rorke FitzWarren, The sword, he knew, waited in the past. The past that he was part of and to which he must return.

"I give it to you for safekeeping, warrior," Arthur told him.

"It will be here, at Camelot, where it belongs," Rorke assured him.

Arthur nodded. Seizing the reins of his horse, he swung astride, wincing slightly from a minor wound. He looked across at the man he had made his counselor, his mentor, and his friend. An immortal, older than when they last spoke with each other in that time five hundred years in the past.

"Ride with me," Arthur said, with that authority of command that came so easily to him, then added, "please, old friend."

And so they rode ahead of that vast army of ancient warriors and knights, whose places were recorded in legend and myth. And the two spoke of things there had been no time to speak of in the past.

"I was angry when you left," Arthur said thoughtfully. "I thought you had betrayed me."

Merlin's gaze sharpened. So carefully had he guarded against Arthur ever finding out the truth, for he could not bear the thought that he might cause this man whom he loved as a brother the pain of knowing what had passed between he and Guinevere. In having the ability to know the future, he had also known that he and Guinevere could never remain together.

There was a certainty of history that had been set in

motion. They were part of it and for a moment, might have changed that history. But in the end he had left her, hoping to preserve the dream of Camelot.

But he had loved her before she went to Arthur. Then he had let her go because he knew it was her destiny. In all truthfulness he was able to say, "I left because I could not betray you."

"I felt as if you had taken a knife and cut out my heart," Arthur admitted freely for the first time what he had never been able to tell another living soul.

"And she felt your loss just as keenly."

Startled, Merlin searched his friend's face, then his thoughts for the truth behind the words. Was it possible Arthur had known all along!

"You were friend to both of us. You made it possible for us to be together."

And in that moment, even with his powers, Merlin could not be certain what Arthur spoke of—that first meeting between a young noblewoman and the king, arranged by her father; or the last time he lay with Guinevere and then left, freeing her to follow her destiny as queen.

"What of the past?" Arthur asked, his gaze sweeping to the wide, low hills that surrounded the valley and the shining castle—Camelot—that lay nestled there like a crown jewel.

"I have seen the ruins. I have heard Lord Stephen's men speak of the end of Camelot."

Merlin knew he risked much in telling Arthur anything of what would come to pass in his own time when he returned, as he must. That future time that lay beyond Camelot as he had known it when he last left, in the time preceding the fall of the kingdom.

Gareth was dead. An embodiment of the evil of the Darkness, born in this present time of 1068, a minion of the Darkness used to lure Truan into the past with the purpose of destroying him—and thereby destroying the future as they knew it now, where hope survived for Camelot in Lord Stephen, and the future generations, his own grandchildren, who had already been born. The heirs to the powers of the Light.

But he could not let Arthur return without some knowledge of what awaited. He owed him that much. Such was the bond of their friendship. And so he tried to explain as much as he could.

"There will be a great cataclysm."

"Can it be vanquished?"

In his voice, Merlin heard the fierce strength and resolve of a mortal man, a warrior, who had built a kingdom and would not easily let it die.

"It is already part of our history," Merlin answered.

Arthur nodded. He knew there were things that could not, must not change.

"How will it happen?"

And this much Merlin too would tell him. "You will be betrayed by someone close to you."

The muscles at Arthur's cheek spasmed. "Will we meet again?" And in the question, Merlin sensed the one that went unasked, knowing that he could not lie.

"We will not meet again," Merlin said with certainty, and saw Arthur visibly relax. The king nodded. And the unspoken thought that passed between them—that Arthur could not bear it if Merlin had betrayed him.

"What of Guinevere?" Arthur then asked, and in the way he said her name, without the use of her formal title, or referring to her as his queen, Merlin sensed the depth of love that grew even now for her. Two strangers, brought together in an arranged marriage of title and wealth, according to history.

"She waits for you, milord."

Arthur looked at him then and for a moment a deeper truth passed between them, unspoken, unformed even by thought, perhaps only something that Arthur once guessed at.

"You have a fine son. A son that a king would be proud of. If I were to have a son, I would want such a man as he. You must say goodbye to her. She will never forgive me if you do not."

Then Arthur looked once more at Camelot, that symbol of dreams in the distance, yet as near as the gathering mist that formed even now, waiting to take them back.

"I will miss you," he said, "all the days of my life."

Then without looking back, he gave the signal to his men and led them forward into the mist—back through the portal that linked their two worlds together for that brief moment in time, back into that time that waited for them. Into legend and myth.

Guinevere waited for him on the other side of the portal. She extended her hand to him and Merlin took it, feeling once again that wild stirring of passion with just her touch, remembering all the ways they had touched as they came together as lovers, then locking it away deep inside the memories of the past where they belonged.

"You will not stay," she said with certainty and a sadness in her eyes.

"I cannot, dearest love," he said, holding her as he once had, feeling it to the depth of his soul, feeling too the whisper of that other love that waited. In the future.

"I hated you for a while," she said, laying her head against his heart. "At the same time I loved you. Feeling our child grow inside me, wanting you there with me, hoping you would return. But I think even then, I knew you would not."

"I did not know," Merlin whispered against her hair. "With all my powers I did not know! If I had . . ."

"If you had, the future would have been different. Your guilt would have consumed you, and in the end I would have lost you anyway." They both knew she spoke the truth.

He released her then, and they walked for a ways, hand-in-hand, as they had so many times as young lovers.

"Arthur cares deeply for you," Merlin told her then. "You must build your future with him." He did not tell her that her time with Arthur would be brief, as their time together had been brief.

She nodded, accepting his words, but not yet letting go of his hand. "Will I remember any of this? Will you at least leave me with that much?"

He could not give her what she asked, for even these moments that they spent together might yet alter things further. And that they must not risk.

"You will know that you were loved deeply, by two men, who wished only to share your life."

She knew he would not, dare not promise her more. She accepted that, for it was more than he'd left her with in that before time.

"I would like to see our son once more."

" 'Tis dangerous, Gwen."

"Please."

He took her into his arms and gently cradled her head within his hands. In the connection of their thoughts and a last parting kiss, he gave her the vision he saw as Truan returned to that place apart, returned to his own lost love.

* * *

The forest was as it had been that time when he and Amber had lain together, their bodies joining in passion and love that needed no words. And he found her there, exactly as he had left her, so still and silent, as if she lay dreaming, as if he had only to touch her and then feel her come alive once more with passion beneath his caresses.

Had it been days, hours, or only minutes since he laid her there until he could return to her? In this place time ceased to exist. In this place, he held death at bay, refusing to let it claim her.

He had wiped the blood of battle from his hands and reached for her, gently pushing aside the edges of his mantle.

Her lashes were dark golden crescents that lay against her cheeks. Her lips were softly parted, as if she took shallow breaths while sleeping.

As he had in that other time when he had brought her there and they had become lovers, slipping beneath the surface of the pool, and he had taken her breath within him, then given it back to her in soft stirrings of air that filled her lungs and gave life back to her, he now lowered his mouth to hers.

In those dying moments, mortally wounded, she had given her life and soul to him. He had taken her soul within and joined it with his. Now . . . pain tore through him, as if his soul was being cut in two, twin halves of one that could only go on living if the other lived. He gave her soul and her life back to her, drawing it from that place within his heart where he had kept it sheltered and protected until this moment, willing her to open her eyes, to live. For he had no life without her.

Like bursting the surface of deep water, air filled her lungs. Painful, wrenching, pulling her back, willing her back from the cold and darkness toward the light and warmth. The warmth of Truan's mouth against hers, the warmth of his love, filling her, wrapping around her, protecting her.

Her eyes slowly opened. She saw only him. Then reached for him.

"I thought I had lost you."

"Never!" Truan whispered fiercely as he tasted the tears at her cheek, then tenderly at her lips.

"Never."

Epilogue

The sun slanted low behind Amesbury Abbey, casting long shadows across the garden and the slender woman who stooped there, working against the fading light and the fading season as an autumn chill stole away the heat of the last day of summer.

The old monk grumbled, rubbing his eyes as the light faded, then feverishly reading those last lines of ancient Latin text.

Poladouras looked up as he finished, easing the ache of too much close reading by staring into the distance. He shaded his eyes with a gnarled hand, squinting against the glare of the setting sun. One moment he saw nothing, then he saw the outline of a man astride a horse. As if he had ridden right out of the sun.

He carried himself like a warrior, but with the bearing of royalty, tall, lean, gaze fixed steadily forward, the wings of his mantle billowing gently about him.

Poladouras moved slowly, the pain of years having settled in his bones through the long hours of the afternoon as he watched her painstakingly gathering the precious herbs and healing plants—enough to last the winter through. He grunted to get her attention.

She looked up then a frown of concern forming tiny lines at her eyes and mouth. "Are you all right?"

"It's grown late," he commented, jabbing at the pale sky overhead with his walking stick as blue faded to twilight. "The cold settles into my bones."

" 'Tis a wonderfully mild afternoon," she said, coming to him with concern.

"Bah! Mild if you are young. Tell that to my bones!"

She smiled gently. "I do not think there is that much telling in all the world. Your bones are far too stubborn." Then she laid a soothing hand on his arm.

"Do you wish me to come with you? I could brew you a soothing tea."

He waved her off. "You've not finished your gathering. Later will do. And I would not have a woman harping at me because her herbal medicants sat too long in the sun, or got frostbitten on account of my suffering."

Ninian smiled indulgently. There was a familiar pattern to their conversation. His grumbling, her consoling. Her tears, his gentle words in response. Always willing to listen, even as she poured her heart out. Willing to sit silently while she harvested her garden and wondered what the future held.

That pattern had defined the passage of days since she'd come here, needing to find some measure of peace in her life, a place, a haven where she could find refuge from the pain of her parting with her husband.

"Finish, woman!" Poladouras scolded. "Or I shall have no peace." And he shuffled off into the tumbledown abbey that was in desperate need of repairs, a fact he refused to accept, saying it had a certain charm.

Ninian tried to understand how any charm could possibly be found in stones that threatened to tumble down on their heads at any moment, or gaps in the walls that would freeze them out when winter came. She would have to ask her daughter if something might not be done about it before then.

She went back to her harvesting, working against time, the change of the seasons, the fading daylight, and the pain that was always present deep inside, like a wound that would not heal, but lay forever open where her heart had once been.

She had found a measure of solace here, and Poladouras had accepted her, taking her in as he had once taken her daughter in, raising her to be a fine young woman who now had a child of her own.

It was then she saw that lone rider as she reached for the basket. He was framed against the setting sun, tall and imposing as he sat astride, the fullness of his mantle stirring the cloud of mist that gathered at the end of the day. There was a familiarity to him, something she sensed, or perhaps felt or hoped for. A stirring that began at the sudden lurch of her heart, and then continued in its fierce beating as he reined the horse in and then swung down.

He was handsome. Before even seeing his features as he stepped from that golden glare of light into the soft shadows at the garden, she knew he would be. It was something she knew in her heart, just as she had seen him countless times in the past. Their shared past.

"Ninian," he said, slowly walking toward her.

She wanted to turn and run—she wanted to run into his arms. But she did not. Instead she clung to the pain of his leaving, knowing that he had gone to another. She held it like a battle shield before her, her only defense against having her heart broken all over again.

"How did you find me?"

Was it really her voice that spoke. It didn't even sound like her. And then she almost laughed. How had he found her? Of course, he would know just where to find her, without anyone telling him of it. Just as he knew all things. Including the depth of her love for him. Still.

Then, "Why did you come here?" because it was the only question that mattered, and his answer the only answer that mattered.

He breathed then, as if he had forgotten to, or perhaps had been holding his breath, waiting for her anger. She was beyond that now. And then he answered simply, "Because you are here."

Had he spoken the words or merely thought them? In that way that had once flowed so freely between them. She did not know. She only knew that it was not enough.

"And what of Guinevere?" she said softly.

"I love her," he said with brutal honesty, because he could not lie, then said gently, "I will always love her with that first stirring of passion that a young man finds with his first love. I cannot deny that, Ninian. Nor would you want me to."

He knew her so well. Her thoughts, her heart.

"We share a child. I will not deny that, any more than I could deny the daughters you bore me, for they are as much a part of my blood."

She threw down the spade she had been working with and faced him then, in all her radiant, smudged beauty. Forever young, passionate, filled with anger, pain, and love.

"I do not ask about the blood you share. I ask what is in your heart."

"You are my heart."

Ninian was stunned. He had ever been a passionate lover, but never passionate with words. He never saw the necessity of them, when he could give her his thoughts. She sensed his thoughts now, even as she heard the words he spoke and knew them to be true. She felt his words with all the passion she had brought to him then given to him in those days and weeks when he was first banished to the world between the worlds and no longer cared if he lived or died.

She had healed him with her gentleness and her spirit. Then she had healed him with her body and her heart, giving him back his will to live. Giving him back his passion. Even now she felt herself losing her battle to hold onto her pain and anger. She turned away from him, fearing he would already see the answer he sought in her eyes. She wanted more and she wanted him to say it.

"Your heart is not enough," she said with aching sadness, despairing that he would understand, or could ever say the words. She felt him standing behind her, his warmth holding back the cold of the evening shadows as he had a thousand times. If he touched her she was lost. But he did not. Instead, he gave her words of passion that she had longed a lifetime to hear.

" 'Tis all I have left to offer, you already have my soul, the air I breathe, all my hopes and dreams for the future. As you have from the moment you came to me. I do not wish to live without you, Ninian."

She turned to him then and Merlin thought she seemed hardly changed from that first time he looked up and saw her, a slender girl, a changeling who appeared in the mist, carrying a brilliant sword in her hand, with the hope of love in her eyes. Or in the months that followed, the first time when she had lain with him, rousing his mortal body in passion when he had believed none remained, joining with him, giving his life back to him as he felt himself reborn within her.

"It cannot be the same," she said, slowly letting go of the pain.

"It will not," he said, reaching up to tenderly cradle her face, half afraid she would pull away from him. She did not, and as he lowered his mouth to hers, he whispered a solemn promise, "It will be far more than you could ever dream."

Clouds of mist wrapped around the trees of the forest and purled across the floor of the clearing. The wolf ran through the mist in great bounding strides, urgency rippling its muscles beneath the gleaming black coat. Then it gathered its strength. The powerful muscles bunched as it leapt through the prism of light. It emerged from the other side in long-legged strides. Not a wolf, but a man, lean and tall, the thick folds of his mantle swirling the currents of mist.

The mist still clung to his mantle as he mounted the steps of Camelot. The oil lamps on the passage wall quivered, then seemed to burn brighter, banishing the shadows from the walls. He turned his thoughts from that inner place and sent them afar, his senses expanding with the power of the Light that flowed through his blood.

He sensed the young woman's approach and the undercurrent of urgency in her own thoughts. Then he saw her as she opened the door to the chamber having sensed his approach. Her hair was the color of brilliant flame, her eyes the color of the heart of a flame, bright blue, golden at the edges. The color of their eyes, a bond that connected them, through the blood of their father.

There were deep lines at his mouth and eyes that had not been there before, Vivian thought as she welcomed her brother with a gentle touch. But it only seemed to add to his handsomeness, the lean features, the preda tory way he moved like a creature that roamed the forests, his lips set in a hard line.

Pain and sorrow had transformed him from a young man into the man who stood before her, his features haunted by remnants of that pain and sorrow, along with the fear.

Then he looked to the pallet across the chamber and the slender young woman who lay there. No longer the girl he had first loved, but a young woman whose body was swollen with the child she struggled to bear. His child. A mortal child conceived in love and passion. A gift he'd believed no woman would ever be willing to give him.

The lines at his mouth and eyes eased as he went to her, going down on one knee beside the pallet, reaching for her in a way that was both tender and possessive, as if he would hold her back from death itself if necessary. As he once had.

He had spoken of it to no one. Vivian had no idea what he had done, what wondrous powers he possessed. Surely as great as their father's. Perhaps greater. For he refused to let death take Amber, carrying her to a place apart, there reclaiming her life, returning to their own time and place only those few months past.

They were both changed. It was as if neither one could exist without the other, with a powerful love Vivian had experienced with her own husband, but which seemed somehow to pale in comparison. It was as if Amber only truly came alive when Truan was near, and her brother could only be at peace with that part of him that was mortal when he could touch Amber once again. Otherwise, Vivian feared, he might become a mindless wraith that roamed the world, incapable of being either truly mortal or immortal.

She laid a hand on her brother's shoulder. "It began after dawn. It will be soon."

Truan nodded. "Leave us."

"She will need someone . . ."

He looked up at Vivian then, and his expression was transformed, tender, youthful once more and filled with love. "Please leave us," he said gently.

She did leave then, because she could not have done otherwise. There was something in his voice and his thoughts that was far too intimate and passionate for her to be part of.

"I thought you would not come," Amber whispered to him. "I dreamed that I was lost. But you found me."

"You will never be lost," Truan whispered against her lips, feeling his soul reborn in the sweetness of her kiss.

He sensed when the next pain began. It moved through her like a fist, as if she was being torn apart. She clenched the sides of the pallet, bracing against the pain as her body fought to bring forth their child. A mortal child with immortal powers.

Then Amber felt his hands gently stroking low over their child where it lay within her. As the next pain began and her muscles spasmed, he took the pain away, easing it from her body with tender warmth, taking it inside his own body so that he felt what she felt, her pain, her anguish, the fierce battle that went on inside her body.

And in that bond of touch and thought that connected them as it had from the moment he gave her life back to her, he saw and felt his child, alive, strong reaching out in its eagerness to be born, reaching toward him.

Amber's gaze fastened on Truan's as she felt it begin again. But there was no pain, only the tightening of her muscles, and then his tender words slipping through her thoughts with gentle promise and love, easing her muscles as she gave back this small measure of the life he had given her.

Later as their child lay sleeping at her breast, Truan held them both, and felt his heart beating in the gentle heart of the young woman who lay against him, his soul held within the tiny fist that lay curled within his hand. This was what he had fought for. This was what he could not let go of.

And beyond Camelot, night blanketed the earth. A bright blue star hung suspended between heaven and earth like a brilliant jewel.

A sign, some said, as the star streaked the sky, a fiery beacon that lit a path, a dragon's eye that saw beyond the mists of time . . .

When Nicholas Barrington, eldest son of the Earl of Larcombe, first met Melissa Seacort, the desperation he sensed beneath her well-bred beauty haunted him. He didn't realize how desperate Melissa really was . . . until he found her again at a Newmarket gambling club—being auctioned off by her father to the highest bidder. So, Nick bought himself a wife. With a villain hot on their heels, and a fortune and their lives at stake, they would gamble everything on the most dangerous game of all: love.

A TOUCH OF PARADISE   (0-7860-0271-9, $4.99)
by Alexa Smart

As a confidence man and scam runner in 1880s America, Malcolm Northrup has amassed a fortune. Now, posing as the eminent Sir John Abbot—scholar, and possible discoverer of the lost continent of Atlantis—he's taking his act on the road with a lecture tour, seeking funds for a scientific experiment he has no intention of making. But scholar Halia Davenport is determined to accompany Malcolm on his "expedition" . . . even if she must kidnap him!